I HAVE
TO
SAVE THEM

BOOKS BY ELLIE MIDWOOD

ELLIE MIDWOOD

I HAVE
TO
SAVE THEM

bookouture

Published by Bookouture in 2024

An imprint of Storyfire Ltd.
Carmelite House
50 Victoria Embankment
London EC4Y 0DZ

www.bookouture.com

ISBN: 978-1-83790-962-9
eBook ISBN: 978-1-83790-961-2

To the medical workers—the healers, the guardians of life.

PROLOGUE

The sanatorium is particularly silent today. The only sounds you hear are your own steps muffled by the thick green runner, but audible nevertheless in this unnatural serenity of the first morning of the year. At the nurses' station, the only nurse on duty is still slumbering at her desk, her head resting atop her folded arms. The rest of the medical staff have gone until tomorrow. Only you haunt the sanatorium hallways, like a Victorian specter doomed to eternal limbo.

You should have been home with Lotte, but instead, you left her to sleep off her hangover and slipped out of bed and into the early new-year morning. The streets were so devoid of any life, they looked almost eerie. Only the colorful confetti and celebratory hats scattered like feathers of an exotic bird hinted at the earlier festivities.

Yesterday, you promised your patient's husband, Eduard, you would check on her first thing in the morning, even though he assured you that it was unnecessary, that she would be perfectly fine. But something kept gnawing at you the entire evening and sleepless night and here you are, in your white medical gown, knocking gently on her room's door because you feel that you owe it to her, this constant vigil you imposed on her in spite of her gentle reproaches and even gentler protests.

Because, some twenty years ago, she kept that vigil for those in Auschwitz, and it eventually broke her irreparably. You and Eduard—her kind, devoted Eduard—were left to pick up the pieces. Not that either of you mind.

You gently knock on her door, but you're greeted with silence. No matter her mental state, she always minds her manners and opens the door, even if just to tell you to please leave her alone for she simply doesn't have enough energy at the moment. You call her name and listen again, holding your breath—she had tried taking her life before, more than once, and even jokes about it now, saying that she's just as bad at dying as she is at living—and gently turn the handle, already suspecting the worst and yet praying for a miracle.

Blast it, Orli! Just as you suspected, she's face-down on her neatly made bed, a handkerchief covering the spot on the rug where she must have been sick. No wonder, judging by the number of empty pill containers lined up in immaculate order on her nightstand.

With your heart in your throat, you turn her over, feel for her pulse, first on the wrist and then, after finding nothing, on her neck. You think you feel something, fluttering as erratically and weakly as the wings of a battered butterfly and rejoice, for there's still a chance. She's not gone just yet, you can bring her back, because you're not only her psychiatrist but a physician and a guardian, just like she once was for all of those people she cared for—

It is then that you notice a small note in her other hand. Your heart sinks, already knowing what it's going to say, and consider pretending not to notice it; saving her first and then dealing with the consequences. But that feels too much like a betrayal.

Time is running out, but you unravel it slowly and read the

words full of kindness and heartache. She thanks you for everything you've done for her but insists that it's time to let her go now and you shouldn't try to save her. She made the same mistake back in Auschwitz, trying to save some against their wishes, and suffered a guilty conscience her entire life—and you're so very young and have such a promising career in front of you—she'd never wish anything of the kind on you.

Even in her final moments, thinking of others. You feel a lump in your throat and crush the note in your hand. You can still save her. The trouble is, unlike in the beginning, when you had just started treating her, you don't think she can recover from this. Her past that won't let go. She may have left Auschwitz's walls, but the walls of Auschwitz have never left her. They have kept her prisoner day and night, tormenting her with nightmares of the past.

You can still save her.

Or you can set her free.

You hold her pale hand and ask yourself, what she would have done. A few seconds pass and you have your answer.

ONE

AUSCHWITZ. MARCH 1942

Through the wooden planks of the cattle car, golden slivers of light probed the darkness. Standing, all of them, shoulder to shoulder in this unbearable, tense silence for hours on end, swaying as one organism whenever the train took a sharp turn. Every such turn was accompanied by the groans of those smothered against the planks and was inevitably followed by the stench of the refuse splashing from the overflowing bucket in the corner. Not a single curtain to preserve one's dignity when using it. Cattle—that's what they'd been reduced to. Meat for slaughter and little else. Sweat and fear. The entire car stank of it. There was no escaping this rat trap, no losing herself in the past. That very past was the reason she'd ended up here.

Orli closed her eyes, trying to pinpoint the moment when her life had taken a wrong turn and set her on this path leading straight to the bowels of hell, judging by the looks of it. Was it her joining the German Communist Youth? Or marrying Fritz, that two-faced Nazi swine... Though, in her defense, when she had married him, he was a fellow Communist Youth member, just as bright-eyed and idealistic as she was. No one could have predicted that he would shift his support from trade unions and the Women's Lib movement to a brown SA uniform and a baton to go with it. No one could have imagined he would report his wife and former friends to the Nazis for an NSDAP membership pin.

During her first year in Ziegenhain women's prison, Orli had still wondered how her scum of a husband lived with himself. By the time she'd been transferred to Ravensbrück some four years later, she had ceased thinking of him altogether. She had only muttered an indifferent "hm" when one of the camp's overseers had informed her that Friedrich-Wilhelm Reichert had divorced her and gone on about her business in the camp infirmary. Good riddance to bad rubbish, as far as she was concerned.

Now, she could hardly remember what his face looked like. With a chilling lack of any real interest, Orli wondered if she would recognize him at all if she saw him again.

What a hoot it would be if once again he had switched uniform, only this time from a brown SA to a gray-green SS Totenkopf one and would meet her on the platform of whatever new camp they'd been shipped off to.

Orli swayed as the cattle train finally rumbled to a stop. For an instant, there was nothing but frantic running to and fro outside, with an occasional shout and the hiss of a whip. At last, with a resounding clang, the door was unlocked and pushed open by several pairs of grimy hands. Half-blind and momentarily disoriented, she stumbled out of the train car, her legs weak and unsteady.

From the nearby forest, March fog rolled in thick waves. As though ghostly apparitions, prisoners in striped uniforms emerged from it, just to be swallowed by it once more. All around Orli, the air was thick with the stench of death and decay. Under their SS superiors' watchful eyes, black-clad Kapos began prodding the new arrivals with their batons, barking orders at them in their native languages. It was a

Babylon of hellish proportions and made Ravensbrück look like a summer camp in comparison. Orli's heart sank as she realized her worst fears had become a reality—she had been brought to Auschwitz.

In Ravensbrück, she had heard stories of the notorious camp. SS wardens had used it as a means of "raising the morale" whenever the inmates failed to meet production quotas: "Keep being lazy scum. See how fast we put you on a train to Auschwitz, where they shall put you to good use, as oven kindling."

Orli had never paid such threats any heed. The SS needed workforce, not corpses. However, now, as she watched smoke rise from a chimney just visible from the tracks and felt greasy, foul-smelling ash smear on her fingers, she felt cold, primeval fear harden on her like plaster.

Now wouldn't it be ironic if the oven-kindling threats turned out to be true, Orli thought, and felt a lump of terror in her throat. So many years in and out of prisons and camps, so many years of seeing it all, and here she stood, shivering with nerves, together with these innocent Jews still clad in their civilian dress. Hardened criminal, whom the state had refused to let out upon serving out her four-year sentence and shipped off to Ravensbrück on protective custody orders, as someone far too dangerous, far too gone to rehabilitate.

Hardened criminal, my foot...

As she neared the front of the line, Orli could see a large building with a sign that read *"Desinfektionsanlage"* above the entrance. Her heart sank even further as her legs all but refused to move forward. It was much too close to the smoking chimney, much too real, with its red brick that stank of death; Orli could swear it did.

But there was no time to dwell on it as she was pushed inside the building. A group of SS men barked orders at the new arrivals, telling them to strip down and hand over their clothes to the *Sonderkommando*. With stiff fingers, Orli struggled with her Ravensbrück-issued striped dress, suddenly longing for its comfort; longing even for the place that had provided it. It had become a home away from home. She had friends there. Here, everything was alien. Alien and threatening throughout, with unfamiliar faces, unfamiliar barracks, unfamiliar rules of survival—a death camp; not a detention one, not anymore.

More hoarse orders. More cold wooden batons prodding their backs slick with the sweat of utter terror. Before long, they were herded into a large room with pipes running alongside its walls. For some time, there was nothing but silence so thick and palpable, Orli swore she could have sliced it with a knife. Then, something rumbled through the pipes, some ancient beast crawling through the metal, growling its guttural threats as it slithered closer and closer. A sharp smell of ammonia hit Orli's nostrils, twitching like those of a cornered animal.

In their uncontrolled terror, some of the women lost control of their bladders. They, too, must have heard rumors of the gas chambers and jokes of oven kindling. Those who didn't appeared to be more concerned with preserving their modesty rather than freezing with fright in what could have easily been the last moments of their lives.

But then, suddenly, after much rumbling, the pipes sprayed water from all directions, drenching them from head to toe. Orli gasped as the cold water hit her, making her teeth chatter uncontrollably. But at least it was only that—water. Not gas, which the same Ravensbrück wardens had taunted them with. As its rivulets ran down her grimy skin, Orli exhaled a ragged breath and closed her eyes, unclenching her fists in overpowering relief.

Next, another room. They were prodded along at a speed that allowed no thinking, only following the orders barked at them by the SS and their underlings. Orli saw a vat full of a vivid green disinfectant that looked suspiciously like acid, capable of melting one's very skin off the bones. It must have appeared just as questionable to the first young girl in line for she planted her feet firmly on the ground and refused to budge, even as an SS man brandished his gun in front of her face. It took two *Sonderkommando* inmates to grab her and dunk her in the vat as she continued to struggle for her very life. After ten long seconds, they pulled her out. Spluttering and coughing, but very much alive and unharmed.

When her turn came, Orli tried to hold her breath and squeeze her eyes shut as a *Sonderkommando*'s hand pushed her head under, but she still emerged half-blind, coughing and gagging from the liquid so many of them would share that day.

"Enjoying your *mikvah*, my Jewish princesses?" one of the Kapos brayed with laughter as he dunked a girl of barely sixteen into the green sludge.

Orli swiped at her face and turned away.

Another march of their pitiful, naked ranks. This time to a warehouse of sorts, where two inmates hurled clothes and underthings at them seemingly without any rhyme or reason. Orli's dress was a striped one but three sizes too big. Other girls regarded their shirts with unconcealed, alarmed wonder. Khaki green, with high collars, obviously of a military cut, but not German, that was for certain. Next to Orli, a woman put her finger through a hole in her new attire. Orli noticed faded brown surrounding it but said nothing when the woman inquired quietly as to what this was.

"Nail polish, to be sure," the uniform-distributing inmate replied, grinning like a viper. "The Soviet type."

The woman was Jewish, a civilian. She nodded, confused but somewhat pacified, and proceeded down the line.

Orli glowered at the inmate, but he only shrugged, smiled even wider and made a sweeping gesture with his hand.

"To the photo atelier, my lady."

Another barrack, with tables and rows of filing cabinets this time. Bespectacled inmates writing and typing fastidiously as the only SS supervisor smoked, perched atop one of the desks, legs in shiny black jackboots swaying lightly in time with the music pouring from the radio.

An inmate functionary searched for her name and conviction in the list that must have arrived on the same train as Orli did.

"Aurelia Reichert. Political." He nodded. "Number 502."

Another inmate immediately slammed a white piece of cloth with a downturned red triangle and black 502 on Orli's chest. "Sew it on after you leave here."

Then a chair, a metal rod sticking from the wall. An inmate photographer pressing her head against its flat back.

"Face toward the wall. Kerchief off."

A flash.

"Face me."

Another flash.

A young girl, number 503, regarded the white cloth in her hands in puzzlement. She had the biggest eyes, which, framed with long velvet lashes, gave her the appearance of an innocent doe looking lost and visibly frightened without her mother, alone in a forest full of predators, so very tender and so easy to kill. And yet, as Orli looked on, she approached that very predator in his SS uniform, simply because she was much too innocent to know better, and searched for help where only death could be found: "Where am I to get sewing supplies?"

Without removing the cigarette from his hand, the SS man backhanded her with such force, she slammed into the opposite desk, sending a neat stack of papers atop it flying. As she was sliding down to the floor, wild eyes on the uniformed man, a hand holding her broken lips, an inmate functionary was picking the papers up in great haste.

"Kerchief on. Face two-quarters to the side. Smile."

Orli followed the instructions without a single word uttered.

Outside the barrack, she paused. When number 503 emerged, still far too stunned to speak, she pulled her to one side.

"In a camp, and particularly this one, never ask the SS any questions. You're fortunate he didn't shoot you."

As they headed toward the barracks, 503 followed Orli like a shadow on her long, colt-like legs. She stuck to her even as they entered the two-story barracks, in which the smell of stale urine and feces was overpowering.

The bunks were stacked three-high, with barely enough room to sit up. Orli found a spot on the top bunk, and climbed up, her muscles aching and her stomach empty. Quietly, cowering like a pitiful pup, 503 climbed after her and nestled next to Orli's legs.

"What's your name?" Orli asked after a few minutes of silence.

"Miriam."

"I'm Orli."

As she lay there, staring up at the ceiling, Orli realized that she had entered a world of madness. A world where human life had no value, where cruelty was the norm, and where death was a constant companion. She knew that she had to fight to survive, to cling to her humanity in the face of such brutality.

Orli closed her eyes, her mind reeling with the events of the past few days. She had been torn from the world she had known for the last four years; she had been thrown into a nightmare, a place where the only certainty was suffering. Why now? Was she truly becoming such a threat to the Ravensbrück authorities? True, they had formed a sort of a clique, she and a few other political inmates, but it was nothing but ordinary friendship. They minded their own affairs at the infirmary and didn't antagonize the authorities. It was the Soviet Red Army women who were a veritable thorn in the SS wardens' side. It was they who marched in their prideful military formations to work details and back, and sang their defiant songs and spoke Russian among themselves, even after being whipped multiple times for not using German. But it wasn't them who'd been transferred. It was she, Orli.

"Damn it all to hell," she muttered under her breath and wiped her hands down her face.

She was exhausted beyond any measure and yet refused to give up. They wished for her to roll over and die? Hard luck. She would fight tooth and nail to survive. She would cling to hope, no matter how dim, and she would hold onto her humanity, no matter how much they tried to take it from her.

As she drifted off to sleep, Orli knew that the road ahead would be long and treacherous. But she also knew that she was not alone, that there were others like her, fighting to survive; she only had to find them. And she swore to herself that, somehow, some way, she would make it out of this hell alive.

TWO

Orli had never been trained as a nurse, let alone a doctor. But it had mattered little to the SS at Ravensbrück, who had assigned her to the infirmary with the same indifference they assigned inmates to other work details. When she had tried to explain her lack of qualifications, she'd been slapped across the mouth and that had put an end to the discussion. That was all she had brought with her to Auschwitz: knowing when to shut her mouth in front of the authorities and her Ravensbrück "medical degree." Two years of residency, courtesy of the Third Reich.

Perhaps that was the reason why she stepped forward when an inmate with a harassed look about him called in a hoarse voice for anyone with medical experience. Perhaps that or the fact that the alternative was an outside construction crew allocated to building the second concentration camp, and Orli knew from experience that their life expectancy was a month at best.

She didn't speak much; never had. Observed a lot, took it all in, just as she did during her very first roll-call here at Auschwitz. One ear attuned to the *Blockälteste*—their block leader—calling their numbers out and the other listening closely to the banging just outside the camp perimeter, opposite direction from the entrance and the train tracks.

As they stood under the dome of the heavy gray sky, trembling uncontrollably in their thin dresses, Orli roved her gaze around the *Appellplatz*. Each brick block was two stories high, and mostly men surrounded her, their numbers going up in thousands, compared to her 502. Their women's transport must have been one of the first, if not *the* first. But there wasn't enough space here; Orli was sure they must be expanding.

It was then that the harassed medic stepped forward and interrupted Orli's inner monologue.

"Anyone with a medical degree?"

Women looked at each other, but no one stepped forward. They were convicted felons—prostitutes, that was, or sheltered Jewish women who were raised to be homemakers instead of workers. No nurses among them.

Orli regarded the man in his striped uniform and white armband with pity, threw another glance at the back of the camp from where the sound of sledgehammers carried far and loud in the crisp morning air and pushed her way forward between the rows of women.

"Two years of infirmary experience, Herr Doktor. KL Ravensbrück."

He didn't question her further; only nodded, with apparent relief, to Orli's block elder and looked up at an SS man supervising the assignment of work details. A sort of silent exchange passed between the two men. During this time, the inmate shifted nervously from one foot to another, pleading with the SS silently with his red-rimmed eyes. The only reason why inmates were called to such "kosher" positions was to become someone's replacement. Someone who was no longer among the living and definitely not due to natural causes.

In response, the SS man cringed, gestured to Orli's dress as an indication of her gender. No women were permitted in men's details; Orli knew that much from her experience as a "hardened criminal." And yet, the situation must have been dire indeed for the inmate infirmary, for the SS man in charge shook his head but eventually nodded his consent.

Orli suddenly wondered if it was he who had shot the previous assistant medic or sent him to the gas chambers and now had to face the music. He had that look about him, of someone who killed easy and without mercy yet slept like a babe at night, not a shadow of remorse gnawing on his rotten soul.

As soon as he waved them off, Orli hurried after the Auschwitz physician, hoping not to lose her camp-issued shoes that were two sizes too big. Men's—further evidence to support her theory that women hadn't been incarcerated here before.

The infirmary was a small, cramped building that was located toward the edge of the camp. Seemingly indistinguishable from the other brick barracks but with a wooden cart parked outside. Even if the physician noticed Orli's eyes dart toward it, he made no comment. Nor did he need to: Orli had spent enough time in Ravensbrück to identify a death cart when she saw one.

Questions burned a hole in Orli's chest. *How's the mortality rate? How many days do patients have to show improvement before the SS strike them off the list? Is this a true infirmary or another "rabbit farm"?* Yet, she knew to keep her mouth shut. At a new camp, it was of paramount importance to be on one's best behavior if one wished to last longer than a month.

Inside the infirmary, the stench of sickness and death hung heavily in the air. The walls were lined with rows of narrow cots, each one occupied by a sick or injured man. Orli could see that many of them were emaciated, their skin stretched tight over their bones. Some were covered in bruises and cuts, while others had deep, infected wounds that were oozing pus.

At the sight of the physician, many hands reached out in silent pleas. He let them brush his prisoner uniform but kept moving forward, eyes straight, mouth a sharp unyielding line preventing the scream of desperation from breaking out. At least, such was Orli's impression.

"This is the medicine cabinet," he said, yanking a thin curtain away from the wall. A lone wooden cupboard stood there with a simple red cross painted in its middle. Only the very first shelf was stocked, and hardly at all. Orli counted several rolls of aspirin, exactly nine rolls of bandages and two lone bottles of iodine solution.

"No alcohol?" she asked, her voice just above a whisper.

"There was a bottle, but one sod sold it to someone for two pieces of bread." The physician regarded the cupboard through his spectacles.

"One of the patients?"

"Patients?" The physician snorted softly. "No. Look at them. They're in no condition to trade anything. My former assistant."

"He won't do it again, will he?"

"The Kapos bashed his skull in, so I would say no. And please, don't do anything as foolish either." He slightly inclined his head. "Finding trained personnel here is a headache. I'd appreciate it if you spared me the pains."

Orli understood then her previous convictions were correct: the reason she'd lucked out in being assigned to the infirmary that morning. Someone had to die so that she could take his place. Grim Auschwitz reality, staring her square in the eyes.

"Don't worry, Herr Doktor. I like my skull intact."

. . .

As the day wore on, Orli followed the physician like a shadow, absorbing, learning, and listening to the list of instructions that came from his permanently exhausted voice. It soon became clear that Auschwitz infirmary differed from Ravensbrück. Instead of women, men regarded her either with ill-concealed mistrust or embarrassment. Instead of scabies, broken bones or flesh slashed open by a horsewhip only the SS carried. The physician could do little more than clean wounds with water, apply iodine and tell them to rest. Whether they healed or grew infected was anyone's guess.

"The SS *Doktor* comes for inspections every morning and evening," the physician told Orli while tending to the men. "Your task is to follow him closely and take down numbers for him, if I'm not here. There will be three columns: one for the discharged, one for those who are to remain here and one for the difficult cases."

If Orli hadn't been a camp old-timer herself, she wouldn't have caught onto the slight change in the physician's voice.

"Those, Herr Doktor sees himself," he proceeded. "In a separate room. Orderlies will carry those unable to walk there."

Orli nodded, asking no further questions.

The inmate, whose buttocks the physician was presently tending to—all purple and angry-red splotches of flesh beaten until the Kapo's hand had grown tired—issued a certain chortle. "Since when have you become so impossibly formal, Mark? Difficult cases, my ass! Unable to walk, unable to work. Phenol to the heart and off to the crematorium they go on a cart pulled by two merry ponies." Twisting himself to see Orli better, he pointed a grimy finger at his chest, not embarrassed by his exposed state in the slightest. "One of the ponies."

"It's not for her benefit that I'm so 'impossibly formal,' you feebleminded donkey," the physician hissed, annoyed. "I have other patients here besides you, you know. And I wouldn't like them agitated."

The cart-puller shrugged. "They know where they are. They see the smoke as well as we do."

"Keep at it and I'll personally put you in the third category at the evening inspection."

"Ha, no can do, Herr Doktor," the cart-puller laughed, tugging at his uniform tunic. "I'm a political just like you are. It's against their racial policies, killing their own stock."

"How would you know? Have you written the laws?" the physician mocked.

"I read newspapers."

"Bare-assed intellectual."

"One yourself."

At one moment, Orli was grinning, listening to similar exchanges, and in the next, a work gang marched through the gates and brought with them one of their own, crushed by machinery or beaten by the ruthless Kapos—the first victim followed by a crushing tide of others, threatening to overwhelm their tiny hospital. All at once, the infirmary was an inferno of screams, moans and pleas—a cacophony of horror accompanied by a camp orchestra playing a brassy march outside. Orli's limbs were hanging limply by her side.

"Sorry, girl," Mark said, spreading his arms in a helpless gesture, indicating the veritable sea of people. He needed a fellow physician, not a student. "You're on your own."

With a rush of anxiety in her chest, Orli turned to the nearest man. He was sitting on the floor, his face white as chalk as he held onto his shoulder.

"What happened?" Orli asked, all business now. She would digest all of this later, back at her barracks.

"I'm from the carpentry detail. We carried a log, my partner and I," he breathed, visibly in pain. "It was much too heavy for him. His legs gave in. Crushed his chest instantly. When I crawled from under it, I managed to roll it off him, but there was nothing doing." He gestured vaguely around his mouth with his good hand. "Bloody foam, gushing and gushing... He expired within moments." He lowered his eyes and suddenly added, "Lucky sod."

Orli made no comment. Just hoped he wouldn't notice how her fingers trembled when she moved to undo the buttons on his striped tunic. "I'll have to remove this."

"Yes, yes, of course." Cringing and gasping in pain, he helped her as much as his dislocated shoulder allowed.

Dislocated shoulder and the arm, visibly broken just below his elbow.

The inmate, too, saw the bone poking through the skin and cocked his head, swallowing several times. "Why, would you look at that," he muttered to no one in particular.

Orli looked at the arm and at the curtain at the end of the barrack, concealing the cupboard with its meager supplies.

"All right." She nodded, gathering herself. First, the shoulder. A simple dislocation—that she could fix. After, she would worry about the broken bone. "Here's the tricky part. Ordinarily I'd have to pull you by the arm to set your shoulder back into its socket, but since it's broken..."

The longer one thought, the darker the thoughts would get as they crept into one's mind on their spidery feet. Orli hated the cobwebs they spun worse than any visible horror she was surrounded with. Anything visible, tangible could be dealt with. It was those webs that she dreaded. They would paralyze and suck the very life out of her if she allowed them.

And so, without any further thinking, she grasped the man by his forearm and yanked as hard as she could, just as Marthe at Ravensbrück had taught her. A shrill scream momentarily silenced the barrack. Orli saw Mark whip around. Her patient closed his mouth and regarded his shoulder in stunned amazement. Mark turned back to his own case once again.

She did good, she read in his back turned to her as a universal display of trust.

She did good, she breathed out in relief and rose to her feet. "I'll be right back."

Her patient nodded. The color was slowly returning to his ashen face. He was almost smiling at her, this angel that had descended upon their cursed land just at the right moment.

More hands reached for her, voices pleading for help, but in Orli's mind, only one thought pounded: the splint. Through the throngs of injured men, she sprinted toward the medicine cabinet and grabbed a roll of dressing. Teeth biting hard at her lip, she looked around frantically, until her eyes returned to the cabinet itself. To be sure, there were no such luxuries as splints or anything to make a cast out of here, but there were empty shelves. If they weren't utilized one way, she'd just have to utilize them in another.

With that, Orli planted her foot at the back of the open cabinet and grasped at the ledge of the lowest shelf. It took all her strength to get the ledge to start budging; whoever had built the damned thing had done much too good a job, but still, tearing her nails to the quick, Orli finally pried the ledge off the shelf and banged it several times on the concrete floor until it broke into two uneven parts. Sharp short nails were still sticking out from both ends, but there was no helping it.

Her patient looked on, bemused, when Orli set her makeshift splint and dressing next to him.

"You'll have to bite into one of these sticks and hold onto something because this will hurt," she warned him.

"Worse than the shoulder?" He grasped onto the edge of the nearest cot and dutifully placed one of the makeshift splints in his mouth.

"You have a bone sticking out. What do you think?" she asked and, before he could reply precisely what he thought, pulled hard at the forearm. The man screamed through his wooden gag and then dropped it as his head lolled to one side.

Passed out and good for him, Orli thought and quickly dug

into the skin near the wound, setting the bone where it belonged to the best of her abilities.

By the time he came to, his arm was already in a splint, tightly bandaged and smelling reassuringly of iodine.

Orli had long moved down the line.

THREE

In the evening, just as Mark had promised, an SS physician made an appearance. Orli was in the middle of cauterizing her patient's wounds—a stitching kit was apparently an unnecessary luxury by Auschwitz standards—when the man pushed her hand away and leapt to his feet, freezing to attention just like the rest of them.

Against the brightness of the entrance, a lone dark figure stood. With a long, still-hot nail in her hand, Orli straightened slowly, suspecting authority but not quite seeing the rank. Inmates jumped in this manner to pretty much anyone higher than them on a totem pole: Kapos, block elders, even some camp functionaries who had made it their business to torment their fellow prisoners worse than the SS just to stay in their higher-ups' good graces. But only when Mark rushed by her and slapped Orli lightly on the back of her head—*Stand to attention, girl; are you mad?*—did it dawn on her that the authority was the dreaded SS.

As the man glided into the infirmary barrack, Orli studied him discreetly from the corner of her eye. A middle-aged man of average height, bespectacled; hair—she couldn't tell. He never bothered removing his uniform cap, just as he didn't bother speaking with inmates. A single glance over and a number of fingers raised for Mark to write down in the list on his clipboard. Orli saw him pause by her carpenter fellow and regard his arm in a splint. Her heart jumped into her throat when the SS physician asked him in a soft and almost kind voice to which commando he belonged.

"Birkenau carpentry, Herr Untersturmführer," the carpenter reported, eyes gleaming wildly, all enthusiasm all of a sudden. "I'm heading back to work tomorrow."

To Orli's astonishment and horror, the SS physician smiled. Those were the worst kind, the sweet chameleons who hid their true nature behind such theatrics; that much she'd learned by now. She'd take the screaming ones, the insulting ones, the brandishing-whips ones, instead of these smiling ones, any day. From the screaming ones, one could walk away with a split lip but their life intact. It was those soft-gloved types that pacified one into blind trust, then plunged the knife, deep to the very hilt, into an exposed back as soon as it was turned on them. "But, my good fellow, just how are you planning to work with a broken arm?"

"I saw wood, Herr Untersturmführer. My right hand is perfectly intact to hold my end of a saw. And besides, the bone will heal in no time. The broken part shall calcify and will be even stronger. Nothing will be able to damage it then." He was blabbering now, also painfully aware that his very life was at stake.

It was strictly verboten, speaking when not spoken to, and to the SS even more so, but there was no stopping him now. Like a fish on a hook, he was thrashing in front of these cold, calculating eyes, and the sight of such sheer desperation churned acid in Orli's empty stomach, awakening something primal and very dark at the furthest corner of her mind.

The physician cocked his head, suddenly interested. "Have you studied medicine by any chance?"

"No, Herr Untersturmführer. I read it in some paper."

The physician nodded pensively, and slowly, like a Roman emperor, raised his hand to Mark.

Orli released a tremendous breath when she saw him holding only one finger up. The first category. The ones fortunate to be discharged.

He was almost away from him when suddenly the SS man swung round on his heel and took a second look at the carpenter's arm.

"Where did you get the splint?" His eyes were on Mark's now, narrowed ever so slightly.

Orli saw him open his mouth and close it slowly as he stared at the splint, as if only now realizing that it was there. Naturally, he had not the faintest idea where it had come from; nothing to say to the SS man impatiently tapping the tip of his boot shined to mirror perfection.

"It was me, Herr Untersturmführer," Orli said, stepping forward. "I put that splint on."

The SS man half-turned to her, only now seeing her in her full Auschwitz glory: striped dress stained with blood, white kerchief askew about her short chestnut hair, the nail in her hand still smelling faintly of singed human flesh.

"A woman?" he asked Mark.

"Herr Rapportführer permitted it. Only until they open the women's infirmary in Birkenau, Herr Untersturmführer," Mark added hastily, inclining his head.

"Since when is Palitzsch in charge of infirmaries?"

There must have been some power struggle going on between the two men, or one simply didn't like the other, it occurred to Orli. Just their luck, it would be them, the inmates, paying the price, as always.

"I asked you a question." His tone was casual, but Orli still saw a tremble slowly taking over Mark's entire body.

"It was my mistake, Herr Untersturmführer." Mark was a question mark now, hunched so low, his head all but hung on his chest.

"Your colleague made a mistake two days ago. Where is he now?"

"Dead, Herr Untersturmführer."

The SS physician nodded, satisfied, and turned to Orli, suddenly losing all interest in his latest victim. "Where did you work previously?"

"Ravensbrück, Herr Untersturmführer." Orli stared at his feet as prescribed.

He chuckled softly. "I mean, before your incarceration. Which hospital?"

For a split second, Orli thought of lying, but devil knew where this sod worked and who he knew. Being caught lying was a much worse offense than simple inexperience.

"Nowhere, Herr Untersturmführer. I was assigned to the infirmary once I arrived at Ravensbrück and learned from their physicians there."

"Field experience then, eh?" He smiled again. "All right. Sometimes it's even better. Where did you get the splint?"

Orli's eyes traveled slowly to the curtain hiding the medicine cabinet.

The SS man arched his brow, walked slowly past her and, with the very tip of his gloved finger, moved the curtain away, uncovering the bastardized piece of furniture.

Seeing its state for the first time, Mark slowly closed his eyes. *Didn't pay enough attention to the new girl. Didn't explain; didn't warn in time and now, tomorrow, he would have to head back to the Appellplatz and ask Herr Rapportführer for yet another medical worker, for this one would be dead, to be sure she would.* Orli read it all in the tragic lines creasing his kind, exhausted face.

"Breaking camp property for splints?" The SS physician was all smiles now, almost amused by such antics.

All Orli saw was the death's head insignia atop his uniform cap. Explaining anything, let alone talking back, would be sheer suicide. She'd heard precisely how Mark had talked to this man and adopted the same humble posture, lowered her eyes in the same expression of utmost servitude. "Forgive me, please, Herr Untersturmführer. I wasn't thinking of it that way... I only thought that my patient needed the splint. It was my mistake. I'll repair it, first chance."

"And what's with the nail?"

"For cauterizing wounds so that infection wouldn't set in. We don't have any stitching kits here; else, I would have used them, Herr Untersturmführer."

He regarded her for what seemed to be an infinitely long minute.

"Put in a request for restocking next time. If you continue with your improvisations, we'll be left without bunks or walls by the time they transfer you to Birkenau."

"*Jawohl*, Herr Untersturmführer." Orli beamed her widest, silliest grin.

"Told you they don't dispose of Germans as easily as they do of other races," the very first patient who Orli had seen Mark tending to that day winked at her once both Mark and the SS physician had moved into a room at the back of the barrack. Orderlies were presently bringing inmates there. Not a single one had walked out so far. "Had you been a Pole or, heaven forbid, a Jew, you would have been the first in that line," the man proceeded almost merrily. Now, with the SS physician gone, he was lying with his bare red buttocks in the air once again. "And ask Mark for a double dinner ration. He owes you that much."

"For what?" Orli asked.

"He knows," the man replied with yet another cryptic grin. "And now, go back to work, little doctor. Remember why you're here. You're here to help these people, to ease their suffering in whatever way you can. That's all that matters."

Orli nodded like an automaton, not quite expecting such profound insight from a bare-assed inmate, yet somewhat grateful for it.

As the evening wore on, Orli continued to tend to the sick and injured. She gave out more aspirin, bandaged and disinfected whatever she could and tried to comfort those who were in pain. She felt as though she was starting to get a better handle on things, that she was making some progress.

As the banging outside signaled dinner and the inmates with cauldrons hurried inside the infirmary, Orli collapsed into a chair at the physicians' station, utterly exhausted. She had worked from dawn till dusk, barely taking a break, and her body was screaming for rest. The SS physician was long gone.

Mark lowered himself heavily onto a stool opposite her, handing her two pieces of bread and some blood sausage to go with them: "Your share."

Despite her utter exhaustion, a starved animal reared its head inside of her at the very sight of food. Orli sank her teeth into the sausage first and, only after all of it was gone, leaned back in her chair as she munched on her bread bit by bit to make it last.

"My share for what?" she asked at long last. "Taking the blame for the cupboard? But I did break it. It was my fault."

Mark smiled over his bread. "No, not for the cupboard. For distracting Dr. Kremer. Making him lose count of category three inmates headed for euthanasia. Ordinarily, he counts them himself to make sure I don't 'forget' to put anyone on the list. You saved seven people today."

Orli stopped chewing. She'd thought Mark was a good physician working with an impossibly low inventory, but that was about it. Certainly not some hero who risked his very skin for his patients.

"What's your name?" he asked.

"Aurelia. Orli."

"Pleasure to make your acquaintance, Orli." He shook her hand across the rickety table. "And now, go back to your barrack. It's almost roll-call time."

Orli nodded, feeling suddenly lightheaded and almost punch-drunk from an emotion she couldn't quite identify. She made her way toward the door of the infirmary, her steps slow and unsteady.

As she stepped outside, she took a deep breath of fresh air, feeling the crisp chill of the March night on her face. She knew that she had a long way to go, that there would be many more long, exhausting days ahead of her. But she also knew that she was doing something important, something that mattered.

And for the first time since she had arrived at Auschwitz, Orli felt a glimmer of hope.

FOUR

Morning. Still so dark, it might as well have been night, but here their *Blockälteste* was, banging on a metal pipe and screaming at them to get their fat tails up before she did it for them.

"Up, up, lazy cows! Enough lounging about. Time to make yourselves useful to the Reich."

"Good morning to you too," Orli grumbled under her breath, causing Miriam to smile as she hustled down from their bunk.

In the few weeks that she had spent here, Orli still couldn't understand the nature of inmates such as their block elder, Johanna. They were both German, she and Orli, both appointed to somewhat privileged positions upon arrival, but it was precisely there that their similarities ended. Whereas Orli did her utmost to soothe and help not only her patients but the inmates around her—if not with actions, then with a kind word whenever she could—Johanna had made it a point of honor to degrade and abuse women under her charge worse than any SS could. Perhaps, it was a mere survival tactic. Or perhaps, Auschwitz had simply revealed her true, ugly nature—Orli had no sight into Johanna's heart. But, for some reason, this unnecessary abuse coming from the inside of their own barrack hurt worse than the abuse the Kapos and SS showered them with.

"Ten minutes until breakfast," Johanna continued to bellow as she stalked along the barrack. "I want this bedding in perfect order before you go wash your filthy mugs. Well?" She yanked some unfortunate girl down by her ankle, causing her to tumble onto the floor from the second-tier bunk. "Do you need a special invitation, or what?!"

"Johanna, you're just an image of motherhood, aren't you?" Silke, another German prisoner marked with an antisocial black triangle, called to her in a singsong voice. "How you remind me of fine Sunday mornings, when my *Mutti* would wake me up in the same gentle manner."

"Shut your trap, Silke." Johanna glared but didn't swipe at the cheeky girl.

Rumor had it, Silke was back at her old profession in the camp, only now she was trading favors with Kapos instead of regular customers.

Johanna was smart enough to know making an enemy out of someone without knowing just who was sweet on them was dangerous business.

Silke knew it too. As she was passing Johanna by, she blew a theatrical kiss to her, much to Orli's quiet satisfaction. Silke shared whatever treats her Kapos showered her with. She was an all right girl.

Achy from sleeping on wooden planks covered only by a thin straw-filled pellet, Orli and Miriam twisted their cracking backs this way and that as they waited for their turn in the crowded washroom of Auschwitz. It was a dimly lit affair, filled with the stench of human waste and sickness and mold decorating the walls in elaborate black and green designs. There was only one pipe, with several rusty faucets attached to it, a row of filthy sinks along the wall and, sardonically, a sign above all this indecency: *Cleanliness prevents diseases. Keep yourself clean at all times*. No soap. No towels. Only dozens of inmates crowding around the faucets, jostling and pushing each other in a desperate attempt to wash themselves before roll call.

It was there, in the blinding light of the overhead lamps, that Orli saw just how much Miriam had changed in the course of a few short weeks. The difference between a privileged detail and an "outside" construction detail reflected on the girl's drawn face as in some demented mirror as Orli stared at her, unable to keep her expression neutral. Instead of her former lean but strong physique of a typical teenager, with her gangly limbs and facial bone structure she was still growing into, Miriam now looked exhausted and sick. Her face was ashen and drawn, with lines etched into her skin that had aged her far beyond her years. In sunken sockets, two black eyes gleamed feverishly as she passed her hand over her thinning hair, suddenly self-conscious.

"What? That bad?" she asked Orli and broke into a fit of forced laughter that soon turned into coughing.

Orli shook her head. Her lips trembled as she forced them into a smile of encouragement. "How's work?" she asked.

Miriam shrugged, all mock nonchalance. "It's work."

"What do they have you do there?"

Another pitiful shrug. "Haul logs from one place to another. Mix concrete sometimes. Whatever occurs to them." She suddenly grinned and Orli couldn't help but feel horror wash over her as she saw that leathery skin stretch over a skull visible underneath it in what used to be a sweet, girlish face less than a month ago. "The good news is that we're building the women's infirmary. I've already claimed the first bunk once we finish. If I make it that long, that is."

"What nonsense! Of course you will," Orli said, all assurance on the outside and cold, sticky fear deep in her guts.

"Don't get me wrong. This," Miriam said, gesturing toward her Soviet-tunic uniform dress hanging off her as though there was nothing, no flesh, under it at all, only bones, "this is not contagious. But my coughing is. The authorities don't take too kindly to it. Spreading disease and all that. And besides, I'm Jewish. We're expendable. They've made it clear enough to us already."

She tried to smile once again, the brave girl, but Orli saw tears, big as pearls, standing in those deathly frightened, black eyes.

"I'll try to get you some medicine," she said with a determination she didn't quite feel.

Miriam smiled weakly, grateful for Orli's kindness but not quite believing in the possibility. Hadn't Orli told her, each night just before they would drift off to sleep, just how tough a job it was, begging literal crumbs out of Doktor Kremer? Hadn't she admitted that only ten percent of requested medicaments were approved by the SS physician, and the rest vetoed as something much too expensive to waste on human scum like them?

And yet, Orli refused to lose this battle to the Grim Reaper already hovering just over Miriam's shoulder with his scythe, no matter how uneven such forces were.

"I'll get it," she repeated, pushing Miriam to the sink that was now free. Herself, she'd just have to wash in the infirmary during lunch break. "You just wait and see."

The new nurse's name was Zuzana. She was a new arrival, a Slovak girl with close-set eyes and freshly shorn hair under a blue kerchief. They had begun the practice recently, as the conditions in the camp were growing progressively more cramped and lice infestation took on epidemic proportions. Being among the first female arrivals, Orli had been fortunate to avoid such a fate and still had all of her thick, dark hair about her, and yet it was Zuzana who had greeted her, an old-timer, as though she was a novice as soon as Orli stepped through the doors of the infirmary.

"Good morning! I'm Zuzana," she chirped, hugging a box of supplies to her side. "I'm a nurse here. I suppose we'll be working together?" she finished with a questioning tilt of her head.

Something about her manner rubbed Orli up the wrong way. An old camp instinct, developed through the years in captivity, set off a series of alarms in her mind. She eyed the box she'd practically begged from Doctor Kremer, all of the necessities nestled comfortably under the crook of the girl's arm, and felt a sudden urge to make a grab for it. Instead, she raised her eyes back to the new nurse and forced a smile, which no doubt came out dark and crooked. When all one thinks of is survival on a daily basis, one doesn't have much strength left to feign well-bred smiles for a stranger.

"I'm Orli. I'm a physician's assistant here. Do you have any medical experience then?"

From Zuzana, a crafty grin. "I told them I did."

"Do you?" Orli repeated.

"What's the difference? They didn't gas me like they did with the others, did they?"

The nonchalance with which she uttered those last words and, even more so, Zuzana's giddy, self-congratulatory chortle turned Orli's stomach. An opportunist, just as she suspected. Someone who'd step over still-warm bodies just to ensure her own survival, the worst kind of inmate one could wish to share working quarters with. Of course, Orli could report her to Mark, or Doctor Kremer even, but then Zuzana's death—lying was a capital offense here—would be on Orli's conscience.

To hell with her. They'll find her out sooner or later and then it won't be my business what they do to her.

"I'll take it." Orli reached for the box.

"Oh, it's no trouble at all. I can sort it out myself."

So could Mark's former assistant, who was missing a good chunk of his skull after Palitzsch was finished with him, Orli thought but said nothing. The idea of letting Zuzana get caught trading medicaments for food on her very first day was tempting indeed. But then someone's voice called out to her from the depths of the infirmary, asking if she'd managed to procure the sulfa drugs she'd been promising him for almost a week now, and, reluctantly, Orli dismissed it—patients came first.

"Not allowed. Only physicians and their assistants can sort the medicaments." This time she made a no-nonsense grab for the box and felt instantly better once it was secured in her own embrace. "But thank you all the same."

"Of course." Zuzana smiled slowly. "Always ready to help."

I'm sure you are.

Orli was about to take her leave when the new nurse caught her sleeve, pulling her close with a conspiratorial look about her. "What is the main doctor's name?"

"Mark," Orli replied, somewhat confused.

Zuzana waved her reply off and rolled her eyes expressively. "No, not him. The SS Doktor."

"*Ach.*" Orli stared deep into the girl's eyes, but the black pools betrayed nothing. "Doctor Kremer."

"Doctor Kremer," Zuzana repeated, committing the name to her memory. "What kind of man is he?"

Orli glared at her. "He's an SS man," she replied and, after freeing her sleeve, walked away from the new arrival.

The further, the better.

FIVE

Orli tried to focus on her work in the infirmary, but her mind kept drifting back to the events of the past few days. She couldn't shake the feeling that something was off, that there was something sinister brewing just beneath the surface.

Ever since Zuzana had joined their infirmary staff, things had been different. Orli couldn't quite put her finger on it, but there was something about the new Slovak girl that made her uneasy. She seemed too eager to please, too willing to do whatever it took to curry favor with the SS physician. The worst part was that she diligently monitored all the numbers Dr. Kremer designated to the doomed category three.

With mounting horror, Orli watched Zuzana point an eager finger at an unfortunate patient Mark was risking his very life to save.

"I gave you twenty numbers." Dr. Kremer shifted the gaze of his cold, bespectacled eyes to Mark after checking his clipboard. "There's only nineteen here."

As it was, nineteen barely-breathing, gray-skinned apparitions were already lined up near Dr. Kremer's "exam room."

"Phenol room is more like it," Mark had grumbled one day and Orli couldn't agree more.

Now, all of her hackles stood to attention as she watched Zuzana reach for the list, so very eager to "help," just as she'd promised.

"Herr Doktor, allow me?" she addressed the SS physician, ignoring Mark altogether as though he didn't exist, despite the fact that it was him holding the clipboard. "I have a very good memory."

A quick scan of the numbers; an even quicker scan of the inmates looking anywhere but those beady black eyes.

"Ah, found it!" Zuzana declared victoriously, pointing at an elderly man all but invisible behind the protective backs of his two sons.

They'd been unfortunate to catch typhoid, all three of them. The sons had already pulled through and were recovering; it was the father who needed more time, just a couple more days till his fever broke. Better yet, Orli and Mark had just been celebrating obtaining apple cider vinegar for him to mix with his water to help restore his liver and intestinal functions. But Zuzana was already at his bedside, pulling at the man's frail arm with all the cheerfulness in the world.

"He can't stand," the eldest son tried to protest gently, his entire body pulled tight as a string ready to snap. "He's delirious; very high fever—"

"Well, don't just stand there!" Zuzana dropped the man's arm and stepped back. "Help him up. Carry him to Herr Doktor's door."

"Please," the youngest son whispered, barely moving his lips. Orli's chest clenched at the sight of tears filling the young man's eyes. "He's our father..."

"So help him then!" Zuzana looked at him as one would at a silly child. "That's the very reason Herr Doktor put him on the list—to give him a shot to make him feel better! Go on, get him up!"

The fact that Dr. Kremer looked on without interfering didn't escape Orli's attention. She was the best little helper he could count on, no doubt about it, a bitter, sardonic thought crossed her mind.

Certainly, the SS man must have thought the same.

"I think it would be best if you were in charge of the list from now on," he told Zuzana without taking his eyes off Mark.

Defeated, life itself gone out of him, Mark surrendered the clipboard to the triumphant nurse.

Should have reported her, Orli thought in anguish as she watched two sobbing sons carry their father to imminent death.

Should have reported her, she would keep berating herself every evening thereafter when even more men followed the old man's fate.

Should have reported her when she had the chance, but now it was too late.

Orli could only hope it wasn't too late for Miriam. Something told her that now, with Zuzana around, smuggling medicine for the girl would amount to a small miracle.

"How could she?" Orli kept muttering under her breath like a broken record.

The day was rolling to its early grave, twilight creeping from the woods to shroud its body in darkness. On the physicians' station's table, a single candle burned, throwing frantic shadows all over the cubicle. Like the souls of the dead trapped here, desperate to get out, prisoners even in death.

"You aren't new here." Mark pushed Orli's two pieces of bread and some sausage toward her. "Eat and don't ask idiotic questions."

"That's precisely it." She picked up the bread and stared at it as if searching for answers in its grainy texture. "I'm not new and I still can't get it into my mind, how can one just—" She dropped the bread and gestured desperately toward the ward, quiet as a graveyard behind the closed doors. At mealtimes, no one spoke a word. All the mouths were much too busy eating. "He was just an elderly man. A recovering man. He had his sons there."

"Do you have children?" Mark asked.

Orli couldn't see his eyes behind the spectacles, only the fire reflecting in their glasses.

"No." A grim grin twisted her mouth. "Fortunately for those children, I didn't have."

"How so? I watch you take care of your patients—you'd make a wonderful mother."

"I'd still be in jail, thanks to my *Arschloch* of an ex-husband, and they would be stuck with him, and heavens know what he would have turned them into."

"I want to ask and I don't."

Orli smiled in gratitude at the physician and his polite ways. Once again, she wondered which cosmopolitan city he had been plucked from and exactly how he had ended up here, and for which sins. But, just like him, she didn't pry.

"There's no secret about it." Orli tore a piece of a bread and put it into her mouth. "Everyone in Ravensbrück knew my story. May as well tell you."

"Only if you wish."

"I fell in love with a comrade."

"A fellow communist?"

Orli nodded. Swallowed hard. The bread was suddenly scratching her throat that would always feel sore from the infinite tears of betrayal she'd cried all those years ago. "We were so young and naïve. Wanted to change the world for the better. No more Kaiser and no more elites plundering the money from the working class." A dreamy smile transformed her face, softened its features in the candlelight as memories flashed like an old movie with every blink of her eyelids. "We marched for unions and women's liberation and for a world in which everyone was equal and working for the common good. Fritz was such a brilliant orator. He was always the first to climb the truck bed and grab a megaphone and pour his entire heart into words like only he could. People loved him and followed him—so did I."

"What happened?"

For a few moments, Orli sat still as a granite statue of some glorious past, just before the sledgehammer of a new regime crashed into it. "The Nazis."

Mark nodded knowingly, sympathetically. *Should have guessed*, his expression read.

"I was so in love with one side of him, I completely ignored the other. I only saw how brilliant a leader he was and didn't wish to acknowledge that he was only so good because he loved power. I listened to his impassioned speeches and didn't realize he was in love with the sound of his own voice and the adoration of the others. I admired him for the ease with which he could adapt to anything and didn't see that it was only for his own advantage. Refused to see the power-hungry, ambitious, cruel, heartless politician-in-making until he showed up on the doorstep of our apartment in a brown SA uniform. And even then, I stared at him and smiled like an idiot and thought it was all just some stupid joke I couldn't get through my thick skull—" She stopped abruptly there, buried her face in her hands, wiped them down her cheeks and tossed her head in annoyance, at herself more than anyone else. "He did give me a chance to renounce my 'wayward ways'; I ought to give him that," Orli added with great irony. "It all went south quickly after I spat at his new shiny jackboots and told him to go hang himself. He went and reported me instead. That was back in 1936, I've been an inmate ever since."

"Six years," Mark whispered incredulously.

"Six years." Orli nodded and buried the almost-untouched rations in her pocket—for Miriam. "Six years and I still can't believe what she did today. Should have learned better from Fritz's example, but, I suppose, I'm just as much of an idiot as I used to be."

"You're not an idiot." Mark's words stopped her, already at the door. "You just want to see good in people even if they're rotten to the core."

Orli made no reply; just walked out of there, feeling lighter somehow.

It was summer solstice—the perfect night for what Orli had in mind. The SS had been celebrating since early morning. Half of them were on leave; the other half, drunk and merry, entertaining themselves with throwing bits of blood sausage into the dust and watching inmates fight for them like starved dogs, as a Kapo, appointed specifically for such a mission, wrote down bets and kept score.

Mouthwatering smells of roast meat and freshly baked bread wafted from the SS canteen, penetrating even the usual stench of the infirmary. But it wasn't roast duck that Orli was thinking of. Ever since early morning, her eyes had been trained on the thin curtain hiding the treasure itself—sulfa drugs, courtesy of Dr. Kremer. He had finally seen reason, once typhoid began to spread not only all over the camp population but to Kapos and SS who came in contact with them. Orli had begged and pleaded with him for weeks to stock the infirmary shelves with the lifesaving drugs, but it was only after she'd changed tactics and voiced concerns for his health—"Rapportführer

Palitzsch got it too and he's so poorly; we can't have that happening to you, Herr Doktor"—that he finally conceded.

"I know he's doing poorly, no need to remind me," he'd barked, but then must have ordered the drugs all the same. For, the very next day, an orderly had been waiting for Orli at the infirmary doors with boxes of medicaments stacked neatly on a small cart.

"All accounted for," the inmate orderly had said in a voice that suggested that the warning was not his, but Kremer's.

Orli had nodded. She hadn't expected anything less for such a treasure.

Now, as the evening rolled in from the forest and colored the camp in shades of rust and blood, Orli couldn't help but count down the minutes till she heard the dinner gong. She'd gone without food since the morning, feigning stomach sickness just to have a few minutes to herself while Zuzana and Mark ate their meal.

Sure enough, Zuzana didn't refuse the second helping when dinnertime came. Orli left the physicians' cubicle starved but exhilarated all the same. For Miriam, her poor Miriam who she'd watched wasting away day after day, she didn't mind sacrificing her entire day's ration.

Disappearing behind the curtain, Orli quickly pocketed a small roll of sulfa drugs from the very back so that it wouldn't be noticeable at first glance. And later tonight, Mark would strike it off the list, writing a report to Dr. Kremer in his neat, calligraphic handwriting, explaining that the drugs went to typhoid case number so-and-so—they had agreed upon this already. After the evening they had spent trading memories or, rather, Orli offering hers, she felt the camaraderie with Mark grow by the day. He could rely on her and she on him, and neither would think twice of risking one's hide for the other; Mark had let Orli know that much when she'd asked him to take this risk for Miriam.

But as she was turning to leave, Orli heard footsteps behind her. She whirled around, her heart racing, and saw Zuzana standing in the makeshift doorway.

"What are you doing here?" Orli asked, trying to keep her voice steady.

Zuzana looked at her with a strange expression on her face, a mix of curiosity and suspicion. "I could ask you the same thing," she said, her eyes fixed on the cupboard behind Orli's back.

Orli felt a surge of panic wash over her. "I was going over the inventory to see if I need to put anything on the list for Herr Doktor," she said, keeping her voice as steady as possible.

Zuzana studied her for a moment, then nodded slowly. "Inventory, is it?" she said with half a grin, her voice low and conspiratorial.

Orli released a breath she was holding as she made her way out of the infirmary but she couldn't shake the feeling that Zuzana was up to something, that she was playing a dangerous game.

Later that night, as they stood for their evening roll call, Orli discreetly pushed two pills into Miriam's palm. It was wet with sweat; she'd been burning with fever for several days now, barely standing on her own two feet, swaying with the slightest gust of wind as though it was more than enough to move her bony frame.

Miriam regarded the offering with glassy, empty eyes.

"I told you I'd get it for you," Orli whispered, unsure if Miriam heard her at all. "Well? Go on. Take them, quick. It's sulfa drugs. Only the SS used to have access to them, but I made Dr. Kremer stock the infirmary because—"

Because she promised she would. Orli's voice, full of tears, broke off as she watched Miriam dry-swallow the pills with an indifferent expression on her face. She didn't even have the strength to thank Orli, let alone look at her...

Wrapping a protective arm around Miriam's waist so that she wouldn't fall, Orli could only pray to whatever higher power there was that it wasn't too late.

SIX

Two months before New Year's Day

You knock on her door and, when she doesn't answer, gently push it open. No wonder she didn't hear you; she's all but buried in the mounds of paper stacked on her desk, windowsill, and even the floor around her chair. Her hair is in disarray. In her trembling fingers, a cigarette is smoldering—one of the many she must have smoked in the past few hours. You clear your throat but not because of the haze hanging in the air. She startles easily, and particularly these days, her head once again in the past, former nightmares coming to life when you've been struggling so hard to keep them banished to the furthest corner of her mind.

You told her it was a damned idiotic idea, her testimony at the upcoming Frankfurt trials, as of now scheduled for 1963 while the prosecution gathered their evidence. Reliving Auschwitz once again, day by day, crime by crime, brutality after brutality, medical experiments that gave you night terrors when you first heard of them. Facing her former tormentors, now on the defendants' bench, sans SS uniforms but recognizable still. Recounting what she saw, what she endured, what she was helpless to stop. But there was no reasoning with Aurelia Wald once she got something into her head.

You smile when she, without turning around, tells you to quit fidgeting—she heard you the first time. Hoped you'd take her silence as a hint, but she guesses no such luck. Pushes your arm away when you try to open the window to ventilate the room at least a little. It's much too windy outside today. She can't risk sending all these papers flying. Took her all morning to get them sorted.

Since that fateful phone call from her fellow Auschwitz survivor (Lang-something—Langmann? Langheim? With the best will in the world, the name keeps escaping you), the documents began arriving in thick envelopes on an almost daily basis. At first, you were glad to see her occupied, but now she looks manic, forgets to brush her teeth or wash her face if the nurse doesn't remind her. Her entire world has been reduced to this room, much like it used to be reduced to Auschwitz's walls some sixteen years ago.

Voluntarily, in front of your very eyes, she's slowly descending back into the extermination camp's hell. And it's anyone's guess if you will be able to pull her out this time.

SEVEN

"Did you order the administration of sulfa drugs to him?"

Orli shifted her gaze from the tip of Dr. Kremer's pencil to the inmate's hand he was currently pointing to. It was swollen twice its size after an infection had set in and was smelling of rot. One idiotic scratch with a rusty nail at the construction site, so minor that the carpenter himself didn't pay any heed to it for the first few days. Then, all at once, he was bedridden and delirious with a fever so high, he wasn't recognizing where he was any longer.

"I did," Orli admitted at last. "Three times a day at six-hour intervals. Zuzana is administering them—"

"How long ago?" Kremer interrupted her explanation with an impatient flick of his hand. Like some dark, demented shadow Zuzana hovered just behind his shoulder, her expression perfectly blank.

"Three days," Orli replied, more and more at a loss. "By the time he arrived here, the wound was so infected, it was all I could think of to prevent amputation."

"So, three days, three times a day, that makes it nine sulfa pills." The SS physician stared at her.

"Eleven," Orli said quietly. "I personally gave him two as soon as I cleaned the wound—"

"Eleven!" Kremer's eyes were mere slits now. "Better still. Eleven pills wasted on a carpenter—not even a valuable inmate, but a carpenter. This camp has a dime a dozen, and does he look like he's improving to you?"

Frankly, all Orli could think of was Miriam and the fact that she was still alive, still stumbling her way to work and back, and not struggling for each breath at night but sleeping, actually sleeping now. But she couldn't admit that to the SS man, could she now?

"I haven't finished my morning rounds yet, Herr Doktor," she confessed softly. "I can't tell you yet if—"

"Oh, but *I* can. I can tell you right now that this man won't make it through the night. And you keep wasting precious resources, which, I shall remind you, were only provided to this infirmary to stop an actual epidemic. He needs a bullet to the neck to put him out of his misery; not sulfa drugs."

Confused, unable to control the trembling of her ice-cold fingers, Orli unraveled the dressing and nearly gagged at the stench of rotting flesh that instantly filled the air. Along the neat stitches, red, angry flesh was bursting like cauliflower, seeping foul-smelling, yellowish pus. The tips of the man's fingers were already turning black. The gangrene had taken hold, spreading further, poisoning his blood itself.

Shaken to the core, Orli stared at the wound in stupefaction. "It's not right..." she whispered. The drugs would have stopped the process in its tracks; she'd treated far too many similar cases to know that much from experience.

"Is it now?" Kremer barked, holding the pristine white handkerchief to his nose. "What gave you that idea?"

With that, he swung sharply round and stormed off, Zuzana following him close on his heels.

Orli was still cleaning out the moaning man's wound to the best of her abilities when Zuzana returned.

"Any further administration of sulfa drugs is to be authorized by Herr Doktor personally," she said. "His orders."

Orli raised her gaze to the Slovak girl. In it, a storm was slowly brewing.

"Did you give him the drugs at all?" she asked at last. She would have asked the man himself, but thanks to Zuzana—or at least such was Orli's suspicion—he was presently on death's doorstep, much too delirious to understand anything at all.

From Zuzana, half a shrug and a grin. *Maybe I did and maybe I didn't.*

All the blood instantly drained from Orli's face. "Why haven't you said anything?"

"Why should I? You helped yourself to a couple of rolls. Why shouldn't I? I thought this was how it worked here."

It took Orli all her willpower not to hurl herself at the nurse and rip that serpent's tongue straight out of her lying mouth.

"I took them to help a girl who was dying," she hissed through clenched teeth. "Not to trade them for the extra rations you're always stuffing your greedy face with!"

"And here I thought we were friends," Zuzana said with a sugary smile.

"*Friends?*" Orli nearly choked with indignation. "Because of you this man will die!"

Zuzana suppressed a yawn, looking bored with the conversation. "Big loss. Transports are arriving daily, we're overpopulated as it is. I bet his bunkmates are happy."

"You're not a nurse, you shouldn't even be here." Orli's blood was all fire now, singing right through her veins. "I should just go and report you to Palitzsch for your lies."

That got her attention, but only for a moment. The next second, she was smiling again, that cat-got-the-canary smile Orli had grown to loathe with every fiber of her soul. "He has no authority here. Dr. Kremer does. And he doesn't like you lately."

"What is that supposed to mean?"

Zuzana only shrugged enigmatically again and danced away, swaying her hips that had never lost their roundness. Orli thought about Miriam and her twig-like limbs, clenched her jaws and returned to draining the pus out of the man's purple palm.

Over the next few days, life at the infirmary turned into a surreal version of its former self. Despite Orli's best efforts, the patients who had been improving suddenly took a turn for the worse, and with the best will in the world, she couldn't explain why. Mystified at first, Mark soon voiced the idea that Zuzana was deliberately sabotaging Orli's endeavors.

"I know you. And we both know her. Something doesn't add up."

Cold creeping up her veins, Orli shook her head in denial. "Harming people just to spite me? That's too much even for her."

"Is it now?" Mark arched his brow. "She did put the old man on the list," he reminded her.

Orli winced. The memory still hurt.

With a wistful smile, Mark pressed her hand in a fatherly gesture. "You're your own worst enemy, Aurelia. Pitying the beast that's sinking its teeth in your flesh, making an excuse for it and calling it hunger."

Deep inside, Orli knew he was right. It had been the same with Fritz, the same blind denial until the very end.

"All I'm saying is, watch your back, girl."

He'd watch it for her, but how could he—the only physician to hundreds of inmates, who scarcely slept at night because there were so many of them and only one of him? Orli read it all in his gaze full of sympathy, worry and regret before he hurried off back to his patients, working himself to the bone like the rest of them, until he, too, would end up on a death cart from exhaustion or a broken heart—whichever came first. Orli followed him with her eyes and made a silent prayer for all the saints like Mark who walked the earth until the SS would slaughter them all.

The sun was rolling westwards and the inmates talked animatedly about dinner, when, suddenly, just before his evening rounds, Dr. Kremer called Orli to his office. With a sense of dread washing over her, Orli made her way to his door, already suspecting the worst. She knocked softly and waited for him to invite her in.

As she entered his office, she saw him sitting behind his desk, a cold expression on his face. He gestured for her to approach him.

"*Ach*, there you are, 502," he said, his voice like ice. "I have been watching you closely lately, and I must say that I am not impressed with your work."

Orli felt her heart sink. She knew that this was not going to end well.

"I have received reports from other staff members that you are not following proper procedures when treating patients."

Orli felt a surge of anger at the accusation. She had been doing everything in her power to help the patients under her care and the said "staff members" knew it, would have sworn to it, if only he'd asked Mark. But it was Zuzana whom the SS physician listened to. It was finally time to acknowledge the truth.

"I assure you, Herr Doktor, that I am following all of the proper procedures," she said, trying to keep her voice steady.

The SS physician leaned forward, his eyes locked on hers.

"Are you now?" he mocked. "Why does it look like you're trying to undermine the work of this infirmary then? I think one can go as far as calling it outright sabotage even."

Orli stared at him in disbelief. How could he think that she would do such a thing? She had dedicated herself to healing, to helping those who were suffering. "I would never do anything to sabotage the work of this infirmary," she said, her voice shaking with emotion. "I am here to help the patients, not to harm them." *Unlike someone we both know.* Orli bit her tongue before the words she'd regret slipped off it.

"And yet, they're dropping like flies." The SS physician stood up and walked around his desk, his eyes fixed on Orli. "Not that I personally care, but you waste medicaments and dressings on them and they don't recover."

Orli's worst suspicions were brought to life with Kremer's own words. *If I just come out of here, I'll strangle that bitch with my bare hands,* she thought, blood rushing to her temples, pulsating wildly with every beat of her heart. *Killing men, innocent men, just to curry favor with the SS—what soulless creature does that?*

"I think you would be of more use at some other work detail," Dr. Kremer said, his voice cold and menacing. "Construction, perhaps. Then wasted resources shall be their problem, not mine."

Orli felt a surge of panic as she realized what was happening. She was being dismissed, thrown out of the infirmary and sent to Birkenau, where she would likely be assigned to the stone-and-wood hurling crew—a grueling and deadly task. But it wasn't hard work that weighed so heavily on her mind. It was the fact that her and Mark's patients would be left alone with the woman who cared not if they lived or died as long as her stomach was full. Orli had to rid the infirmary of Zuzana. Then, she would willingly go not just to Birkenau, but to the devil himself if Kremer wanted.

"Herr Doktor, I must stay here." To keep her patients safe, Orli was not above begging. "I'll do whatever needs to be done. I can work through nights too, instead of Mark. I can live in the barrack if needed—"

He waved her off, too busy lighting his cigarette. "You're fortunate your assistant Zuzana asked for you," he said, his voice low. Immediately, Orli felt tiny hairs rising all over her neck at the mention of the hated name. "But you must prove your loyalty to the Reich and to this infirmary."

Orli waited, a growing sense of dread turning her stomach.

"Whatever you need me to do," she said, her voice barely above a whisper.

"Zuzana, she's a good nurse, but clumsy with certain things. I asked her, and she tried to, but she can't find a heart in a living patient with a magnifying glass," he snorted softly, amused. "So, she suggested you assist me with the category three patients," he said, voicing what Orli had dreaded hearing. "You will help me prepare phenol shots and administer them to the inmates to euthanize them. I used to do it all myself, but now, there's just so many of them..."

In Orli's mind, his words whirled, dissonant, dissolving into a black pool of utmost dread. Her stomach turned at the thought of being complicit in such heinous acts. The category three patients, those very unfortunate ones she and Mark tried so hard to save. The ones taking too long to recover, the ones deemed unfit for work, too sick or weak to be of any use to the SS.

"No, Herr Doktor... Surely, you don't mean that. I can't do that," she said, her voice shaking with emotion. "I became a nurse to help people, not to harm them."

The SS physician leaned in closer, his face contorted with rage. "You want to stay here," he said, his voice low and menacing, "you do what I tell you to."

Orli opened her mouth and closed it again, her head swimming, drowning with despair. Put a needle straight through a beating human heart and feel it cease to beat... No. Anything but that.

But what of Zuzana? Just how many corpses would she walk over to keep her kosher position? And how many minions would she assemble around herself, who would keep their mouths shut whenever lifesaving drugs were pocketed by her greedy hands instead of being administered to the patients? Orli had seen it firsthand, the things Zuzana was capable of. If she could just last a few more days here while she and Mark came up with a plan of how to get Zuzana transferred somewhere —*anywhere*—but away from vulnerable people she could feed off like some bloodsucking vampire.

It took Orli all her power to will her lips to move: "I have no experience in this, Herr Doktor."

"Oh, nothing to be worried about. I'll teach you in no time."

I'm sure you would. Orli wiped her hand across her forehead. "But can I still treat my patients during the day? I'll ask for your approval before administering any medication—"

"No need to." All of a sudden, his goodwill knew no boundaries. "You can have Mark sign off on that. He was some hotshot professor at the Charité hospital in Berlin. Before he went and opened his big mouth on account of our Führer and the war, the pacifist pig." He snorted.

Orli felt a sense of resignation wash over her as she made her way out of the SS physician's room. She knew that her fate was sealed, that she would likely never make it out of here the same person she had walked in. She would be a killer, a death dealer's right hand. One didn't walk away from such things with their soul intact.

As she lay in her bunk that night, she thought about all of the patients she had tried to help, all of the lives she had tried to save. She knew that she had done everything in her power to make a difference, but it had all been for nothing.

. . .

The next morning, as she made her way to the infirmary, she saw Kremer standing in the distance, watching her with cold, dead eyes.

She knew that she would never forget the look on his face, the cold, calculating gaze that had condemned her to a fate worse than death. But, despite everything, Orli refused to give up hope. She knew that even in the darkest of times, there was always a glimmer of light, a way to hold onto the humanity that made us who we were. And she vowed never to give up that hope, no matter what horrors lay ahead.

EIGHT

The boy couldn't have been older than fifteen but was tall and lanky. Some kind soul on the platform must have whispered in his ear to claim to be older, and so here he was, gliding like a sad apparition along the infirmary's floor and peering into the sick inmates' faces with his doleful eyes. In the twilight of the descending night, he didn't see Orli sitting with her back against the wall, but she saw him, moving among the shadows, almost a shadow himself.

"Can I help you?"

The boy jumped with fright at the sound of her voice and dropped something on the floor. A piece of salami, wherever he'd squirreled it from. It rolled slowly in a wide arch and came to a halt by Orli's feet. For a few moments, she stared at it without any expression. Breathless, the boy waited, all angular limbs with a sweat of sheer terror hanging about him like a cloud.

Pushing herself off the wall, Orli picked up the piece of precious dried meat and handed it back to the youth. "Here, put it in your mouth before others will. We're not all so charitable here."

She was in a bad mood and, frankly, didn't care for first impressions.

"I know," the boy said in a voice that didn't belong either to a child or yet to an adult. "And thank you." He didn't eat the sausage, though. Only pressed it harder against his chest—Orli saw that much out of the corner of her eye.

She didn't want to see anything any longer. She closed her eyes, banishing the boy from her view, together with his damned contraband. Something dreadful had happened just hours before. Something her brain still refused to process.

He shifted from one foot to another. Orli could just discern the rustling among the quiet coughs and whispered gossip the inmates exchanged in that hour that balanced precariously on the verge between dying light and approaching darkness.

He cleared his throat. Orli's limbs were much too heavy to move. In fact, they didn't feel like hers any longer. If they were hers, they wouldn't have done what they had. Her entire body wasn't hers anymore.

"Are you a nurse?"

After an infinitely long moment, Orli forced her eyes open and glared at the boy. Wide-eyed and trembling like a newborn fawn, he was staring at her armband with the cross on it.

What a joke.

Orli closed her eyes again. It was better in this darkness. If only she could have silence as well...

"She's a doctor," the inmate growled from the nearest cot. "Leave her be. Can't you see she's not feeling well?"

Only then did it dawn on Orli just how quiet the infirmary had stood ever since she'd returned from Kremer's exam room. How perfectly still. They were mourning the Orli she had been before; because whoever had walked out of Kremer's exam room wasn't her any longer.

She'd expected curses hurled her way. A beating would be even better, but instead, there was this collective silence, acknowledging innocence forever lost, as though the SS physician had claimed not seventeen but eighteen victims that evening. For Orli was now a dead woman walking—her body still there, but the soul already gone, gone to a dark place from which there was no return.

"I'm sorry..." The boy again. The boy and his pitiful whimpers, as though they mattered at all. "I'm looking for my father. We have arrived together today, but they took him to the infirmary..." His voice trailed off, laced with uncertainty.

Orli opened her eyes and caught the boy staring at the sausage in his hand. *Came to share it with his father.* Her teeth were aching from her gnashing them without noticing for the past couple of hours. Her entire jaw was one big deadlock, barely holding her screaming mind from exploding.

"Did they assign your father a number?" Even her voice sounded alien. Hollow and dead, just like everything else inside.

"They did." Eagerly, the boy recited it.

With an inhuman effort, Orli pulled a clipboard from under her legs. At the physicians' station, a candle was burning, but all of a sudden, she couldn't bring herself to use it. This was what purgatory must have felt like, when one's soul was suspended in the unknown.

Instead of the list, she searched the boy's face for clues.

Have I killed your father? Have I put the needle through his heart as I was ordered?

And, all at once, as though broken by an invisible force, the walls of a dam burst open, flooding Orli's mind with images her brain so desperately tried to block from her memory in order to protect its sanity. Snapshots at first: Dr. Kremer's gloved hands. Hers, trembling violently. Then, the sensations returned and they were even worse: the rubber of the SS physician's glove atop her wrist. The heaviness of the syringe with liquid death itself dripping off its needle, sharp, gleaming, lowering slowly away from an inmate's chest. Then, sounds. Blood pulsing violently in her ears, her ragged breathing just at the very top of her lungs, the air didn't reach any deeper. Dr. Kremer's hissing, hot in her ear: "Whatever are you doing, you daft cow? These are the new arrivals. They think it's vitamin infusion, they don't know anything about phenol. It's either this or gas. Do you wish them to suffer?"

No. Of course she didn't. Phenol was a fast, merciful death.

Orli had repeated it to herself seventeen times as she had found the spot in between the ribs behind which a heart was steadily beating. She had smiled at them reassuringly, their unwilling executioner, and promised that everything would be all right. Most of them had smiled at her in return just before gasping momentarily and collapsing against an inmate orderly's awaiting arms.

Dr. Kremer had been right: those were the new arrivals, they didn't know about the phenol.

Dr. Kremer had been smart, too. Made her practice on the innocent ones until she'd grow thick-skinned enough to euthanize old-timers like sickly dogs.

Only she never would...

In Orli's hands, the clipboard was shaking, the trembling growing more and more violent until the list attached to the board clattered to the floor.

At once, several pairs of feet shuffled all around.

"Here, Doktor Orli, let us look."

"Go back to your barrack, Doktor Orli. It won't do you any good to miss the night roll call."

But the death she'd administered had finally caught up with her. Whatever temporary blissful forgetfulness had clouded her mind fell from her eyes like a shroud, revealing its horrible grinning skull staring her square in the face. She pressed her hands against her lids to block it out, but the image was still there, cackling, pointing its skeletal, accusing finger at her. Screaming,

"*Murderer! Murderer!*" so loudly, Orli couldn't hear her own weeping behind it.

Even the inmates' hands and words didn't break the spell right away. It took them a good few minutes to pry Orli's hands from her face and shake her back into reality with grins and pats on her backs she couldn't at first comprehend.

"It's all right, Doktor Orli. He's alive."

"The boy's old man is alive."

"He's right here, on the list, in the discharged category."

But the seventeen weren't.

Orli tried to explain it to them, tried to make them see reason, but all she got in exchange was more compassion she knew she didn't deserve.

"Don't blame yourself. It wasn't your invention, Doktor Orli. It's the SS."

"Think of Doktor Mark. You spared him the misfortune."

"Yes, he got his day off away from the phenol duty today."

"And you smiled at them, Doktor Orli."

Through the wall of tears standing in her inflamed eyes, Orli saw the face of the inmate orderly who had assisted her that day in her ghastly duty.

"You smiled at them and they died happy," he said. "It's better to die easy while seeing a friendly face than under an SS boot or facing a brick wall with a gun against your neck. They didn't even know what was happening. You saw to that. And in a place like this, if you can't stop death, stop unnecessary suffering at least. And you do it, Doktor Orli. Like Doktor Mark. You're good people."

Orli didn't believe the words but nodded nevertheless. He was doing it, too. Easing her suffering if he couldn't stop the death already breathing over her shoulder.

Orli felt its shadow follow her all the way back to her barrack. Felt it and, for the first time in her life, welcomed its presence.

NINE

SEHNDE, GERMANY. NOVEMBER 1961

One and a half months before New Year's Day

Huffing and visibly annoyed, she sits in the chair opposite you. She used to love these therapy sessions with you. Used to jest in her lighthearted manner that you were her favorite psychiatrist. And she should know, too; she's an experienced self-declared mental case. The others broke their teeth on her. And you are still holding, look at you! Stubborn one, aren't you?

Now, all the playfulness is gone out of her eyes. In its place, there's something dark smoldering, much like the inevitable cigarette in her hand.

You tell her she smokes too much.

She tells you to go to hell and blows the smoke out of her flaring nostrils.

You know she would have missed the session entirely if the nurse didn't drag her out of her room and back into the real world, which she wished to have nothing to do with these days. Her attention is needed elsewhere. There is justice to be finally served, and here you are, worrying about her depression. Do you even know what depression is?

You let her vent and curse at you and snarl because she wasn't allowed to do so in Auschwitz. Now, she can finally fight back. Good. Let her.

She runs out of steam soon enough. Passes her bony hand over her wild hair to smooth it out. Apologizes.

It's not your fault. It's just... they have uncovered the films at long last. Remember the films? Sure, you do. Well, Langbein had them developed. She saw what was on them today, for the first time.

TEN

AUSCHWITZ. SUMMER 1942

With summer came the heat. Not the good, dry kind that gilded the skin and made one feel indescribably lazy and rich in its embrace, but the wet, oppressive kind, which coated the skin with its grime and filled the lungs with moisture. It drowned the inmates slowly during the day, draining them of sweat—the last precious drops of moisture—and broiled them alive under the unforgiving sun until the evening gong announced the end of work. The night didn't bring relief either. Heat deprived them of their sleep or smothered them altogether, adding more corpses to the next day's tally.

As a child, Orli used to love summer. Its freedom—from everything: school, layers of clothing, parental supervision even. For three full months, she could roam free: the streets, the countryside, the lake, and the forest looming behind it. Everything was hers: every blade of grass that tasted the sweetest in June, every drop of July's downpour, every wild cherry and raspberry and even sour green apples dropping all around her as she lay in the orchard's shade with a book, lost to a world that was hers and hers alone.

Now, Orli was convinced that summer was a Nazi. Ruthless in its green uniform, with only torment on its mind. It refused to let go, even when inmates dropped like flies—always in the afternoon when the sun glared down on them from its highest point like an SS sentry in his guard tower—and cared not that there was not a drop of water to be had. Sometimes, after a rare thunderstorm, the inmates crawled around hollow ravines and drank brown puddle water until they sucked the whole thing dry. Sometimes, there was no time to fish drowned rodents out of it. After thunderstorms, the infirmary was always full of dysentery cases.

"Wash your hands," Mark reminded Orli on an almost hourly basis. "I don't want you catching it."

Orli nodded absently and washed. He had to remind her about many things now. She didn't think for herself and, frankly, didn't seem to care for her own well-being, or survival for that matter. Her brain was all thick fog now, with reality losing itself gradually in its grayness. Her self-imposed starvation certainly didn't help matters.

At first, shortly after Dr. Kremer had forced a phenol syringe into her hand, Orli had begun sharing her bread with her patients. Next, she had started spoon-feeding her soup to whoever needed it most that day. By the time Mark had noticed a frightening skeletal outline forming in place of Orli's face, she was surviving on morning black ersatz coffee and the hope that the devil would take her soon.

"God, He has no business with murderers," she had explained to the former Charité physician with an astounding indifference about her. "And that's what I am. A murderer."

Nothing could persuade her of the opposite. She had sentenced herself to death for crimes committed by others. No guts to throw herself against the electric wire; she would have to taint this earth with her existence for a bit longer, but starvation would take care of it soon enough. With that reasoning in mind, Orli would tuck another piece of bread under a sleeping inmate's straw pillow. They were good people, innocent people —they deserved to live much more than she did.

The door flew open and slammed into the wall—kicked by an SS boot, no doubt. Sure enough, here he was, Rapportführer Palitzsch himself, stalking along past the inmates who were desperately scrambling to attention, with Kapos slamming their batons into the necks of the slowest ones to move. Orli, too, dropped the wet cloth she was holding and froze next to Yakov —the patient she was washing.

"Search!" Walls themselves seemed to tremble at the sound of the report leader's voice. "All bedding—on the ground, now!"

Too sadistic, too eager to aid their superior, Kapos threw themselves upon the patients, who were trembling with fright. In front of Orli's eyes, hands tore thin straw bedding, groped skeletal men and disrobed them in the beastliest of manners without any regard to their injuries or dressings.

She made the mistake of stepping in front of Palitzsch's underling to protect her current charge—the dysentery case wasting him down by the hour—and tried to protest, "No, no, he's too weak to—" only to be backhanded by the Kapo with such force, her entire body flew aside like a mere rag doll. She tried to stand up, mouth full of blood, ears ringing, just to be clubbed along her back until forced back onto her knees and, soon, into a ball, with bloodied hands atop her head.

Assured that there would be no more protesting, the Kapo yanked Orli's patient down by his foot. The entire barrack winced at the sound Yakov's skull made as it hit the ground. And the Kapo, victorious, doubling and wavering in Orli's bloodshot eyes, held aloft a piece of bread Orli had placed under her patient's pillow mere hours ago. Despite his state, she had been certain he'd pull through. With enough bread and water, he would have. She'd have seen to it, if it was the last thing she did. But not now—now she could do nothing for him.

"Well, what do you know?" Rapportführer Palitzsch produced a handkerchief and used it to take the bread from his underling. He held it with two fingers like a dead rat and, after another smirk, threw it to someone: "Your share for reporting theft."

Orli's eyes widened as they traveled from the feet to the striped skirt and apron of a camp medical worker: Zuzana. Grinning, round-faced Zuzana, a new blue ribbon in her hair.

Silently, Orli spat the blood on the ground. It tasted like arsenic. Like the deadliest betrayal.

Around Yakov's head, the man who she'd been tending just minutes ago, a small puddle of blood was slowly pooling, the richest burgundy spilled just for the thrill of it.

Unperturbed, the Kapos uncovered more foodstuffs— broken into halves, hidden for tomorrow or the middle of the night when the pain would grow unbearable and there would be nothing else to stifle it with. More skulls bashed in, more bread thrown Zuzana's way, into her plump, awaiting hands.

With acidic hatred burning her heart, Orli wondered what she would trade the goods for this time. More ribbons? A compact mirror to admire her rosy cheeks? A nail file to manicure the hands that hardly touched a patient these days?

As soon as the report leader departed, his minions in tow, Orli pulled herself up, swayed on her unsteady legs and turned to Zuzana.

"Whatever did you report him for?" Every word echoed back in her head, all but splitting in two but surprisingly still intact despite the Kapo's baton. "You know perfectly well that I gave him my bread. He's been delirious for two days now, he's in no condition to steal anything. And they..." Her hand made a helpless arch in the air, indicating the broken bodies scattered for her and Mark to gather onto the death cart. "They break their own bread in pieces to eat it later. You know this. Why would you..." Her voice trailed off, broken just like Yakov's neck.

Zuzana smiled and gave a shrug. "For fun." Watching her step so as not to muddy her footwear in blood, she headed for the exit. To trade the pile of goods, no doubt. "Don't look at me like that," she said over her shoulder, laughing. "I'm joking. A post office orderly has a box of Belgian chocolates someone sent their relative incarcerated here. For all this," she said with a nod to the bread, "he can make it disappear. I said, don't look at me like that! It's chocolate. I haven't had it in forever!"

Chocolates, Orli repeated to herself in hateful astonishment as she mopped the pool of Yakov's blood off the floor.

Chocolates, a demented echo pulsed in her temples as she crossed murdered men's numbers off the infirmary list.

Chocolates, something hissed, coiling and uncoiling in her chest as she pocketed a few extra valuable medicaments early the next morning.

Mark saw and said nothing. The same vengeance-craving snake was hissing in his ear too.

They were conspiring to murder without a single word shared, and for the first time in both of their lives, the murder tasted sweet on their tongues. Justified.

"You're early today," Mark noted the following morning. The sun was just emerging from the black expanse of the forest looming in the distance when Orli walked into the physicians' cubicle. In her eyes, steely determination shone.

"Lots to do," she said.

Mark understood the unsaid. "Yes. Indeed." He nodded slowly. "Anything you need help with?"

"Yes," Orli replied and pulled the cubicle door closed. Such conversations demanded privacy. And with Zuzana, they only had one good chance: failure was not an option.

When Zuzana sailed into the infirmary that day, late as always, arrogant in her knowledge that no one would say a word to Dr. Kremer's favorite, she was met with dead silence. Oblivious to eyes glaring at her from every corner, she went about her business, humming contentedly to herself. That business had little to do with patients in dire need of medical help; Zuzana much preferred disinfecting, cleaning, and arranging Dr. Kremer's instruments and personal effects in his exam room. He would be arriving to do his morning rounds soon.

"If only Herr Doktor took his coffee here," she said, noticing Orli standing in the door of the room. She must have had her damned chocolates already, it occurred to Orli. Something had sweetened her mood, turned her uncharacteristically chatty with people she considered well beneath her on Auschwitz's social ladder. "I'd make it for him better than they do in the officers' mess."

"I bet you would." Orli smiled, glanced over her shoulder and nodded to Mark imperceptibly. He, in turn, nodded to Ari, the boy recently employed as an infirmary runner. The "salami boy", as Orli and Mark good-naturedly teased him. The son of the father whom Orli hadn't killed on that very first death duty day of hers. Ever since Orli had helped him locate his only surviving parent, the boy had refused to leave her side, sticking to her and Mark as his new adoptive family, devotion and eternal gratitude burning in his bright, amber eyes.

As soon as the youngster set off, Orli pushed herself off the doorframe. "Your apron is a bit askew. Here, let me help you retie it."

"Is it?" Zuzana instantly dropped her polishing cloth and

began turning this way and that, much more concerned with the state of her attire than the sight of men beaten to death just so she could have her Belgian candy.

"Stand still and don't wriggle, will you?" Orli began fussing over her with an exaggerated sisterly benevolence. "Here, it's all better now. Don't you just miss mirrors?"

For an instant, Zuzana regarded her closely.

Orli feigned an embarrassed chuckle as she passed her hand over her kerchiefed head self-consciously. "I must look a fright. And you, you're always so well put together, so clean and you smell so good."

Zuzana's suspicions melted under the heap of praise Orli poured on her like warm honey. "I can get you soap, if you like," she said. Her sense of superiority was tickled pink. Just as Orli had hoped, it blinded Zuzana to any possible suspicion. "Just give me your rations instead of feeding them to that scum. I know you have a big heart, but you're not too savvy, Orli. You give and give, and what do you get in return? Human waste you have to clean off their filthy buttocks—that's where your rations go. And in the end, they die of dysentery anyway so what's the point?"

Orli pretended to consider. It was important to keep Zuzana talking—it would take Ari some time to get to the SS quarters.

"I know you think me to be a self-serving swine," Zuzana continued. "But in this kind of place, it's each person for themselves. Survival of the fittest. If you're not a predator, you're prey. It's simple nature, Orli."

Orli nodded several times, slowly. "I'll give you my rations today."

Zuzana flashed a bright smile. "I take a percentage for my services. Four pieces of bread for soup, the fifth one—for me."

"Have my sausage, too. I don't have the appetite for it lately."

"Suit yourself."

"Help me with rounds, can you?"

Zuzana was about to scrunch her nose, but Orli caught her wrist and pleaded with her the best she could only muster.

"Please, Zuzana. Mark is such an insufferable, self-important raven! I can't have him breathing down my neck any longer."

"And here I thought you were such good pals."

Orli gave a guilty half-shrug. "I only keep in his good graces because he's the head physician here."

Once again, Zuzana grinned like a Cheshire cat. "Oh, Orli, you have so much to learn yet. The head physician here is Dr. Kremer. Mark, he's just an inmate. A nobody. Disposable."

Like the men you sentenced to death for your blasted chocolates.

Orli smiled through clenched teeth and put her arm through the crook of Zuzana's. "I'm sorry I was such a bitch to you."

Zuzana broke into chuckles. "I didn't know you had such words in your vocabulary."

You don't know many things about me, Orli thought as she steered Zuzana into the barrack.

They were just in the middle of swapping their charges' bedding when Rapportführer Palitzsch stalked inside, accompanied by an SS private. He was in a terrible mood, their "lovely" report leader, it occurred to Orli as soon as she saw his rheumy eyes with bags under them, the stubble on his cheeks and the collar of his shirt sticking out from under his uniform jacket. Judging by the creases on it, he had slept in it, passed out in drunken stupor, as was his habit—this was no secret to anyone in Auschwitz. Close on his heels, Dr. Kremer trailed. And as loyal as a shadow, Ari hung about the doors of the barracks, Orli and Mark's little co-conspirator.

"What is the meaning of this?" the head physician demanded but wisely recoiled once the report leader swung round to face him.

"You have a big theft problem on your premises, Herr Doktor," Palitzsch drawled and smiled like a snake. "This is the second day in the row I'm inspecting your premises."

Pale in his indignation, Dr. Kremer stepped away. He looked as though Palitzsch had just slapped him. "What nonsense!"

"Is it now?" Palitzsch arched a brow.

Next to Orli, Zuzana was observing the scene with a mixture of interest and confusion. It was the first time that someone other than her had snitched to the authorities.

"Let's see then." With those words, Palitzsch motioned his head to his escort.

In an instant, the SS man was upon Zuzana, patting her down without any ceremony, despite all of her and Dr. Kremer's protests.

"I demand an explanation!" the SS physician gasped. "This is outrageous! She's an exemplary worker and my most trusted —" He stopped abruptly.

In his hand, the SS private held sulfa drugs and morphine— the most sought-after medicine for which a human life could be easily traded.

Theatrically slowly, Palitzsch turned to Dr. Kremer. "You were saying?"

But Dr. Kremer wasn't saying anything any longer, only staring at the vials with unblinking eyes.

It was Zuzana who recovered from the shock first.

"It's not mine! I didn't take it, I swear! It was her," she screamed, pointing at Orli. "She must have planted it into my pockets while she was messing about with my apron this morning."

All eyes on her, Orli shrugged calmly. "I was here, inside the infirmary, the entire time, Herr Rapportführer, tending to my patients."

Palitzsch thrust his chin at Mark. *Well?*

"It's true, Herr Rapportführer," the inmate physician confirmed. "She was here, where I could see her, the entire time. It's Zuzana who always stays in Herr Doktor's office. It's also she who restocks the shelves according to Herr Doktor's orders. We barely see her here."

Zuzana, her face ashen, swallowed hard. Like a cornered animal, she was shaking her head. "It's all lies. They conspired against me, these two!"

"Doktor Orli was with us all morning," one of the inmates said, stepping forward. Risking getting shot for speaking when not spoken to, but he did all the same. "The nurse was in Dr. Kremer's room by herself, that much is true."

Murmurs followed from all over the infirmary, heads bobbing in agreement. *Yes, yes, this was God's honest truth; they could all swear to it.*

"They're all lying!" Zuzana's tone was turning hysterical. The direness of the situation was slowly dawning on her. "They all conspired to get rid of me because... because..."

"She's been known to steal supplies before," Orli continued, going for the kill. It mattered not what happened to her next. Likely, that very evening, Dr. Kremer would jab her with phenol or just with air—to make her suffer—but that wasn't her worry any longer. The important part was that Zuzana would be gone and her patients safe, and that was all Orli cared about. "She trades on the black market. With someone from the post office. They had Belgian chocolates there. I'm sure they still have the box somewhere if you search the premises."

"Oh, that'll be our next stop," Palitzsch assured her with a grin that promised death. "Why haven't you reported her earlier?"

"She was under Dr. Kremer's protection," Orli replied. "Thanks to her scheming, I was almost sent to a construction detail in Birkenau. Dr. Kremer only allowed me to stay on because he knows Zuzana has no medical experience and we're still in dire need of medical personnel."

"Favoring a Jew over an Aryan," Palitzsch tutted.

Dr. Kremer stood still like a statue.

"That's something that smells almost like... I don't know. A race treason," Palitzsch continued, suddenly interested in his nails. "Do you still wish to vouch for your, and I quote, 'most trusted employee'?"

Under Zuzana's pleading stare, Dr. Kremer made no reply.

The SS private dragged her out by the hair. Soon after, a single shot rang out. Without another word, Dr. Kremer proceeded to his office. He locked the door after himself.

"Poor sod is in mourning," Palitzsch made a mock-sympathetic grimace and strolled toward Orli and Mark. "I owe you a share for reporting, but I can't give out morphine vials, as you can well imagine."

Orli nodded. She understood.

"He'll kill you, you know," Palitzsch said.

Orli nodded again. *Let him*.

"You aren't afraid?" He regarded her closely, suddenly very curious.

Orli smelled stale cognac on his breath.

"No, Herr Rapportführer."

He was silent for a while, considering something. "If you were a Jew, I'd leave you here and to the devil with you," he said eventually. "But you're Aryan and it goes against my conscience as an SS man to kill a fellow Aryan. Tell you what, I'll sign a transfer for you. To Birkenau women's infirmary. They're all but done building it. What do you say to that?"

Naturally, he didn't need her answer. Not that Orli could provide one, stunned into silence with such a turn of events. It wasn't every day that mercy came from one of the most ruthless men in the whole of Auschwitz.

Auschwitz. An animal world. And Zuzana had been right: it was survival of the fittest.

ELEVEN

The following morning, after swallowing her "coffee" and waiting for the block leader to count their sorry heads, Orli stepped in front of the inmates. On Palitzsch's explicit orders, she called for anyone with medical experience. Miriam had already been alerted to the announcement and it was her little charge's hand that flew in the air before anyone else's. After that, doubtful silence as Orli studied their pitiful military formation.

Somewhere in between the fight for survival and the permanent foggy cloud that had settled over Orli's mind in her self-imposed starvation, the number of inmates had swelled, and the faces were now unrecognizable. It was during that morning roll call that Orli had realized that many of the women who had stepped from the cattle train with her were no longer among the living. Gassed, starved, worked to death, perished on the very steps of the women's infirmary they'd been building—it was anyone's guess what had happened to them. There were no funerals in Auschwitz. People simply vanished, leaving only agonized ghosts roaming this accursed land. It was Orli's profound conviction that centuries would pass and their presence would still be felt here. Too much of their tears and blood and ashes had gone into this earth for it to become anything other than a communal grave for years to come.

"I used to be an obstetrician," a woman stepped forward at last. Her head was shorn under a faded blue kerchief, her face burned to weathered brown leather in the unforgiving camp sun. "Not sure how useful I will be to you."

Wordlessly, Orli motioned her over. She herself had no formal medical training, and now look at her, a big shot thanks to Herr Palitzsch—let him rot in hell—a chief physician gathering a motley crew of anyone who had ever as much as opened a biology book to treat the pitiful wretches the SS would send their way first thing upon arrival.

"Nurse here." Another woman, seemingly identical to the first one. Same face scorched with sun, same deep lines etched into it as though with razors. Same bony frame and shaved skull under a grimy kerchief.

"A former Red Cross volunteer, if it counts for anything." A third woman said, almost indistinguishable from the first two.

Orli asked their names on their march to Birkenau but kept mixing them up and apologizing through the fog of her brain and the ringing in her ears.

"Don't take offense, I'm not usually this obtuse," she said, trying to wet her lips with an almost-dry tongue. "It's this place..."

"You have nothing to apologize for, sister. It *is* this place. They dress us, starve us, and shave us to make us as indistinguishable from one another as possible. So that when one dies, the other steps in their place and it's as if the first one had never existed. When you can't remember someone's face, it can't haunt you at night. That's how they sleep soundly, the SS."

Orli was staring at the obstetrician closely for some time as they marched in neat rows of five to the sounds of the camp orchestra.

"Admiring my ugly mug?" the woman grinned, squinting against the sun.

Orli shook her head. "Committing your face to my memory. So that even if they forget, I shall always remember. You're an obstetrician. Your name is Gerda and you're from Alsace."

Against the blinding sun, Gerda's smile widened. "And just what do you think to do with this valuable information once I croak?"

Orli shrugged. "Tell the others. Scribble it on the wall with a nail. Scream it into the air before they put a bullet through my neck. Does it matter?"

"I'd rather you carve it into the forehead of the SS man who killed me once you have been liberated."

Orli regarded her skeptically. "Do you think we will be? Last thing I heard, we were winning on all fronts."

It was Gerda's turn to shrug. "We have to be. Else, we can just go to the SS, ask them for a rope and hang ourselves collectively, no?"

"Suppose there is some logic to it."

Next to the older women, young Miriam hung onto their every word.

The march to Birkenau was so long and exhausting, Orli wouldn't be surprised if it was already midday by the time they reached the new camp under construction. On Miriam's sweat-streaked face, a painful shadow creased her brow. She'd nearly died building this place—just to call it her new home. Identical barracks in neat rows as far as the eye could see, as though the entire world had been reduced to one big camp. Gray barracks and gray dust—dust everywhere, roused by their shuffling feet and refusing to settle back down, obscuring the sun itself, reducing the day to permanent twilight.

"Birkenau," Orli spat the word together with the sand grinding on her teeth. "Veritable birch paradise, my foot."

They were standing where their SS escort had called them to a halt, waiting for the warden in her tailored gray uniform and the assembling Kapos to divide them into work gangs.

"There used to be many birches here when we first arrived," Miriam said. Her voice, too, was hoarse with thirst and dust. "We cut them all down for the barracks construction."

"What about the grass?" Orli asked. "Where did that go?"

Miriam shrugged. "Stomped to death, I suppose. It just doesn't grow here anymore."

Orli swiped her hand along her arm and for the first time noticed that instead of a dry smear, it left an odd oily residue on her skin.

Miriam caught her rolling the soot between the tips of her fingers and explained in a voice so cool and detached, it sent a deathly chill down Orli's spine. "That's ash. They used to bury people they gassed right over there," she said, pointing in a westerly direction. "But there were so many of them, the ground began rising where they buried them. Sometimes we'd see black hands appearing from the ground as if they had tried to get themselves out, the dead ones. The SS just gave us more lime powder to throw over them but then, local farmers began to complain. The rot began to poison their water. Their cattle began to get sick and die. Many of us got poisoned too, drinking pipe water. The SS, they drank mineral water only, from bottles. But one day they sent *Sonderkommando* here—you know, those men in tall rubber boots, the ones who man the crematoriums. The SS made them dig all the corpses out and burn them. That's where the ash is from. It's been weeks, but it's still here—there were just too many of them."

Orli stared at her in stunned silence and wondered at how fast, in between felling birches and watching the humanity being burned to ash, Miriam had transformed from a frightened young girl to someone who could recount horrors that Dante himself could not imagine in his worst nightmares and not even flinch. But wasn't it she, Orli, who had murdered Zuzana with Palitzsch's hands and didn't lose any sleep over it?

How terrifying it was, what this place was doing to them. How it was twisting them into something they could never imagine themselves to be; turning them on one another, revealing the ugliest sides to them they had never suspected were slumbering in the darkest corners of their souls.

"Thank you, Orli."

It took a few moments for the warmth of Miriam's narrow palm connecting to hers to pull Orli out of her unhappy musings.

"For what?" She blinked at the girl.

"If it wasn't for you, I'd be buried there together with them. Buried and burnt and nothing left of me at all besides this ash. You saved me."

Something caught in Orli's chest. She'd been holding herself so perfectly together this entire time and now, suddenly, after hearing Miriam's simple words and feeling her small hand in hers—life itself, pulsing like a little bird in her palm—it all came crashing down on her and there was no stopping it. Her vision blurred and smeared. Her hand flew to her mouth to stifle the sobs. The SS didn't take too kindly to such emotional outbursts. After working so tirelessly at reducing them to a faceless, mute workforce, they punished any such attacks with whips or guns—depending on their mood that day and on the value of the worker. They saw them as anything but human—it was easier to kill them this way.

Orli didn't care one way or the other if she lived or died, but apparently her new charges did. As she was weeping silently, a protective cocoon formed around her: Miriam shielding her from the warden's eyes, Gerda rubbing her back as she whispered something sisterly and comforting, and two of her new nurses, Velma and Enna.

If this place was digging the most nightmarish parts of them out of the depths of their psyche, it also brought out something else in them. Bravery in circumstances that would send entire armies running for cover. Fierce protectiveness that knew no rivalry. Selflessness and love that knew no boundaries, when one shared their last meal with someone they scarcely knew just because it was the right thing to do and to the devil with the fact that they, themselves, were slowly starving to death.

It was in the arms of those women around her that Orli took a silent oath that day to tear her own heart out to share it with those in need. Auschwitz had all but broken her, but in Birkenau she would rebuild herself into something much stronger, something that could withstand the most violent storms in order to remain a beacon to the others. On the ashes of all who had fallen, Orli had sworn herself to it.

TWELVE

Despite being a new construction, the Birkenau hospital presented a frightful sight. By midday, it was overflowing with prospective patients. Those already admitted occupied not only every bed but the floor as well; they lined the walls, some standing and some sitting with their legs crossed to allow passage for others, in the hope of if not a cure, at least some respite from the murderous pace of work and unmerciful sun that had burned their scalps to painful blisters.

"See that no one with a temperature lower than 38°C is admitted," Dr. Kitt, their new SS physician, instructed before setting off in the direction of the officers' mess. There, ice-cold beer was being served. Here, only sooty-faced inmates loitered, scratching absently at their lice-bitten heads, and the air stank of sweet female sweat and menstrual blood. Their communal stench must have offended his delicate senses.

During the first week, Orli still instructed Miriam to take every single prospective inmate's temperature. On week two, in view of having far too many critical cases and only one thermometer, she abandoned the practice altogether.

"What do I do if they don't seem to run any fever?" Miriam

asked after Orli commandeered the thermometer from her. "Turn them away?"

Orli saw Miriam search her face, holding her breath as she awaited the answer. The answer that would decide someone's fate; it was obvious to everyone present. To the inmates who sat silently, without breathing, waiting for Orli's capable hands to tend to their battered bodies, thanking providence no doubt for making it inside the infirmary. To Gerda, bandaging a woman's toe, half-eaten by a rat at night. *However didn't you feel the beast gnawing on you, Mother?—I did, love. But we sleep five to a bunk. When you're pressed from both sides as though in a vice, you can't rise every two minutes to chase it off. And besides, I was so very tired, I fell asleep.* To Enna and Velma changing soiled sheets from under the dysentery cases. To Orli herself.

"Let them in," she said at last and could swear she heard the entire infirmary sigh with relief. "Let them sit a few days out, it won't hurt anything."

And so they hid, scattering like mice at Miriam's warning whistle—SS inspection!—but remained alive and that was all that mattered to Orli and her crew.

Another blazing August afternoon. Another lunch she chose to go without. Orli gazed out of the small window of the infirmary barracks in Birkenau. The air was thick with despair, and the stench of suffering hung in every corner. The Nazi regime had taken hold of their lives, reducing them to mere shadows of their former selves. But amidst the darkness, there was a new plague lurking in the shadows—malaria.

Ever since her arrival in Ravensbrück, Orli had made it her mission to alleviate the suffering of her fellow prisoners. She had seen countless lives snuffed out by disease and malnutrition, but the Birkenau malaria outbreak was a new level of horror.

At first, no one had noticed the invisible threat that hung in dark clouds over bogs bordering the camp's vicinity. Swiped their hands at the buzzing annoyance, scratched at the bites without giving them any second thought. After all, why would they bother with something so trivial? Mosquitos were just as synonymous with summer as sunburnt noses and humid heat. It was in that deceiving lull of familiarity that the disease spread with astounding speed, aided by the overcrowded and unsanitary conditions of the camp. Before Orli realized what precisely they were battling, they had a full-blown epidemic on their hands.

Startling Orli out of her black reverie, Gerda marched in and deposited a pot full of used syringe needles next to a small iron stove.

"Have you eaten yet?" Orli asked her trusted aide.

"When would I do that?" Gerda snorted with goon-natured contempt and passed the back of her hand along her forehead. "Just finished making my rounds."

"Go eat then. Soup will get cold."

"In this heat? Fat chance!"

"Still..."

From Gerda, an obstinate toss of the shaved head—a mannerism Orli was growing more and more fond of. "Need to disinfect these first."

In an instant, Orli was on her feet, taking the matches out of Gerda's hands to light the stove. "I'll do it myself. Go."

Gerda's eyes narrowed suspiciously. "Have you eaten?"

"Yes, yes, I have." Orli waved her off, purposely occupying herself with the pot full of water and contaminated needles. It would take the small stove forever to boil the water to a suitable degree—the only disinfection method available to them in this hellhole of a place—but Orli didn't mind the wait.

"I haven't seen you by the soup cauldrons."

"You were busy."

"Liar." Gerda prodded Orli's ribs. "You think I haven't noticed? You're not eating. Look at you, a veritable bone-bag!"

"One yourself," Orli muttered, placing the pot atop the stove.

"Do you think you'll be of any use to anyone dead?"

"I'm not dead."

"You will be soon if you proceed in this manner."

"Aren't you an optimist?"

"I'm a realist and you have a mental disorder."

"What are you, Dr. Jung now?" Orli scoffed. "I'm not hungry is all. A blessing in this place, if you ask me."

"You're not hungry because your body is consuming itself to sustain itself for a few more weeks. It has grown so used to you starving it, it has learned to sustain itself on its own resources. That is, muscle mass—or what's left of it. Fat, it burned for energy a long time ago. Now, the question is, why *are* you starving yourself?"

No one had asked her that before. Dr. Mark, he had begged her to eat but never wondered why she wasn't eating—here of all places, where everyone either talked of food, dreamed of food, tried to steal food or died for food.

"Don't know," Orli said at last. The water had been boiling for a good ten minutes. All the remnants of malaria were surely annihilated. "And to hell with you and your psychoanalysis. We have patients to tend to, in case you forgot."

Gerda took no offense at the reproach. In Auschwitz, outbursts like these were nothing new. She, herself, was prone to them.

In their absence, a new batch of patients had been admitted inside, their bodies shivering and weakened from the fever. Tangling in their scattered limbs, Miriam and Enna ran along the narrow corridor left between the bodies lying there like a human carpet. The backs of their uniform dresses were drenched with sweat. Today, more than ever, the barracks were filled with moaning and the cries of pain—a constant reminder of the suffering that surrounded them.

Swaying from side to side, picking her way among women's bodies on the floor, a frail young girl approached Orli. If Orli hadn't known any better, she would think that the girl had just taken a nice cooling shower somewhere. But it wasn't rivulets of refreshing water that were streaming down her face and soaking her thin dress with its faded stripes until it stuck to her bony frame. Life itself was draining out of her by the second.

"Sit, sit here, don't exhaust yourself." Orli grasped the girl's hand and nearly dropped it that very instant. It was almost as hot as the pot with syringes she had handed Gerda mere moments ago. "Let me grab some wet cloths and a thermometer. I'll be with you in a second—"

"No, no, Doctor, I'm fine," the girl interrupted her, her voice barely audible above the cacophony of suffering. The heat of her feverish breath nearly singed Orli's lips. "It's my mother. Save her, please! She's the only one I have left..."

Another Ari, their beloved "salami boy," the Auschwitz infirmary runner, only in female form. What was this world coming to when children were pleading for their parents' lives when their own were hanging by a thread?

With the girl's burning hand clasping at hers, Orli followed her outside the barrack. In the narrow strip of shadow provided by the roof, more women lay—some in fetal positions, some splayed out, delirious and talking to loved ones who had long gone up the chimney.

Velma ran frantically to and fro with a small basin of water and rags swimming in them. "I don't have any sulfa drugs! Doctors Orli and Gerda prescribe them. I don't have any! Here, put this on your forehead and wait for the doctor..."

Guided by the girl, Orli stopped and paused beside a middle-aged woman who was sitting propped against the barrack wall. On her lap, her lifeless hands held onto a bent

aluminum bowl filled with what looked more like water than
soup. At the approach of her daughter, her eyes, even though
glazed with fever, focused and creased in the corners in the
faint semblance of a smile. "Here, Birdie," she said in a voice
that was much too weak to belong to anyone other than a phan-
tom. "Saved for you..."

"You eat, Mama." The girl lowered herself heavily to the
ground next to her. "Look! I brought the doctor out for you. I
promised I would."

Orli didn't need to measure the woman's temperature to
form a diagnosis. The deathly yellow shade had already crept
into the balls of her eyes, set into the creases of her dust-specked
skin. With the woman's liver on its last dying breath, there was
only so much that she could do.

"How are you feeling, Mother?" Orli asked in a voice that
was purposely bright with optimism.

"Not too bad, Doctor." The woman was breathing heavily
as she gazed at her daughter. "Help my Birdie. She's young and
she's a very good worker—"

"I'm not the SS, Mother," Orli interrupted her, feeling the
woman's wrist for the fluttering of a pulse. Just as she'd
suspected: irregular, faint and yet desperate, like the wings of a
butterfly caught in a spider's net. "I don't value my patients'
lives based on how useful a worker they are."

With her last effort, the woman nudged the plate toward
Orli. "Make her eat, please. It's a miracle no one stole it
from me..."

Her voice was fading. It took too much for the woman to
speak.

Orli took the plate out of her hands with the utmost care,
only to see Birdie, whatever her real name was, shaking her
head at it.

"No. She should eat, she's sicker than me."

So she was. But she was also dying, and no matter how

much it pained Orli's heart, feeding the dying woman soup would be wasting it, and the girl could still pull through. Rotten, cynical thinking to be sure, but that was Auschwitz for you. With the best will in the world, she couldn't help them all.

"In your mother's condition, it would actually harm her," Orli said, gently placing the plate in Birdie's hands. White lies for the noble cause, and to hell with the black hole of despair that kept growing in Orli's chest, threatening to consume her whole. "She needs to be on a water-only diet until her fever breaks a little. You eat and I'll go get some sulfa drugs and water for you and your mother. I want the entire plate gone by the time I'm back."

Birdie smiled feebly and began slurping from the plate.

With a heavy heart, Orli headed back inside, before reappearing minutes later with a water carafe.

"Two pills for you," she said, pouring the water into the plate that was now licked clean. The girl was hungry still. Good sign. "And two for your mother."

In her feverish state, Birdie didn't notice that Orli produced the pills from two different pockets. She could only spare sulfa drugs for those who could still make it. Birdie's mother, she got morphine. Another rarity she shouldn't be parting so easily with, but now at least the woman would slip into death as though in a warm bath, and her suffering would be colored with all the shades of a rainbow. And what more could one wish for in their final moments?

Birdie's mother died that night. Orli discovered her enclosed in her daughter's arms the very next morning, sightless eyes gazing up at the sky where the dawn was just breaking, a faint smile permanently frozen on her bloodless lips. Death was kind to her in her final moments. It smoothed the lines on her face and saw her off in peace, under a starry sky, in her loving daughter's embrace.

Still, Birdie refused to part with her body when the corpse carrier detail pulled up at the infirmary with their cart. Herself burning with fever, she clutched her mother's body to her chest and pleaded with them not to burn her, because then nothing would be left of her and she needed a grave to lay stones on, to weep at and to speak to when... when...

"It's all right, Birdie," Orli said, lowering down on her haunches next to the girl. "They won't burn her. There's a Polish village nearby and there's a gravedigger there who can bury a body for a bribe. We'll bribe him and he'll bury her in the village cemetery. And after you get better, after you come out of here, you can go and visit her there. He'll show you the grave."

A meaningful look passed between Orli and the corpse detail men. They were young and still strong. They had lost their own parents to the Auschwitz chimneys too.

"Don't you fret, sister," one of them said, squatting next to Birdie. "We've turned this trick a few times already. Your mama will be laid to rest under the best apple tree one can find."

"Cherry," Birdie rasped at long last. Slowly, her grip on her mother's frame was loosening. "She liked cherries the best."

"Cherry, it is," the second cart puller agreed without batting an eyelid. "Tomorrow, we'll give you the name under which she will be buried. They have to use Polish names there, you know. You take care and remember it, so you know where to find her later."

They were lying so convincingly, even Orli began to wonder if there was indeed a Polish gravedigger who could bury a corpse in a fresh grave for a vial of morphine, even though it was she who had invented the entire story just moments ago.

"I'll take care," Birdie promised solemnly and surrendered her mother's body to their hands with a final kiss.

With the utmost care, they lowered it onto their death cart.

Orli blocked Birdie's view so that she wouldn't see all other corpses stacked there like firewood. "Come with me now, we'll find you a bed inside."

As they stepped through the doors of the infirmary, Orli threw a glance over her shoulder. The corpse carriers were stacking more bodies into their cart. Only those perished ones had no one to worry about them going up the chimney. All of their relatives were already dead.

The following week, August bled into September, and the death cart was coming by four times a day instead of the usual two. Birdie was finally showing signs of getting better, thanks to Orli's regiment of sulfa drugs and her own generously donated rations. Her fever had broken. She was still much too weak to be released back into the camp population, but insisted on helping Orli as much as she could.

With the same gentle care as she had been tended to, Birdie spoon-fed the patients much too weak to hold their own bowl of soup and washed those who had soiled themselves in their delirium without a single complaint. In her hazel eyes, just days ago veiled with unspeakable tragedy, a renewed sense of purpose had ignited.

"Alicja Kamińska," she muttered when she carried soiled garments outside to wash under a single rusty faucet.

"Alicja Kamińska," she repeated as she waved the wet cloth in the air to cool it before putting it back down on yet another burning forehead.

She had a name now, she had a reason to live, and did it really matter that the name was Orli's invention as much as the entire grave ruse?

"Alicja Kamińska." Birdie smiled and Orli nodded to her, grinning like a conspirator as well.

"Don't forget it now."

"I will never!"

The patients and the nursing staff paid no heed to Birdie's obsessive mutterings. In this communal madhouse, a Polish name wasn't the most insane thing to utter.

Only Dr. Kitt scrunched up his face as he heard Birdie repeat the name during his daily inspection. "What is she saying?" he asked Orli.

With as much nonchalance as it was possible to summon, Orli shrugged her shoulder. "Her mother's name—she passed away about a week ago."

He narrowed his eyes at Birdie's yellow star sewn onto the left breast of her dress. "Isn't she Jewish?"

"A *mischling*, Herr Doktor." Lies slipped easily from her tongue. "Her mother was a Polish gentile."

"A shame," he said.

Certainly, he wasn't sorry that a young girl had lost her mother. A shame that the gentile woman had passed, and the Jew was left to live. That's how they viewed it, the SS.

"At any rate," Dr. Kitt was all business now, having forgotten both the girl and her mother in an instant, "hand me all of the lists that you have and have all the medical staff wait outside."

In spite of herself, Orli blinked at him like an idiot. "The lists with which category, Herr Doktor? Recently admitted?"

He checked them daily, making Orli or Gerda strike the numbers of the deceased from them so that he could submit it to the administration. They weren't technically lists now but books, albums thick like medical encyclopedias. There was only a short list for the discharged now and Orli considered it to be a good day if it was half-filled by the end of it.

"No. All the lists. All of those you currently have here in the infirmary."

Orli stiffened but rushed to retrieve whatever lists she had from their physicians' cubicle. Upon her return, she saw Gerda watch Dr. Kitt gather them, without once looking at them, under his arm.

"Is that all?" he asked Orli as he scanned the infirmary with his glacial gaze.

"Yes, Herr Doktor."

He nodded. "Take your staff outside."

Like a flock of frightened sheep, they filed outside by the wall, eyes trained on the main camp thoroughfare. There, on the horizon, clouds of dust were rising from several transports heading their way.

"What is this now?" Gerda whispered, her shoulder pressing instinctively against Orli's.

Orli made no reply, only pressed her lips into a thin line so that they wouldn't spell disaster. They had all grown superstitious here. Naming death was the same as summoning it.

By the time the first truck with a red cross painted on its side pulled up by the entrance, Dr. Kitt had come out and scanned the sky.

"Looks like it's going to storm," he said to the SS men jumping off the back of the truck and disappearing inside the infirmary. "Make it snappy, will you?"

Preoccupied with watching the truck procession, Orli and her girls failed to notice the heavy purple clouds gathering above their heads. When the first patients began stumbling out of the infirmary barracks, a sudden gust of wind tore into their clothes and threw handfuls of sand into their faces, temporarily blinding them.

The SS eyed the sky as well and bellowed at the women to move *faster, faster, you lazy scum!*

The electricity in the air was almost tangible.

Holding onto her kerchief, Orli approached Dr. Kitt.

"Where are you taking them?" she asked. Her breathing quickened in panic. For the first time in her life did it occur to her that the air tasted almost like blood—sharp, metallic.

He looked at her as though she'd asked him something incredibly idiotic. "An SS man got it. This epidemic has gotten out of control, we can't have it spreading further."

"But, Herr Doktor..." She watched the SS men lash at the women who didn't move fast enough despite the fact that they, sick themselves, carried those unable to walk to the trucks. "They're not contagious on their own. The disease, it's transmitted by the mosquitos."

He swung round to face her, suddenly enraged. "Do you think me to be an idiot?"

At the sight of his eyes, Orli felt a terror wash over her like a torrent of water thrown out of an ice bucket. It only took one flick of a hand from him and she'd be thrown into the back of one of those trucks as well. "No, of course not. I would never—"

"Do you wish to educate me on the subject of malaria and how it spreads?"

"No, Herr Doktor, forgive me, please, it was never my intention to insult you..."

Whether it was her visible terror or the pleading in her voice, Dr. Kitt's face softened a tad. "I know perfectly well that they're not contagious on their own," he said. "But their blood is. A mosquito bites one of them, then heads outside and lands on one of the guards' exposed hands or face, and there you have it—a sick SS man. And the more patients you have, the bigger the chance more mosquitos will bite them and transmit the disease to us. As I said, we can't have it." He was silent for a few moments. "Myself, I'm not afraid of it. Haven't I been in the infirmary every single day since the outbreak?"

Orli nodded, still too afraid to open her mouth.

"Herr Kommandant's orders," the SS physician explained and shifted the lists from under one arm to another. "He has a responsibility to his men. You must understand it as a leader yourself."

"Yes, but—" Orli saw his warning glance, but there was no

stopping her now. Among women frantic with fear, Birdie was moving with a reassuring smile, helping to the back of the truck those who couldn't climb there themselves before climbing up herself. "Can't we spare those who are on the mend though? I have at least fifty girls I was about to submit for your inspection for discharge today—"

A shake of the head from Dr. Kitt and, just like that, their fates were sealed.

"Everyone must go. Herr Kommandant's orders."

From the back of the truck, Birdie waved at Orli. Orli waved back, barely seeing through the wall of tears.

The trucks had long departed. It was pouring something frightful outside, with raindrops as big as pebbles pummeling Orli and her staff's shivering frames. The SS physician had long dismissed them, but for some reason, none of them moved inside, even when the first lightning strike slashed the sky in two and tore the clouds into shreds, soaking them to the bone. They stood there, the sorriest funeral procession in the world, with their faces wet with rain or tears—no one could tell. Wet like drowned rats, feet drowning slowly in mud, and yet, it was still somehow better than going into the barracks that stood so deathly still that silence screamed louder than a thousand voices and nothing, not even the severest of storms, could drown it out.

Orli couldn't possibly tell how long they stood there. The storm eventually passed, and the sky was once again salmon-pink. A new truck pulled up, *Sonderkommando* men spilling out of its belly with canisters in their hands and gas masks hanging from their elbows.

"Go home, sisters," their leader called without meeting their eyes. His team worked the gas chambers and crematorium. He, better than anyone, knew what had just transpired. "We're going to fumigate the premises. Not good for you to breathe the toxic fumes."

Oh, the irony, Orli wanted to cry but instead only motioned for her girls to follow her. One by one, they peeled off the wall and headed north along the road without looking back.

"You asked me why I was starving myself."

Gerda started when she heard Orli speak.

"That's why," Orli said with a soul-crushing finality and gestured toward the empty barracks left behind. "It's all point-less. Everything that we do. In the end, we can't save anyone."

"Not pointless in the slightest." It wasn't Gerda who argued this time, but Miriam, Orli's little shadow. Miriam, who Orli had all but forgotten in the thick of things. But Miriam hadn't forgotten her. "What about me? Do I not count? You saved me, didn't you?"

Orli came to a sudden halt and stared at Miriam as though seeing her for the first time. It took a full minute for a faint smile to warm her face as she studied the girl's stubbornly drawn brow. "Of course, you count, my little one," Orli said.

"Well then, start acting like it," Miriam threw over her shoulder and set off in front of the group, her wooden clogs squelching in muddy mess.

That evening, Orli ate her bread and a piece of blood sausage—the entire thing—for the first time in months.

THIRTEEN

BIRKENAU. WINTER 1942

"Funny how one's perception changes once they're removed from normal life, isn't it?" Orli said, her gaze riveted to the snow falling in great flakes outside the window.

In the physicians' cubicle, it was not much warmer than outside its frostbitten walls. A small iron stove could only do so much against the onslaught of the freezing temperatures that had descended on their forsaken quarters in December. During the day, with the pale sun peering blindly through the anemic clouds, it was all right. It was as soon as the grinning skull of the moon took its place that their breaths began showing in translucent clouds. And against it all, only a few layers of newspaper insulating their bodies and feet from cold.

Sometimes, the *Sonderkommando* felt charitable and threw a few stacks of old papers to Orli and Gerda whenever they stopped by with their death cart to collect their macabre harvest. Sometimes, transports were delayed and there were no newspapers to be had. Then, they had to trade them with the other inmates for a piece of bread or, in Enna's case, for her young body. Neither Enna, nor Orli nor Gerda ever kept all the papers to themselves. Just a couple of layers was enough; the rest—for their patients. It was they who were immobile and sick. They—physicians and nurses—they were moving around. They were keeping themselves warm with work.

"What do you mean?" Gerda asked above the rim of her metal plate with the soup that had gone cold long before the kitchen commando had a chance to distribute it.

As always, they took their lunch in turns. Only two persons per cubicle; the rest tending to the unfortunate ones confined to this communal coffin they called an infirmary. After the SS had gassed its entire population mere months ago, its nursing staff only referred to it as such.

"When I was a free woman, each season was marked by something special and exciting," Orli explained, tracing frosty designs on the window with her index finger. "Spring meant bicycles and hair flowing in the wind and the smell of blooming lilacs in the air. Summer had its lakes and sand between the toes and sweating beer mugs in open cafés. In autumn, new coat and hat collections in the department store windows and golden leaves everywhere and Oktoberfest and rainy days on which brandy tasted the best. And, in winter, everything drowning in tinsel and the sharp scent of trees for sale and children on sleds and skiing in the Alps and the fireplace the landlady had burning in the evenings. When everyone would go to sleep, I loved sprawling on the rug in front of it and I would read until I'd fall asleep, right there, in front of the fire..." Her voice trailed off, full of dreamy recollections of the past that was no more.

"And now?" Gerda asked, despite knowing the answer.

"And now I distinguish the seasons by outbreaks. Malaria in summer, typhus in the fall. Without a calendar, I could tell it was December because the first frostbite cases began to arrive. It was the same in Ravensbrück. The SS are sending them to the forest to cut the trees for their barracks and mess halls. Minus thirty outside and they're stomping through that snow in their wooden clogs. Poor wretches."

"You're just a regular philosopher, aren't you?" Gerda smirked, but the teasing came out good-natured, softened somehow with their shared plight.

"I suppose I am. They sent me to prison for reeducation and, I'll be damned, they saw to that. I had entered the cell as an ordinary typist and now look at me, a physician of the first sort and Kant's follower if ever you saw one."

They laughed about it because there was nothing else to laugh about and when the laughter died, just like everything else did in Birkenau, they went about their work, accursed tending to the damned in that seventh circle of hell created by men on earth.

Orli didn't exaggerate when she shared her musings with Gerda. In the heart of winter, the Birkenau infirmary was a macabre theater of human suffering, a place where the grotesque and the tragic danced in a grim waltz. The air was thick with the stench of decay and whatever meager disinfectants were allotted to them, the walls echoed with the cries of the dying, and the ground was stained with the blood of the fallen.

All of Orli's staff moved in the midst of this hellish landscape like forsaken apparitions. Their hands, cracked and raw from the biting cold, trembled as they moved from patient to patient, administering what little aid they could.

Just a day ago, Dr. Kitt had unloaded an entire truck of women in front of astounded infirmary staff. "Would've gassed them all had they not been from the leather factory detail," he grumbled as he'd shoved the list with numbers into Orli's hands. "A new decree demands we preserve skilled workers at any cost. Easy for those Berlin pen-pushers to issue all of those decrees, they're not the ones who're risking their skin if the epidemic jumps from those skilled workers onto them."

He was still muttering under his breath as he set off in the direction of his staff car, soaking his gloved hands with alcohol and swiping at them furiously with a pristine white hand-kerchief.

"See that it doesn't get out of hand like malaria did!" he'd thrown over his shoulder before disappearing into the comfort of his car.

Orli had looked at the list, then at the feverish women shifting nervously from one foot to another in front of her and motioned them silently in after herself.

Typhus, a specter that stalked the camp with a relentless fervor, had already laid claim to many. It snaked its way through the barracks with ruthless efficiency, leaving a trail of fevered bodies in its wake. Orli would often find herself staring into the glassy eyes of the afflicted, their bodies convulsing as they were consumed by fever-induced delirium. But now, with these new women in her charge, things were different somehow.

"You're prohibited by the SS from dying, hear me?" Orli addressed each one of them during her rounds, much like she was doing now. "So, do whatever you want. Cry, vomit, soil yourself, curse me in words your mother would slap you for, but don't you dare die."

"What if we do?" one of them asked when she was lucid enough to talk. Red was her name; not the real name, of course, but the nickname given to her by her girlfriends. At first, Orli thought it was due to her hair (the stubble that was growing out was indeed a strawberry blonde color), but as soon as Red was well enough to talk, Orli realized that it was due to her flaming temperament and smart mouth that just didn't know when to shut up.

"You'll be in a lot of trouble," Orli replied with a straight face as she stuck the thermometer under Red's armpit.

"Such as? Can't kill us twice, can they?"

"Can kill off the rest of your barracks in retribution. Hold it for ten minutes and call me or a nurse when you're done."

"How do I know when it's ten minutes?"

"Here, take my watch," Orli said with the same impenetrable expression, feigning removing an invisible wristwatch from her hand. "Count to sixty ten times in a row, Red, and stop asking idiotic questions—I have enough work without you."

"I *am* your work."

"You're work, all right. A piece of it."

Orli grumbled and swapped sarcastic comments with those who were well enough to indulge in that word-sparring with her but threw her all at each of them, because she would drop dead before she'd see the entire population of the infirmary go to the gas chambers like before.

As well as typhus, there was the frostbite. The winter in Birkenau was cruel, its icy winds gnawing at the bare flesh of the inmates. Orli lost count of the blackened fingers and toes of the victims she had examined just this past week, the necrotic tissue a stark contrast to the pallid skin. It was frostbite she loathed the worst, and just her bad luck, Miriam was now leading yet another woman up to her with telling signs of it on at least four of her digits.

"Doctor—" was all she said, holding her hand in front of Orli's grim face with an expression that was a mixture of frantic worry and puzzlement.

"Work detail?" Orli asked, probing the tissue next to the blackened flesh.

"Sewing factory," the woman replied.

Orli looked up at her sharply. The sewing factory, much like any other detail that kept inmates under a roof during the coldest months, was considered to be a kosher duty many of the inmates coveted yet only a few were fortunate to secure. "Were you exposed to any negative temperatures for a prolonged period of time?" Orli asked.

For a moment, the woman appeared to consider. Suddenly, her face brightened. "Frau Aufseherin's dog lost the tag from his collar somewhere in the snow. She made me look for it. It would have been easier to find if it was day, but she only saw that it was missing in the evening and wasn't even sure where the dog had lost it... At any rate, I was at it all night, pretty much. I did find it after all, though," she added with pride that tore at Orli's very insides. "Did I get into something while digging in the snow?"

"No, my good woman. It's frostbite."

A glance passed between Orli and Miriam—a glance during which nothing was said and yet everything understood. With a slight nod of her head, Miriam set off in the direction of their makeshift operating room—just a cubicle, really, with a wooden table and a bright bulb dangling above it from a single black cord.

"Frostbite," the woman repeated.

"Yes."

"Is it dangerous?"

Kosher detail employee, to be sure. Orli sighed. Had she been from the outside detail, she would have known all about frostbite and what sentence it carried for its unfortunate owner.

"Fingers will have to come off."

The woman started, went very pale, and stared at Orli for an infinitely long time.

"No," she said at last. "Why would they have to...? No! There must be treatment options. I'll just boil some water when I'm back in my barracks later tonight and keep them warm until they thaw off."

"They won't thaw off," Orli explained patiently. Denial was always the hardest part of the process. Some women refused to believe altogether that there was no turning back from the deathly black flesh. "The flesh is already dead, the process is irreversible. If we don't amputate now, gangrene will set in and then your entire hand will have to come off."

"No!" The woman sounded hysterical now. She stared at Orli as though she was the enemy of the state, trembling with her whole body. The damaged hand she held close to her chest as if afraid that Orli would grab it and hack it off if she weren't diligent enough. "They warned me about your infirmary. A band of butchers is what you are. All you know is how to amputate something. Is there a real doctor here?" She whipped around, searching the barracks with her wild eyes.

From their beds, women looked at her apathetically. One of them called for her to just shut her beer trap and let them sleep if she knew what was good for her.

"There's an obstetrician I can call for a second opinion," Orli suggested in the mildest possible tone.

"Obstetrician?" the woman barked a laugh. "What good is that going to do? I need a surgeon. A real one!"

"Hard luck then." Orli shrugged and turned to Red, who was watching the entire scene with an amused look about her. "Your fever is going down. Good news."

She shook the thermometer to reset it and moved to the next bed, purposely ignoring the sewing detail woman.

"Wait!" the latter called.

Orli turned to her, all infinite patience.

"My fingers can't be dead. I can move them just fine—see?" She proceeded to wiggle her black digits in front of Orli's face. "I was working just fine today until our Kapo sent me to the infirmary. I can go back to work this very instant, they don't even hurt."

"They don't hurt because your pain receptors are dead as well," Orli explained. After the first shock and denial, there always came negotiations. "You can go back to work—it makes no difference to me personally. But the Kapo will only send you back here again. And if you're unfortunate enough to encounter Dr. Kitt when he makes his rounds and he finds out you're from the sewing detail, he'll strike your number off the list before you know what's hit you."

The woman's brows knitted in apparent confusion.

"You're from sewing detail," Red chimed in from behind Orli's back. "Fingers must come off. A sewing detail inmate without fingers equals gas. Understand now?"

"Red." Orli regarded her with reproach.

"What? I'm trying to help her. If Dr. Orli treats you now, you'll be gone without any paperwork. Kitt will never even know that you were here. And then your Kapo will reassign you to a detail where you don't need too many fingers."

"Like what?" With the resignation, the tears always came.

"Like the Kanada, for instance," Orli said. "The warehouse complex where the new arrivals' belongings are processed. You don't need all ten fingers to sort shoes from clothes and personal items."

Finally, surrender. "Will it hurt?" the woman asked, holding her hand before her as though saying her final goodbyes.

"It will," Orli admitted. There was no point in lying. "We have no anesthesia here, but we do have rubbing alcohol. I'll mix it with water and it'll numb you enough to get through it."

She followed Orli like the condemned, sniffling quietly behind her back.

"It's all right, sister," Miriam told her as she helped her onto the operating table. Enna and Velma were already there as well —human restraints in the absence of chloroform. "They make such fancy prosthetic limbs now. Have you seen the Dublin hand? The fellow who invented it had an entire arm missing just below his shoulder. And what do you know? The thing works off the remaining muscles in his arm. He can grab a glass, drink from it, empty it, wash it—you name it, it works just as well as your ordinary arm!"

"And you'll only have four fingers missing," Enna cooed as she lay her entire body across their patient.

Orli prepared the scalpel as Velma grasped the woman's legs.

"Perhaps, you can even find a good prosthetic in the Kanada," Orli feigned cheerfulness when everything inside of her was screaming. "There's an SS man who supervises it and I hear he's very kind. Maybe he'll allow you to keep it."

She was still talking as she sliced just under the blackened flesh, louder and louder to drown out the woman's inhuman screams, until Orli herself was screaming—screaming until her voice was hoarse—about prosthetic limbs and kind SS men and the world that waited for them just outside the gates and the champagne they would open one day to celebrate their freedom and the countries they would all visit together and the mountains they would climb and the oceans they would cross because the world was their oyster and there was nothing impossible for them because they were good and strong and much too young to die.

The pallid winter sun was setting by the time Orli finished bandaging the woman's hand. Only a thumb was left intact and the rest—lost forever to Auschwitz, and all for some blasted dog's tag.

"Thank you, Doctor Orli," the woman said, ashen-faced and punch-drunk from both alcohol and the torturous operation she had had to endure.

"You're welcome. Stay here until four. Dr. Kitt never arrives earlier than five, so that'll give you plenty of time to make yourself scarce before he sees you."

Before parting with the woman, Orli gave her the names of the *Sonderkommando* men who knew the right Kanada girls, who knew the kind SS man in charge. Only after she left did Orli realize that she had never asked the woman's name.

FOURTEEN

"First, typhus and now this!" Gerda cursed quietly, helping Orli prop their latest admission against the wall.

Both knew she had been brought in much too late, when her fever had climbed to the point of her blood nearly boiling, with her lungs so filled with fluid, every breath she took was a struggle for survival, each exhale a desperate plea for mercy.

Pneumonia was their newest visitor. It swept through the crowded barracks already weakened by cold and malnutrition, with ferociousness rivaling that of the SS. Just as mercilessly, it harvested its human crops, but not before it tortured them until the will to live had abandoned them entirely. The infirmary was full of them now, their rattling cough a cacophony of communal suffering.

"And just our luck, it's the contagious type," Gerda hissed under her breath, annoyed by her helplessness to the point of distraction.

Orli replied nothing; only coughed into her fist away from her colleague and the patient and wiped her hand on the hem of her dress. The relentless onslaught of disease and death took its toll on even the strongest of spirits. That day, she felt particularly tired and out of sorts. Even talking consumed too much of her energy and she had so many patients still to tend to.

Gerda's head shot up instantly, her sharp eyes narrowing on Orli. "You aren't sick, are you?"

Orli could have lied to anyone, but not to Gerda or Miriam. Among the medical staff, the three shared a bond forged in the crucible of shared suffering; a bond that was often the only thing keeping them sane amidst the madness. It was pointless to try to conceal anything from the other two. Whenever one of them suffered, two of her sisters felt the pain in their very bones.

"Just a little bug. I took my own temperature, it's just a bit elevated: 37.2."

"Stop faking it then and go back to work." The corner of Gerda's mouth lifted in a grin.

Orli, too, was grateful for the inside joke—the Auschwitz kind regular civilians would never understand.

"Nurse!" their patient suddenly cried, her dull eyes shining brightly with an almost frightening gleam in them.

At once, both physicians went silent. With such cases, the moment of sharp lucidity came in only one case—just before the very end.

"Nurse, I need a priest," she said, grasping Orli's wrist in a surprisingly strong grip. She spoke German, with a strong Polish accent, but very correct German nevertheless—a political prisoner just as they were. A red triangle: either Polish intelligentsia or a teacher, or, even worse, a journalist who just wouldn't stop writing her liberal truth under the Nazis' very nose. There was no chance of asking her now.

"I'm sorry, sister," Orli said, feeling words rolling in her own chest almost in time with her patient's. "There's not one to be had here. Men aren't allowed in the women's camp. *Sonderkommando* only and the carpenters, but I know of no priest among them."

The dying woman nodded, her breath rattling loud in her

throat. "It's all right then. I'll confess to you. God will forgive me, due to the circumstances."

"He most certainly will," Gerda agreed and pressed her lips into an unyielding line. Orli knew by now that it was Gerda's profound conviction that if whatever higher power indeed existed, it owed them all heavenly bliss of the highest order for the eternity to come just to make up for what they'd been put through on this earth.

"Whenever my husband would get drunk, he'd beat and rape me," their patient breathed, her hand a vise on Orli's own wrist. She was straining to talk, to get all the words out in one last breath. "One night, I couldn't take it anymore, so I waited until he passed out in his drunken state, took his gun out of his drawer, put it in his hand, put his hand to his temple and pressed the trigger."

After delivering her confession, she slumped against the wall and froze there, as though awaiting her sentencing. And in those last moments, two women, who had never asked to fulfil the duty of a priest nor a judge, took her by her hands and stroked her hair and tear-streaked cheeks.

"Good for you, sister. That pig deserved it."

"Go in peace now. You are forgiven."

As though granted permission by God Himself, the woman smiled with an inexplicably blissful expression about her, closed her eyes and released her last breath.

She was still smiling when the *Sonderkommando* came with their death cart for their daily collection.

By the next morning, Orli fell ill. Fell in the true sense of the word: one moment, she was up from her cot, and the next, down on the ground with the world upside down, twisting and twirling like a demented carousel around her, only the alarmed faces of her girls around her keeping her from losing consciousness entirely.

"Aurelia Reichert, what kind of a joke is this now?" Gerda was the first one upon her, touching Orli's clammy forehead and prodding her body shaking with chills. "Have you gotten enough of doctoring and decided to take a break in a contagious ward cot? You could have just asked for a day off, you know—we would have covered!"

Gerda was the most collected one of them, stoicism personified, and judging by her shrill babbling, Orli realized that things weren't looking good. As though the racing carousel of her surroundings and the bile rising in her throat wasn't enough of an indication.

Twisting to one side, she spat a few times, apologized, tried to hold it by clenching her teeth the best she could, but it came gushing out of her, this greenish something Miriam set on cleaning up right that instant.

"Don't touch," Orli tried to stop her. "May be contagious."

"So all of us will get sick then," Miriam declared and renewed her efforts with doubled determination.

"Let's get you back to bed," Enna suggested and produced a piece of bread from under her apron. "I'll put it under your pillow. For later. For when you feel hungry again."

"I'll boil water and bring it for you to drink once it cools down," Velma said and was gone before Orli could tell her not to worry.

Her tongue, just like all of her gestures, was much too thick and sluggish, too alien for her own body, as were her arms and legs that didn't fit right into their joint sockets anymore and ached dully, together with her teeth and her eyes and even her hair that couldn't possibly hurt but hurt nevertheless. She wanted to lie down, but Gerda propped her against the wall, awakening the memories Orli didn't want to have awoken, and told her to stay still and no funny business.

"I'm bringing you sulfa drugs."

"Save them for the patients."

"You are a patient now."

There was no arguing with that logic, and besides, Orli couldn't argue even if she wanted to.

The patient. The enemy had infiltrated their ranks.

In the feverish beginning of the delirium, Orli wondered if there was something she ought to confess to. She didn't kill her husband, did she? No... It was he who had virtually sentenced her to death by denouncing her and her communist cell to the authorities. And all for what? A dream of a community where everyone worked and everyone contributed and everything was shared equally and every person was appreciated based on their achievements, instead of their race or skin color or religion. Was she a criminal for dreaming? Dreaming...

She was dreaming of an ice-cone melting off her tongue and some gangsters who came to shoot at her aunt's husband... Or was it the aunt's husband who was doing the shooting? He shot just above her head and the marble column which he wanted to crash down upon her fell but didn't hurt her in the slightest. The face of the gangster with a machine gun changed to her husband's. And she was still alive, despite all...

"Here, swallow."

Gerda. Bitter, harsh pills on her cotton tongue. Cool water slipping into her parched mouth. It tasted like silver. Does silver have a taste? It must have...

More dreams. No ice cream this time, but dogs licking her face and her laughing until her stomach hurt. Someone screaming for their mother... Must be amputating frostbite again... How was Red doing? Red dancing on stage dressed like Marlene Dietrich in *The Blue Angel*. Dr. Kitt forcing her eye open and shining light into it. A dream or not? She wasn't unconscious, there was no need in any light, don't you know it? You're a physician trained for these things.

Did she just say it out loud? Was there a difference if it was only a dream?

Contagious ward. Everyone with pneumonia and typhus into it and lock the doors and no one enters except for you. Face masks at all times.

Cool breath in her very ear (or was her ear so hot, it felt cool?): "Don't fret, Orli, you're staying put where you are. He's not coming back with the inspection anytime soon. You should have seen him running out of here as though the devil himself was chasing him!"

Nights came but they were no better than the days. At night, there was no one to check on her position and she gradually slid down to lie flat on her back and woke up nearly choking on liquid in her lungs, gasping for air in the darkness that was about to claim her. She apologized profusely to Gerda and Miriam and Velma and Enna for waking them up and keeping them up because they just wouldn't go back to sleep, would they? No, they took turns boiling water for her and holding her head above the steam and making her take deep, impossible breaths until she would cough up all the mucus there was to cough up into a rag one of them was holding and lose herself to several hours of a fitful dream that was more of a nightmare if she were entirely honest.

They were wrong about Dr. Kitt, too. He materialized out of thin air like some wretched apparition and hovered over Orli, a thick facial mask fitted closely over his nose and mouth.

"She's not contagious, Herr Doktor," Gerda reported behind his back, wringing her hands when he couldn't see her agony. "It's been two weeks and none of us have gotten sick. She's perfectly harmless and getting better already, see? Her gaze is focused and her lungs are clearing up. She'll be on her feet in no time."

"How much is no time?" Dr. Kitt didn't care to inspect Orli himself to hear just how much clearer her lungs had become.

Gerda blinked at his back as though it was the most idiotic thing one could possibly ask. "A week, I would guess."

"Too long. Two days for the entire contagious ward and inmate 502. If there's no improvement, I'm sending the trucks."

He was long gone and Orli still stared at Gerda with mute horror painted on her face.

"Orli, don't take it to heart," Gerda tried to speak, but her own voice betrayed her with its tremoring. In the corner, Miriam was crying silently, her shoulders shaking with mute sobs. "He's just saying that. To scare you into recovery." She tried to smile, but the smile twitched, twisted into a grimace and off she went before Orli could see that she was crying too, the most stoic one of them all.

FIFTEEN

It was one thing to wonder if you were about to die from pneumonia. It was an entirely different thing to have a clock hanging over your head counting the hours till your execution. Forty-eight hours. Forty-eight hours and then there would be no Orli.

"When the death cart comes, call one of the *Sonderkommando* men to me," Orli instructed Miriam later that afternoon.

"Whatever for?" Miriam regarded her, suddenly on guard.

"Want to get some before getting gassed," Orli grumbled in response and lost herself in another fit of coughing. "Just call him and mind your own affairs, won't you?"

Miriam was suddenly all smiles. "You *are* getting better."

Not fast enough, though.

The night had crept up and pulled its funereal shroud over the camp when the *Sonderkommando* man stomped into Orli's makeshift ward. With no light burning inside the physicians' cubicle, his silhouette was black against the yellow light pouring from the corridor.

"Wanted to see me, Doktor Orli?"

Orli recognized Yasha's voice—the tall Jewish youth who had only survived thanks to his physical strength. It was he and his mates who had promised Birdie to bury her mother in a Polish village. Just for his huge heart Orli would be forever grateful to him, and trust him with her very life.

Instead of a reply, Orli patted the bunk bed on which she was half-sitting. "Have you five minutes to spare? Don't fret, I'm not contagious."

With three long strides, he crossed the space between them and perched his hulking frame on the edge of Orli's bed. "How goes it, Doc?"

"It goes," Orli replied and hoped that the rattling in her chest wasn't too offensive. "Tell me about the gas chambers, please."

His eyes glistened in the semi-darkness. "Why would you want to know about them? Not enough nightmares to keep you up at night?"

"Enough," Orli conceded. "Dr. Kitt was here. In two days, he'll be sending trucks for those not up and about. I'm not up and about; hence, I need to know where I'll be heading to."

Yasha released a breath that hung heavy in the air, much like the oppressive silence that followed.

"Damn it all to hell, Doktor Orli," he said at last, shaking his head. "I'm so very sorry."

"Don't be. Just tell me."

"Well, there's not much to tell. People go into this anteroom, where they undress. Everything is very orderly. They're given their time. We're present at this stage, together with supervising SS men, so we can comfort them if needed."

Orli nodded.

"Then they go into the next chamber, which is the gas chamber. Once everyone is inside, the SS man in charge closes the airtight door after them. Another SS man, who wears a gas mask, opens a hatch in the roof and pours these bluish pellets inside. When they come into contact with warm air, they turn into gas. It paralyzes people's airways and they die of oxygen starvation. Once the SS man in charge checks through a peep-hole that they're all dead, he gives us a sign and we put on these industrial fans they had installed there. Once the gas is gone, we take the bodies out and take them to the crematorium..." His voice trailed off. "But I suppose you're not interested in what happens after."

Orli smiled into the falling night. "Indeed. Frankly, it makes no difference what they do to my body after. But do tell me, and be honest, please: is it painful?"

"The gas?"

"Yes."

Yasha was silent a space. To Orli, that was answer enough.

"It's not instant," he said as mildly as possible. "They suffo-cate. Slowly. Call for their mothers, brothers, sisters, wives and husbands. Plead to let them out. Pound on the door and beg to—"

"Thank you," Orli cut him off before he could say more. "I've heard everything I needed to hear."

Orli refused dinner that night. Officially, due to nausea. Unofficially... well, they would understand the next morning and hopefully appreciate her not wasting precious resources when someone with a chance of a survival could use them.

She took great care to thank her girls for everything they'd done for her, for being such selfless workers; held their hands when they approached her cot before settling for the night, but not for too long. Hopefully, they would forgive that too, her not saying proper goodbyes, and wouldn't hold it against her.

Orli waited for the women who had become closer than blood sisters to her to slip into deep slumbers full of blissful forgetfulness—the only escape from the mad world of Auschwitz—and only then lowered her legs to the ice-cold floor. The cold was sobering somewhat. Her head didn't spin as much as it ordinarily would.

As soon as the attack had passed, Orli padded barefoot out of the cubicle and into the infirmary. Without letting go of the wall—she was still much too weak to trust her body not to collapse—she made it to the physicians' station and counted the shelves in the dark. After reaching the one she'd been seeking, Orli probed for the supplies and identified the few rolls of pills they'd been keeping for the particularly severe cases.

Hopefully, they would forgive her for that, too. She was a severe case, after all.

Without wasting another minute, Orli unwrapped the precious morphine pills, threw the entire palmful into her mouth, cringed at the bitter taste but chewed the chalky mass until her tongue began to tingle. It would have been nice to chase them down with water, but oh well... This slight discomfort was still nothing compared to what would have awaited her in the gas chamber. Together with the pasty residue of pills, immense relief slid down her throat and spread into her lungs that expanded somehow with the promise of the end. The end of suffering, the end of witnessing suffering and being unable to help it—Orli couldn't tell anymore which one was worse.

She wiped her face with the back of her hand as she probed her way back along the same wall. Mourning her own approaching death—pathetic, for sure, but didn't she have the right to? She hadn't chosen it on purpose, hadn't decided to off herself *just because*. It was simply the lesser of two evils. So she would cry all she wanted—for the freedom she would never experience again, for the sea that would never roll off her bare feet in summer, for the young lambs she wouldn't hold on her vacation in Austria, for the new dresses she'd never wear, for the friends she'd never hug again, for the movies that others would see and not her. And, the most important, for the war to end and Hitler to hang without her celebrating it with the others until they were drunk with wine and joy and their voices hoarse from singing.

Orli climbed into her bed and curled into a ball. She wept silently and prayed for death to claim her—from the morphine or the broken heart, but just take her already and end this misery once and for all. However, instead of death, nausea came again. Orli sat up as the first wave of it rolled over her and pressed her back against the wall, holding unnaturally still, breathing through this last obstacle between herself and ultimate freedom.

Should have swallowed them one by one, with water, a though flashed in her mind. *Should have known better, you feebleminded cow!*

One of the following waves was so strong, Orli clenched her teeth and moaned with effort to keep the contents of her stomach intact. It must have been that moan, or Gerda's blasted physician's hearing trained on anyone needing aid, but to Orli's devastation, she was suddenly on her feet, awake and alert as though she hadn't just been snoring softly in her cot nearby.

"Orli, what?" she asked. "Are you sick?"

Orli swiped at the hand Gerda tried to test her forehead with.

"Why are you so cold? Orli? Good Christ, your hands are as cold as ice! Here, let me—"

"No." Orli freed her wrist from Gerda's grip before she could check her pulse, but Gerda still caught it and dug her finger into the vein, where life was still fluttering, uncertain and frantic.

"Orli, what have you done?" Gerda demanded in a voice full of steel.

"Must be pneumonia," Orli replied feebly and raised her head as high as possible to stave off another nausea attack.

"This is no pneumonia and you know it. What did you do? Tell me right this instant or so help me God!"

"Gerda, let me be, will you?" Orli's head was swimming, but not with nausea anymore. She was suddenly all heavy limbs wrapped in cotton, losing herself to sleep. "They would have gassed me."

"What did you take, you idiot? Tell me right this instant!" Gerda was shaking her now, slapping her cheeks and forcing her to stay awake. "Morphine, wasn't it? Decided to take the easy way out? Not on my watch, sister! You're not leaving me alone here, you hear me?"

Roused by the commotion, the nurses were up now as well, their frantic movements in stark contrast to the usual desolate nightly rhythm of the infirmary's communal breathing.

"Miriam, salt water here, now!" Orli heard Gerda scream before feeling her jaw being propped open and two fingers reaching as far as the back of her throat, pressing on the tongue until she was gagging and finally expunging the contents of her stomach on the floor.

There wasn't much to purge; there hadn't been anything else in her stomach besides the pills and bile, but Gerda still wasn't satisfied. As soon as Miriam returned with a pot of the vile concoction, Gerda forced the water down Orli's throat until she vomited again and again, until her stomach hurt from spasms and her hands trembled with weakness.

"On your feet, inmate 502. Walk it off."

"Can't..." All she wanted was to be left alone, just to sleep, sleep...

"We got most of it out of your system, but some already got into your bloodstream." Gerda's voice came in as though through cotton wool stuffed in Orli's ears. "Can't sleep now. Need to move to keep you awake, you hear me? Up, up, up!"

With Miriam's help, Gerda hoisted her up somehow and made Orli stumble about in circles. Time seemed to slow, each second a painful reminder of the thin line between life and death, but even in her borderline state, Orli knew that neither Gerda nor Miriam would lose that battle. They were much too obstinate, just as she was. They refused to see reason even when there was reason to be seen; refused to surrender even one person to the Grim Reaper if they could help it.

"Orli," Miriam whispered as she held Orli's elbow to support her, "you can't do this. You can't give up."

Orli turned to look at her, her eyes vacant but at least not closed any longer. "They're going to gas me, you amiable nitwit! You'll only have me for another day and after that—"

Gerda squeezed her hand, the touch a silent promise. "They won't," she said softly. "If you were well enough to make it to the medicine cabinet, you'll be well enough to put on a performance for Dr. Kitt tomorrow. He doesn't stay here longer than five minutes. And for five minutes, you can tough it out, little soldier. I know it gets too much sometimes, but we can't seek an easy way out: we have to fight, for those who can't."

The entire night, Orli's girls cared for her with a fierce determination. They watched their friend fight against the despair, against the dark pull of death. And with each passing hour, they saw a spark rekindle in Orli's eyes, a spark that had been all but extinguished.

The following morning, as Orli looked around the infirmary from the door of their cubicle and saw faces marked by pain and suffering, she realized that they were all fighters. They were more than victims, more than numbers on a roll call: they were survivors, clinging to life against all odds.

And so, as the evening drew near, and together with it, Dr. Kitt's macabre countdown, Orli braced herself, tied the mask around her face to conceal its paleness and, thanks to the morphine still coursing through her body, moved seamlessly among her patients just in time for the SS physician to walk in and stare at such a miraculous recovery with mute astonishment.

He still sent contagious cases to be gassed as he'd threatened he would. Only Orli wasn't among them; Orli and a few women Gerda and her girls had managed to whip into a somewhat presentable state by the time of the SS's arrival. Not even a dozen, but amidst the suffering, amidst the despair, there was still a glimmer of hope, a flicker of resilience. And as Orli met Gerda's gaze, she knew that they would endure. They would endure, for they had no other choice.

As the infirmary fell silent, save for the occasional moan of pain or the soft whisper of a prayer, Orli found herself reflecting on their grim reality. It was a world of constant suffering, a world where death was an ever-present specter. But it was also a world where the human spirit refused to be extinguished, where hope persevered amidst the darkness.

In the heart of winter, in the depths of despair, they found the strength to fight, to survive, to endure. And in doing so, they defied their captors, they defied death itself. For in the end, it was not just about surviving, but about retaining their humanity, their dignity, in the midst of unimaginable horror. Amidst the bleakness of the infirmary, amidst the brutality of Birkenau, they were more than just survivors. They were warriors, each of them a beacon of resilience, a beacon of hope. And as long as they had that, Orli knew, they would never truly be defeated.

SIXTEEN

SEHNDE, GERMANY. NOVEMBER 1961

Five weeks before New Year's Day

She's quiet today and not in a good way. Her silences are always full of screams no one can hear. You recognize the echo of their agony in her dark eyes, but that's all she allows you to see. That, and closed files she hasn't touched in a few days.

Gently, you ask her if she has changed her mind.

About her testimony? Don't be silly, of course not.

What is it then?

One name is missing.

A name?

A name from the list. The most important name of all. The name of the man who'd committed the worst crimes will be absent from the courtroom.

She stares out of the window into the wintery expanse. They called him an angel, you know. But, really, he was the devil. The devil himself, she tells you. So many men looking for him all over the world and no one has uncovered him yet. As though he went back to the Hades from whence he'd emerged. She's not religious, but sometimes one does begin to wonder...

She stops herself abruptly and tosses her head with an embarrassed smile. Is this how madness starts? she asks you. With wondering?

SEVENTEEN

BIRKENAU. SUMMER 1943

The morning of July 23, 1943 dawned with an ominous stillness over Auschwitz-Birkenau. On this sultry morning, the physicians' cubicle was abuzz with whispers of a new arrival, a man shrouded in mystery—Dr. Josef Mengele.

"Have you seen him yet?" It was the question Velma met Enna with every single morning.

"Where would I see him? I've been here with you the entire time, haven't I?"

"You sneak out at night, you minx!"

"Where I sneak out, there are no SS doctors, only inmates like myself, you daft bat!"

"Maybe you caught a glimpse? I heard he's handsome like a movie star."

"I heard he pulled men out of the burning tank on the Eastern Front. A war hero," Miriam chimed in as she boiled the bandages to be dried and reused.

"If he saved lives risking his own, maybe he's a kind one, at last," Velma mused out loud.

"At this point, anyone is better than Dr. Kitt," Gerda muttered.

Orli nodded from her seat at the table, where she was disinfecting the utensils for the upcoming day. "I still can't believe they transferred him away from us. Good riddance to bad rubbish. All he knew was gas. Pneumonia? Off to the chimney with you. A broken finger? To the gas. Lice? To the gas."

"Mosquito bite—definitely gas!" Gerda added with a sardonic snarl. "Who knew if it was a malaria-carrying mosquito? Better safe than sorry."

"SS logic." Orli snorted softly. It was all they could do with all this death around them—laugh at it—for they were helpless to do anything else, least of all stop it.

It was right after the morning roll call that Orli was summoned to the main entrance by an extremely excited Velma.

"He's coming, Orli! Go report to him, now!"

Dropping the bandage she was applying and motioning for Miriam to take over, Orli rose swiftly to her feet. Her heart pounding in her chest, she wiped her suddenly-wet palms on her dress and slipped out of the dim, musty infirmary. Her eyes adjusted to the harsh sunlight, squinting to make out the figure approaching from the distance where his staff car was parked. A man impeccably dressed in a crisp SS uniform, his black boots polished to a mirror finish, his silver insignia glinting in the sunlight.

Birkenau grapevine didn't lie. His appearance was indeed striking, almost enchanting, with his high cheekbones, deep-set eyes, and chiseled jawline. Though, as he approached closer, Orli couldn't help but notice that his eyes seemed cold and distant, devoid of any human warmth. But who knew what horrors he had witnessed on the Eastern Front? Orli's own eyes carried a permanently haunted look about them, two wells of perpetual twilight where no sun would ever reach.

Through the heavy silence, his footsteps echoed ominously

against the cobblestone path, each step a chilling reminder of the power he wielded. Their new supervisor. The man who now held their very lives in the palm of his gloved hand.

Eyes down now, Orli froze to attention as she'd been trained to and saw the tips of his black boots stop within inches of her own feet. Out of the corner of her eye, she saw Dr. Mengele remove the white glove finger by finger, each movement performed with clinical precision.

"Are you in charge here?" he asked, his voice coated with a calmness that was chilling somehow—cool like surgical steel. "It's all right, you may look at me. You're political, aren't you? Aryan?"

Orli looked and was instantly stunned by the warmest smile of such impossible charm she'd rarely seen in a free world, let alone Auschwitz.

"Yes, Herr Doktor," Orli replied, finally finding her voice. She felt odd under that gaze; wasn't sure what to make of that genuine smile and the eyes looking her over, cold and assessing. "Inmate 502, Aurelia Reichert, Birkenau camp physician reporting."

On Dr. Mengele's chest, an Iron Cross for war merits. The rumors had this right, too—he was a war hero.

An old camp instinct sensed something about him, and yet, Orli silenced it on purpose. Most of all, she wished to believe that after years of torture, fate had smiled down at them and sent them, if not a guardian angel to keep them safe, someone who wouldn't threaten the entire infirmary with gas at the slightest provocation. Then, maybe, they'd pull through until...

Orli couldn't tell precisely what that "until" was, only that word was the German army wasn't doing all too well on the Eastern Front after the loss of Stalingrad last winter. Just as with Dr. Mengele, Orli could only hope these rumors were true as well.

"Well, Aurelia Reichert, show me your little hospital. I can't wait to hear my very first report."

The entire barracks grew silent as they stepped inside. Whoever could stand lined by their cots with arms along the seams. The rest stayed in their beds, frozen like rabbits in the hunter's crosshairs. Dr. Mengele's gaze swept over the room, taking in the bare minimum conditions and the sickly faces of the prisoners. Orli noticed that his eyes held an unsettling mixture of curiosity and revulsion, like a scientist observing a petri dish full of bacteria.

"Sad state of affairs Dr. Kitt left me," he said, a hint of amusement playing on his lips. It wasn't a question. Orli herself was well aware how pitiful the makeshift hospital must look to someone not used to such conditions.

"We tried to improve whatever we could," Orli said, her hands trembling slightly at her sides. "But as inmate physicians, we can only do so much."

"Don't let it bother you," he said, his gaze finally leaving her to scan the room. "I have plans for this place."

For some reason, Orli stiffened after that last announcement of his. The room also fell silent; the only sound was the ragged breaths of the ill and dying.

Mengele's gaze landed on Miriam, or, rather, the inverted red triangle overlapping a yellow one on her chest. At once, Orli's protective instincts kicked in, making her step forward before she realized what she was doing. Miriam had arrived on the same train with her. She was the very first person Orli had helped, and who had helped save her, Orli's, life later on. They'd become closer than blood sisters through the horror they'd gone through. If this new doctor wished to harm her little Miriam, he would have to go through Orli first.

As though in response to such a reaction, Dr. Mengele's lips curled into a thin smile as he approached Miriam, his boots clicking against the concrete floor.

"Jewish?" he asked, his voice echoing in the oppressive silence.

"*Jawohl*, Herr Doktor," she answered, her voice trembling.

His eyes narrowed slightly as he studied her, his gaze almost predatory. "From now on," he said, his voice colder than the winter chill, "this infirmary will be separated into two different barracks. One for the Germans, one for the Jews."

The room was silent, the weight of his words sinking into every soul present. The thin veneer of humanitarianism that the infirmary had clung to was shattered, leaving the naked truth of their situation exposed: this was a concentration camp, not a hospital.

"You," he pointed at Orli, "will be in charge of the German section. And you," his finger shifted to Miriam, "will be supervising the Jewish infirmary. We can't have different races mixing together, now can we? Shared syringes, shared bandages —no, this simply won't do."

His words hung in the air like a guillotine, slicing through the already thin hope they had left. There was no room for argument, no room for appeal. Their fates were bound to his whims, and they were left with no choice but to obey.

Mengele turned on his heel, his eyes glancing over the infirmary one last time. "I'm off to the *Kommandantur* to request a separate building for the purposes I've just outlined," he said, his voice shifting to pleasant and almost charming once again. "Big changes are coming. Personally, I can't wait to begin."

Orli nodded stiffly. "Neither can we, Herr Doktor," she managed to say, her heart pounding in her chest. He was separating them, but at least putting Miriam in charge of her own new infirmary. Orli could live with that, for now.

Mengele gave her a nod, his gaze moving to Miriam. She was pale, her eyes wide with fear. "We'll do everything in our powers to assist you the best we can, Herr Doktor," she whispered, her voice barely audible.

He turned to leave, his boots clicking against the concrete floor. The door swung shut behind him, but the old wood bounced off the frame and creaked open again, just halfway, leaving the infirmary in a suffocating silence. The handsome, immaculate figure that had just left was not just a man. He was the embodiment of their deepest fears, a chilling symbol of the power of the Third Reich, its eugenics, its racial policies, whose name would echo through the ages, a grim reminder of the depths to which humanity could sink.

Through the partially opened door, Orli watched as his staff car disappeared from sight, its shape becoming smaller and smaller until it was nothing more than a speck on the horizon. She felt a heavy weight settle in her chest, the cold realization of what her life had become.

Miriam's fingers wrapped around her forearm. "What are we going to do?" she asked, her voice trembling.

Orli was silent for a moment, her eyes distant. "We survive," she finally said, her voice steady. "We survive and we remember. We remember every face, every name. We remember, so the world will never forget."

As the reality of their situation sank in, Orli realized the enormity of the task ahead. They were not just physicians and nurses, they were now custodians of memory, witnesses to the atrocities that were unfolding before their eyes. They were to bear the heavy burden of truth—a truth that the world needed to know.

Thus began a summer that would etch itself into the annals of history, a summer when the Angel of Death came to Birkenau, immaculate and handsome, a terrifying paradox of charm and cruelty. A summer when Orli and Miriam were thrown into the heart of darkness, left to navigate the treacherous waters of survival and resistance. A summer that would change their lives forever.

EIGHTEEN

It appeared Dr. Mengele meant business when it came to the infirmary restructuring. It only took him a couple of days to commandeer a new barracks from the camp administration. Where the inmates from that barracks went, Orli, frankly, didn't wish to consider.

The gray morning broke over the gloomy Birkenau camp as Orli followed her new SS physician supervisor through the muddy grounds toward the newly erected barracks. Towering and imposing, with a new coat of paint on its walls, the structure was in stark contrast to the rest of the dilapidated camp. With a grand gesture, Mengele pushed open the heavy doors, revealing rows of clean beds and a sense of order that had been missing from the camp since its inception.

"Welcome to your new home, Dr. Reichert," he said with a chillingly polite smile. His eyes, as cold as the Polish winter, locked onto hers, "You are now the camp elder of this German-only barrack. I trust you will uphold your duties diligently. The rest of the German physician and nursing staff shall be transferred here immediately as well."

Orli nodded, silently accepting the position. Gratitude and fear intermingled within her. She was grateful for the slightly improved living conditions and the newfound privileges, but terrified of what this might cost her. After all, nothing was free in Auschwitz-Birkenau, she had learned that much by now. Everything and everyone had their price and sometimes that price was one's very soul. Yet, the hope that she could use her position to mitigate the suffering of her fellow inmates sparked within her weary heart.

In the beginning, it was all right. German patients from her former infirmary were transferred into the new one, happy to be reunited with Orli, Gerda and Velma. Velma missed her bunk-mate and fellow nurse Enna, but, as a Slovakian Jew, Enna had to stay in the "Jewish" infirmary, together with Miriam, and there wasn't much to be done about that.

Around Orli's bicep, a new camp elder's armband was now wrapped, allowing her, for the first time in her life, to move freely about the camp—a miracle she couldn't even imagine in her wildest dreams mere days ago. With a silly smile plastered on her face, feeling free as a bird, she all but flew from one gate with an SS guard manning it to another, and not one of them as much as gave her a second glance. She was Dr. Mengele's "little doctor" now. It was truly unimaginable and astounding just how much respect and privilege came with the position.

There were odd things happening, certainly, with Dr. Mengele's quarantine section being partitioned from the rest of the barracks for instance, but Orli didn't concern herself over it too much. Let him assemble his strange collection of inmates with deformities, twins of both genders and even two dwarfs he'd brought with himself from the ramp where he now presided over selection process. After all, it didn't hurt anyone, did it? Dr. Mengele even fed them better than the rest of the camp population, sometimes dictating a certain diet to Orli to request from the camp kitchen. To be sure, she found it odd that he called it a "quarantine" (none of them were sick at the time of their arrival) and he guarded his small collection of oddities fiercely, strictly prohibiting anyone from interacting with them unless instructed otherwise. But as long as they were well looked after and even given vitamin shots by Herr Doktor himself, it was fine with her.

Only Gerda kept shaking her head and muttering under her breath each time Dr. Mengele departed from the infirmary, "I don't like that quarantine business one bit."

"Why not? Makes him happy."

"Something's not kosher about it."

Orli grinned—funny how they all now spoke this peculiar Auschwitz slang that had almost become a language of its own, with its mixture of Yiddish and Polish and German and even a few Slovakian curse words—*for spice*, as Enna used to say.

"He's not harming them," Orli said, more to herself than Gerda. In truth, she had a certain unsettling feeling about it, but ignored it on purpose. Too sweet the newfound freedom tasted. Too clean and well-stocked their new infirmary was.

"Mhm. Just like the farmer doesn't harm his lambs until they grow big and fat enough."

"Do you suggest he's feeding them to fatten them up just to slaughter them later and put them on a dinner table?" Orli exploded at last.

Gerda only shrugged with one shoulder. *We shall soon see,* her gesture expressed what her sealed lips refused to say.

"Fine. I'll ask him if you want," Orli surrendered.

It took Orli two full days to summon the courage to raise the subject with him. Dr. Mengele appeared to be in a particularly good mood that day. Another set of twins from the ramp—and not just fraternal ones, but identical, beautiful boys with chestnut curls and hazel eyes that shone like gold when the sun hit them at a certain angle. The entire barracks seemed brighter somehow when they arrived with the kind Herr Doktor in tow, sucking on cubes of sugar he'd produced from the pocket of his immaculately white coat.

"Herr Doktor, may I ask you a question?"

"Certainly," he replied without lifting his gaze from his pad, where he was scribbling something furiously.

"Why are these people being segregated from the rest of the infirmary population? They're not sick."

He looked up from his paper sharply and broke into a brilliant smile that had become a signature of his. "Very observant of you, Dr. Reichert."

The term of address, not really a sign of respect of any sort but a good-natured teasing he was fond of, was another indication of his good mood. Orli's patience had paid off; she'd caught him on a good day indeed.

Perching on the edge of a table, Dr. Mengele crossed his legs and placed the pad on top of his knee. "I am working on a groundbreaking paper for the Race Institute I used to work for before I volunteered for the army. This camp population provides me with a unique opportunity to conduct research."

"Research?" Orli echoed, her brows furrowing.

"Yes," he said, playing with a pencil in his nimble physician's fingers. "Imagine if we could completely cure certain illnesses, eliminate them from our lives?"

Despite her suspicions, Orli's heart fluttered with a flicker of hope. "That would be a miracle, Herr Doktor."

His laughter echoed throughout the infirmary, a sound as cold and hollow as the barrack walls. "Yes, a miracle indeed." He studied her for some time with his head cocked to one side before asking something she'd never expected: "Want to help me? I'll summon you when the time comes."

Stiffly, Orli managed a nod, not really believing her luck.

"Research, my foot," Gerda grumbled upon hearing Orli's report later that day.

Only, Orli didn't listen to her. He was a decent doctor after all, just as she'd hoped. He wanted to cure humanity, not send it up the chimney like the other Auschwitz doctors did. And perhaps the vitamin shots weren't vitamins at all but some miracle serum he'd been working on and was now testing on these chosen ones and she would be the one to help him, to help them, to help the rest of humanity from behind Auschwitz's walls as she'd always dreamt she would.

Fritz's face suddenly sprang to Orli's mind without invitation. She'd been just as enamored with him and his desire to save humanity from the selfishness of the elites until he'd revealed his true face and turned from savior to beast in the blink of an eye. Was she repeating a pattern of trusting these charming men who wouldn't think twice before plunging the knife into her back? Or, once burned, was she questioning whether to trust someone just because they reminded her of her former husband?

With the best will in the world, Orli couldn't answer herself no matter how hard she tried. And so, at least for now, there was nothing else left to do but go about her daily business and hope time would answer her questions.

It always did.

Only, the trouble with Birkenau was, by the time it did, it could be too late.

· · ·

"What do you make of him?" Orli asked Miriam after she snuck into their former shared infirmary a few days later, bringing a few smuggled supplies under her apron. Not much had changed around the infirmary. Only the contrast had grown starker between Orli's new barracks and the old ones, where the medicaments were always lacking and the permanent stench had seeped into the walls themselves.

"Besides him being mighty keen on racial policies?" Miriam arched an ironic brow as she hid the supplies under a floorboard in their old cubicle.

"Aren't they all?" Orli mirrored her expression from the rickety stool by the barred window.

Having replaced the board, Miriam dusted her knees and pulled up a second mismatched chair. Orli still remembered how a carpenter had fashioned it for the infirmary from leftover supplies in gratitude for saving his wife. Had even carved out a heart in its back and painted the affair in white—the only paint available to his detail.

"You work with him mostly, Orli, not me. He hardly visits us in our little Jewish haven."

Orli lowered her eyes at the wistful undertone in Miriam's voice. How alone she must feel here, how very abandoned, robbed of physicians she could rely on and put in charge of something so much bigger than her tiny self. And yet, she was managing it and so very admirably, this young girl who had lived a thousand lifetimes in the span of only a few short years.

"I don't know what to make of him," Orli admitted at length. "He's certainly much more educated than the SS butchers we used to work with, but that's what scares me sometimes. That, and his peculiar collection in the quarantine section."

Miriam scrunched up her face, mystified.

"He's been assembling all sorts of medical oddities there:

dwarfs, people with disabilities he pulls off the ramp... but also perfectly healthy twins, which makes little sense to me."

"Whatever does he need them for?" Miriam asked, confused even further. "Except for the twins, the SS would gas those categories immediately. Dwarfs, disabled ones, they can't work and therefore are of no use to the camp authorities."

"Beats me." Orli shrugged. "All I know is that he's constantly measuring them to no end and takes their vitals like someone possessed and sometimes gives them shots of God knows what."

"Not phenol?"

"No, not phenol. They're very much alive and fed much better than anyone else. The children, they love him. He gives them sugar and candy."

Miriam blinked at her, perplexed to the utmost. "He isn't spoiling them for nothing, mark my words. The camp administration would never allow it. If they caught wind that an SS man is so kind to inmates, he'd join them in no time. Something is rotten about the entire damned business, I just sense it."

It took Orli one very long minute before she finally uttered, "I was hoping it was just me. Because of Fritz."

Miriam was about to say something, but Enna poked her head through the door and it was time for Miriam to run back to her patients and for Orli to go back to hers with more doubts gnawing on her gut than ever before. Only now, in addition to her worries, she was missing Miriam and Enna and even Doctor Mark and their little runner Ari and the entire old camp life that had been snatched from under her feet like a rug with Mengele's arrival.

Something *was* rotten about the man. She, too, could no longer ignore it.

. . .

One evening, in mid-August, a summons came for Orli. She was to report to Dr. Mengele's office immediately. The air was thick with excitement as she entered the brightly lit room but the sight that greeted her was one she would never forget.

Two small bodies lay on the dissecting table. The twins, the beautiful, cherubic boys the entire infirmary had been admiring for the past two weeks, were deathly pale, their eyes wide and staring into the void. A white sheet covered their lower bodies, but the upper torsos were bare, revealing cold, lifeless flesh. Orli choked back a gasp, her eyes welling up with tears. She clamped a hand over her mouth to stifle the scream that threatened to escape.

"What happened to the boys, Herr Doktor?"

"What happened? Typhus in one case, phenol in the other. Take that notebook, please, and write down after me as I go, will you?" Dr. Mengele stood by the table, his surgical tools neatly aligned. His white coat was spotless, his hands steady. Orli still hadn't recovered from the shock, but he already gestured toward the bodies with a nonchalance that made her stomach churn. "At the moment of death, specimen one was sick with typhus. Specimen two was completely healthy. Specimen one was infected with typhus by a shot containing the virus on August second, 1943. The progression of the disease is described in detail in file... one, I suppose. Our very first one. Something to celebrate, Dr. Reichert, no?"

A realization dawned upon Orli, a horrifying truth she wished she could deny. Dr. Mengele was using these people as guinea pigs for his research. And she—*she* was to be his accomplice.

"Now, I shall make a side-by-side comparison of the specimens' organs and you shall note down the observations," Mengele instructed, his voice devoid of any compassion.

Orli nodded, her hands trembling as she picked up the pencil and paper. Each word she wrote was a testament to the monstrous acts being committed under the guise of scientific research.

Mengele began his macabre examination, delving into the bodies with a surgeon's precision, his voice steady as he dictated his findings. "The spleen of specimen one is considerably enlarged—a common symptom in typhus patients. Specimen two, however, has a normal spleen..."

His words continued, a ghastly narration that filled the room.

The air was thick with the smell of formaldehyde and death. Each incision, each organ that was pulled out for examination, was a grim reminder of the heinous acts unfolding. Beneath the harsh light, Mengele's cold eyes seemed to glow with an unnatural fascination.

Orli felt bile rise in her throat as she forced herself to write down his observations. The pencil felt heavy in her hands, each word proof of the gruesome reality before her. The room echoed with Mengele's clinical descriptions and the scratching of her pencil against paper—a symphony of horror that would haunt her dreams for years to come.

The procedure went on for hours, Mengele's enthusiasm never waning. His fascination and detachment from the horror he was inflicting was as chilling as the act itself. It was as if he was dissecting animals, not humans.

When it was finally over, Orli was left alone with the bodies. She looked at the lifeless forms on the table, their youth and innocence brutally stolen. This was the true face of Mengele's research—death and suffering masked by scientific curiosity.

As she walked back to her barrack, Orli felt a cold weight settle in her heart. She was no longer just a camp elder, she was now an unwilling participant in Mengele's horrific experiments. The hope she had initially felt was extinguished, replaced by a chilling dread. She was caught in a web of cruelty and inhumanity, a pawn in Mengele's game of death.

From that day on, the camp was not just a prison for Orli. It was a living nightmare, a place where humanity was stripped away, and evil veiled itself in the name of science. The new barrack was not a haven, but a house of horrors, a testament to the depths that man could sink in his quest for knowledge. And she, Orli, was trapped in the center of it all, forced to bear witness to the unfolding atrocities.

NINETEEN

AUTUMN 1943

By the autumn of 1943, Orli had grown convinced that Dr. Mengele wasn't a human but something else entirely. There was no escaping him, neither for her nor for the new arrivals he hunted down with relentless energy. When he wasn't on the ramp, flicking his elegant white glove right and left like some ancient god deciding who was to die and who was to continue their torturous existence in the bowels of hell they called Auschwitz, he was stalking the barracks and work details in search of someone—*anyone*—to get his restless hands on.

Sometimes, he appeared out of the mist in the early-morning hours and instructed Orli or Gerda to accompany him to the ramp. "A big transport today. Go through them and find any twins, dwarfs, anyone with deformities, but genetic ones, not sustained during an accident or any of that sort—those cripples are of no interest to me."

On fog-shrouded mornings like those, his eyes shone particularly brightly with giddy anticipation. Orli could scarcely keep up with his long strides and eventual annoyance if the train was delayed.

"They must be letting a troop transport through, Herr Doktor."

"Troop transport shouldn't have precedent over science."

It was best not to disturb him in this state of cold rage. Even the camp orchestra who gathered on the platform to welcome the new arrivals—another diabolical Auschwitz invention—knew not to make a sound until Herr Doktor finally felt the rumbling of the approaching train through the ground under his polished boots and smiled at them brilliantly, the way only he knew how, and asked for "The Blue Danube." Orli would loathe the melody for the rest of her life.

Before the double murder Orli had personally witnessed at Dr. Mengele's dissecting room, she and Gerda would throw themselves on new arrivals with great enthusiasm that knew no boundaries. If they did well and brought him whatever he wanted, it was double rations for everyone in the infirmary—the patients as well, not just the physician staff. Twins themselves would roll caramels in their mouths and sleep in their bunk beds with the toys they were permitted to keep by the kind Herr Doktor and would welcome him with cries of joy as he always had sweet treats for them and promises to be reunited with their mothers and fathers soon.

After Orli had found out what such "reunification" meant, she began cutting through the new arrivals like a knife, with the same steely determination to prevent any more young victims falling into the charming predator's hands.

"Twins?" she called quietly—the same question the Mengele SS aides were calling into the mass of people just spilled out of the cattle train's suffocating confines.

It was a life-or-death matter to get to them before the SS did, and so Orli pushed and shoved and searched the crowd frantically until she would stumble upon some distraught woman with two young girls in tow and physically block them from the vultures already circling much too close.

"Do you have different clothes for one of them?" she would whisper to the mother and wait in agonizing annoyance for her to blink, stare at Orli for what felt like eternity and go through the same idiotic interrogation most of them did. *But having twins was good, was it not? What did she mean, experiments? Weren't they going to some special place?*

Orli would lose it at this point, explain in the no-nonsense terms that "special place" was one of the Birkenau gas chambers. If she knew what was good for her, she would change one of her girls immediately and redo her hair so that she wouldn't resemble her twin sister and let Orli take her as far away as possible and hand her to some other woman, who would nod to Orli's "Save the child, please," and if they were lucky, they'd see each other again.

Some were smart and listened.

Some called her mad, drew themselves up and called for the SS to come and get their twins.

Deformities were more difficult to conceal, and besides, there was little point in doing so. "Unable to walk, unable to work" was one of the infamous Auschwitz mottos. Conflicted and drunk on moonshine, which Slavek, one of the inmates, had bribed them with to hide his beloved in the infirmary for a few days until she was well enough to work again, Orli and Gerda had a discussion about them one night.

"So? What do you think?" Gerda asked.

"What do I think? I think it's a damned sorry choice between gas or phenol is what I think."

"Gas is faster."

"Phenol is less painful. And besides, he doesn't experiment on them while they're still alive—they only interest him as cadavers."

"You have a point there."

"Also, while they're still alive, he feeds them well."

"That, too."

"And feeds our infirmary for bringing them to him."

"Another good point."

"There are no good points in Auschwitz, sister."

"No, there aren't. But you know what I mean."

"I do."

There was a pause. "Pour me another one, will you?" Orli asked, tired to death and looking it too.

"Have mine. I'm sick as it is."

Orli was sick too but going to bed sober after such a discussion was simply not an option that night.

Dr. Mengele was in a particularly bad mood for almost the whole of October. Rumors had it, things on the Front weren't going all that well, but it was Orli's profound conviction that Herr Doktor's bad humor had much more to do with the absence of the coveted twins than the Reich slowly losing its grip on war-torn Europe. October passed by without even fraternal twins to add to Dr. Mengele's macabre collection.

And then, suddenly, he appeared in the infirmary, all bright-eyed and smiling like a boy through the gap in his front teeth, and nearly tore Orli from the woman she was tending to. "Come, come! No time to waste. If it works, it'll be a breakthrough. All those children from the Family Block, they'll make themselves useful after all. And to think of it, Hössler wanted to gas them all, ha! Good thing I petitioned for them before the *Kommandant*. Now he will see, they will all see!"

He didn't explain exactly what it was that the camp administration was supposed to see, but just seeing him all but dance with anticipation instantly alerted Orli to something sinister brewing in Herr Doktor's mind.

By the time they walked through the gloomy, sterile corridor of Dr. Mengele's personal quarters, Orli's heart was pounding in her chest like a bird trapped in a cage. The air was heavy with the stench of antiseptic, overlaid with a sickly-sweet scent that she had come to associate with Dr. Mengele's experiments. A shudder of dread ran through her as she followed him into the room where the notorious "Angel of Death" was preparing for his latest diabolical experiment.

Inside the room, a group of frightened children, their eyes wide with terror, were huddled together. Their skin was pallid, their bodies thin and frail from the harsh conditions of the camp. They were not Dr. Mengele's regular flock groomed to adore him and trust him with their very lives. These were the camp children who had lived through horrors not every adult would even imagine in their lives. Perhaps, that was the reason for the two hulking inmates with the infirmary armbands on their biceps framing the children on both sides. They froze to attention at the sight of the SS physician; the children did as well—the small pitiful army trained so well to fear the gray-green uniform.

It was only a matter of time before they would begin fearing the white coat thrown casually over that uniform, it occurred to Orli.

"You'll be assisting me here, in the laboratory," Dr. Mengele said to her over his shoulder as he turned the key in the lock to his private, smaller office. "They—" he added with a motion of the head toward the men's infirmary inmates—"will be bringing the children in one by one and your task will be to sit them right here on this chair and hold their heads as still as possible. It is of utmost importance that they don't twist and turn; you understand? Else, the dye will spread disproportionally, and the experiment will be ruined."

"The dye?" Orli repeated, her eyes quickly scanning the small medical table set next to the chair on which vials and syringes were laid out on sterile medical gauze.

Dr. Mengele smiled at her kindly as if she were a child

herself, adorable in her ignorance. "Describe to me an ideal Aryan, Dr. Reichert."

"Of tall stature, with hair light and straight, fair skin, light eyes—blue, gray or green, with a strong, athletic build," Orli recited the propaganda that had been shoved down the population's throats even since Hitler and his clique had come to power.

Dr. Mengele's grin turned almost coy. "Do you or I look like that despite our Aryan blood?"

Orli blinked, wondering where he was leading with this and not liking it one bit. "No, Herr Doktor."

"My hair is dark and wavy and so is yours."

"Yes, Herr Doktor."

"You have full lips."

"Yes, Herr Doktor."

"My eyes are blue, but yours are light-brown."

Orli just stared at him now with her "non-Aryan" eyes.

Perching on the edge of his desk, he crossed his legs and wrapped his hands around one knee. "The women of the Reich already dye their hair to better fit the Aryan ideal until we physically breed dark hair out of our gene stock entirely." He paused, waiting for Orli's reaction.

She could only listen, quietly terrified and frankly at a loss.

"But what would you say if I told you that I could change your eye color to a beautiful sky-blue?" he finally asked, grinning wider than the Cheshire Cat.

Orli allowed herself a reciprocal smile. "I would say it's impossible, Herr Doktor."

"That's what most of the scientists say as well, but I'm not most. We're bigger than most because of what we do here. And when, years from now, you walk the streets of new Germany and see not one brown-eyed child, you shall remember this day and our conversation and feel pride for what we did."

Only then did it dawn on her what it was that he was planning for those frightened little lambs just outside this door.

Little, brown-eyed lambs for slaughter.

"Bring the first one in," he called to the inmates.

Before, she had only seen them fleetingly. Now, it was those eyes that would linger like a photographic image in Orli's mind. Rich, warm brown hues, that would remind her of the earth in spring, full of life and promise. Now, those eyes were about to become the canvas for Mengele's sadistic artistry.

One of the inmates walked in with a young girl in tow. No older than eight, bundled in everything she owned and still drowning in layers of clothes, with a permanently dirty face and running nose, but with eyes black and liquid, like those of a newborn calf, long velvet-like eyelashes framing them.

From kind Herr Doktor, a small chocolate dangled like a promise in front of those mistrustful yet hopeful eyes. "If you sit still, it's yours."

The girl climbed into the chair and froze like a perfect little statue, her gaze fixed not on Mengele's hands but on the small square wrapped in foil that he had placed just out of her reach.

Orli hoped her hands didn't betray her by trembling as she placed them on both sides of the girl's head. Under her fingers, lice crawled, but the girl paid them no heed. Just like a starved dog, all her attention was on the promise of the food.

Dr. Mengele, in his unsettlingly immaculate white coat, held a small vial filled with a chillingly icy blue dye in his gloved hand. Orli felt her charge's small body tremble as Mengele leaned in, his cold, steel-gray eyes devoid of empathy; yet, the girl didn't budge.

"Now, *mein kleines Mädchen*, this will not hurt," he murmured, his voice a sinister lullaby. The lie seeped into the room, mingling with the scent of fear and antiseptic.

Without noticing, Orli clenched her hands around the child's head, her nails almost digging into the girl's close-shaved scalp as she watched Mengele holding the child's eye open with one hand and bringing the vial closer and closer to the socket with the other.

Orli felt the girl's body tense ever so slightly as the unnaturally blue dye spread over the surface of her eye but heard not a sound rise from the child's throat. Her heart nearly tore in her chest at the realization of just how used these children were to torture and physical pain that nothing elicited a reaction from them anymore as long as food was promised.

"Good girl," Dr. Mengele commended as he repeated his ministrations with the child's other eye. "Go back to the waiting room and have your chocolate there. Doctor Orli will take you to a different hospital after we're done here. And in the evening, I'll bring you candy when I come to check on you. Now, how does that sound?"

Blinking at him through the film of blueish tears in her red, inflamed eyes, the girl snatched the chocolate and nodded fiercely.

Inside Orli, everything was screaming.

For the rest of the morning, she could only watch in quiet horror as one by one, the children were all subjected to the procedure. After treating half of his human guinea pigs with a vial, Dr. Mengele switched to a syringe—"for the clarity of the experiment." Those children's cries of fear and pain echoed in the white-tiled room and etched themselves into Orli's memory, a cruel symphony of suffering.

Gerda instantly dropped everything once she saw Orli lead her pitiful procession into the infirmary.

"Help me put them in beds," Orli said through gritted teeth, helpless rage boiling inside. "They can hardly see where they're going."

All the blood leaving her face, Gerda could only stare at the little faces stained with blue tears. But once the physician in her had awoken from its stunned state, she grabbed the smallest child and carried her to the children's ward.

"What happened?" she whispered to Orli once they had tucked the last of their little charges in.

Even Mengele's children, usually cheerful and alert, watched the new arrivals in mute fear, their makeshift toys forgotten mid-play. The new children's moans and muffled cries filled the ward, resonating with Orli's own silent screams.

"He put dye in their eyes to make them blue," she whispered back at Gerda.

"He did what?" Visibly disturbed and mortified, Gerda pulled back as she struggled to process something that was surely too awful even for Mengele's sick mind to conceive.

"Put dye in their eyes," Orli repeated, her entire body still trembling with shock and indignation. "Those children for whom he used the dye as drops are a bit better off—I'm much more afraid for the ones he injected."

"Injected as in..." The thought was too atrocious for Gerda to even voice.

"As in with syringe in the eye. Yes."

"Good God."

"Gerda, don't break down now. I know what you're feeling, but I need you, all right? Help me tend to them the best we can and then we'll both get that moonshine from Slavek, we'll get drunk till we're sick and cry all night. But now I need you here with me. I know it's a nightmarish sight but—"

"I'm here." Gerda nodded, her teeth sunken deep in her lip to get a hold of herself. "I'm here."

"He strictly prohibited us from meddling with their eyes in any way, but I'm not leaving them like that."

"No. Of course not."

"Grab me some lukewarm water and..."

For a moment, they looked at each other in shared despair.

There was no precedent in medicine which explained what it was exactly that could help against dye in human eyes. Only in Auschwitz could something like this have happened.

"Lukewarm water. That's all."

Minutes stretched like hours in a place where children's cries meant nothing to their tormentors, only to the doctors who tried their best to help the most helpless.

"I'm here, I'm here," Orli whispered, her voice trembling as she approached the first child. The little girl's eyes were swollen and bloodshot, her warm brown irises swimming in a pool of cloudy, unnatural blue. Orli dampened a cloth with water and gently washed her eyes, trying to alleviate the pain.

But it was futile. Despite Orli's and Gerda's best efforts, the children's vision faded over the course of the next few hours, their world descending into darkness. The room was filled with a sense of overwhelming despair, the painted blue eyes serving as a grim reminder of the monstrosity they had been subjected to. They cried from fear now, not just pain, and groped their way around the ward, stumbling into bunk beds and each other until Mengele's children or Orli took them gently by the hand and led them back to their beds.

"You just rest now. You'll feel better tomorrow, my little one." Orli lost count of the empty promises she dropped like bread-crumbs that day. The Jewish children who spoke Yiddish under-stood her, but the rest of them didn't, and only sobbed and struggled in her arms until Orli was ready to break down sobbing herself.

The next morning, so early it was still dark outside, Dr. Mengele rushed into the ward, impeccably dressed, clean-shaven as always and all but dancing with anticipation.

"Well, well, how are my little blue-eyed angels?" he asked in a singsong voice.

Orli and Gerda, who had spent the night in the children's ward to ease their discomfort and hug them back to sleep the best they could, jumped to attention shoulder to shoulder, two helpless guardians of their precious flock against the ultimate predator facing them.

He pushed past them and grabbed the first child, shining his pocket flashlight in the boy's eyes. Orli didn't need to see what exactly he'd uncovered. The children's eyes were still brown, some with blue dye still floating around, some bloodshot to the point of appearing crimson, but none of them had turned blue overnight. Some, mostly those injected with the syringe, were slowly leaking out altogether due to the damage instead of turning arctic-blue. How could they, after all? Even Orli, without any background in medicine but a thinking brain inside her head, could understand that much.

Child after child, Dr. Mengele checked, growing progressively annoyed. His expression turned into a scowl as he took in the results of his latest experiment. "Useless," he muttered under his breath. "Utterly and irreversibly useless."

"Herr Doktor," Orli called to him softly. "Those whose eyes had drops in them can still see for the most part. We can still help them—"

"Help them?" Mengele scoffed, his cold gaze sweeping over the children. "There's no helping them now. The experiment has failed."

There was a chilling finality in his words, a terrifying declaration of the fate he had sealed for these children.

"Bring them to your physicians' cubicle, one by one."

Orli and Gerda exchanged glances and jumped at the deafening, "Now!" Dr. Mengele threw over his shoulder as he stalked through the infirmary toward the cubicle.

Silent tears streaming down their faces, they began assembling and escorting their tiny flock for slaughter.

In the cubicle, one single light bulb burned. Its light didn't reach into the corners and the room was mostly immersed in darkness—the same darkness the children now saw. The same darkness that reigned in Mengele's soul.

He moved toward a small cabinet where the medicaments were stocked, pulling out a syringe and a vial filled with a clear, ominous liquid. Orli recognized it immediately: Phenol.

"No," she begged, her voice a last, desperate plea. "They have suffered enough."

"Precisely. Time to end their suffering." Mengele spoke in the voice that was once again the epitome of self-possession, his attention focused on preparing the syringes.

Orli could only watch in mute horror as he approached the first child, his movements methodical and precise. The little girl didn't even flinch as the needle pierced her chest, her body too exhausted to react.

The room echoed with the eerie clicks of the syringe as Mengele administered the lethal injection. One by one, the children's bodies dropped, limp and lifeless, into Orli's awaiting arms. Next to her, Gerda stood frozen, her body numb and her heart aching as she watched the life drain from their eyes, leaving them as hollow shells of the vibrant souls they once were.

Mengele discarded the empty syringe into the pot marked "disinfection," his face impassive as he surveyed his grim handiwork. "It's a pity the experiment failed," he said, his voice devoid of emotion. "It only means I'll have to work harder. Refine the dye formula, perhaps... Fortunately, there will always be more subjects."

His words hung in the air, a gruesome promise of the horrors yet to come. Orli stood in the eerie silence, her heart heavy with grief and helplessness. Once vibrant brown eyes, now tinted with a haunting shade of blue, stared back at her, their light extinguished.

As Mengele left the room, Orli sank to her knees, her body shaking with silent sobs.

She reached out, closing the eyes of the nearest child, her fingers trembling. "I'm sorry," she whispered, her voice breaking. "I'm so sorry."

The air was thick with the scent of death and antiseptic, the eerie silence punctuated by Orli's and Gerda's heart-wrenching sobs. They were left alone in the room with the lifeless bodies, the children's eyes staring into nothing—a terrifying testament to the horrors inflicted upon them by the Angel of Death, Dr. Mengele.

TWENTY

SEHNDE, GERMANY. DECEMBER 1961

One month before New Year's Day

You're losing the grip on her. You're losing her and you know it deep inside and there's nothing to be done about it. But, like the obstinate mule that you are, you refuse to give up. There's new medicine in the US. It's in its experimental phase, but the preliminary research has shown a lot of promise.

You rushed to Berlin to the medical conference and snatched the sample from the American psychiatrists' team and raced back to Sehnde, doing over a hundred on the autobahn despite the sleet and warnings of black ice. Your life suddenly means so little when someone else's is at stake.

Like a holy grail, you carry the new medicine in a small paper cup into her room. As always, she's by the window, gazing out of it into somewhere you'll never see, never understand no matter how much you try. She has already explained it to you in the mildest of manners, that one had to live through it to fully grasp the horror of it. On the sill before her, a book, forgotten. She has little concentration these days. Even less interest in doing... anything, really.

You approach her and ask her about her day and offer the small white pill that has cured so many in America. She looks at it apathetically but takes it all the same and swallows it dry and gives you a small, tragic smile. You realize she pities you. You and her husband and your joint woeful attempts to glue together the pieces of her that keep falling apart. She pities you but goes along with your charade and your promises of miraculous recovery because, some fifteen years ago, she, too, was an obstinate mule. She, too, refused to give up.

But she did save lives, you remind her. She saved so many lives, and particularly when she came up with that brilliant idea of the typhus infectious ward.

She considers it for some time, nods slowly, doesn't argue, like she used to do, that half of them have killed themselves and the other half were mad like her and was it saving really or just prolonging their torture? Some of them didn't want to live but she made them—out of vanity, out of a desire to spite the SS and show them that she was stronger than them, smarter than them.

To spite death itself, maybe.

When she succeeded, she felt like God. It's only now she realizes that she was nothing but a fraud who talked people into living—living without their families, without a home to return to. She is a fraud and they must be cursing her still and the world will be better off without her.

She's talking herself out of living before actually going through with it like she has already done so many times before.

You feel like you're too late this time, but you ask her for one more chance, just another day to let the pill do its magic, just to give you a chance to see if it works. You beg like a wino for change and she graciously drops it in front of you.

A few more days. Yes. She can do a few more days.

TWENTY-ONE

AUSCHWITZ-BIRKENAU. WINTER 1943–44

Winter was Auschwitz's most brutally honest accomplice. It peeled away the thin veneer of humanity, revealing the camp in all its raw, skeletal horror. The once-muddy grounds were now stark white, the snow untouched but for the crimson stains marking where the weakest had fallen. Frost kissed the barbed wires, creating an illusion of a winter wonderland, hiding the deadly reality within.

By the fifth year of war, Orli had seen the worst that humanity had to offer. She knew the stench of death, the look of despair in the eyes of those who had given up all hope. She had felt children's bodies grow limp as Dr. Mengele's syringe pierced their hearts. She had looked into their blind eyes and felt like plucking her own out so as not to see the carnival of terror spinning around her for years on end.

It was no wonder that the entire infirmary breathed a sigh of relief when he went on Christmas vacation, leaving Orli and Gerda to their own devices. At the first opportunity, Orli tied her camp elder's armband around her bicep and told Gerda that if the SS came, she was searching the camp for twins on Dr. Mengele's orders.

"I have to check on Miriam. With that beast breathing down our necks for the past few months, I couldn't risk it."

"Go, go," Gerda said without hesitation. "Please, give them all my warmest regards. Find out how Enna's doing."

"That little minx?" Orli arched her brow as she wrapped a rag around her neck as a sorry imitation of a scarf. "As long as there are men in this camp, she'll be fine."

They laughed, but there was a nervous undertone to that laughter. With Dr. Mengele's being virtually everywhere, they hadn't had a chance to see their friends and former barrack mates. It was anyone's guess how they'd been faring there, in their Jewish infirmary.

Out of breath from both her sprint and the negative temperatures outside that stole the very air from her lungs and covered her eyelashes in ice, Orli shook the snow from her kerchief and mentally prepared herself for what lay ahead.

However, the sight that greeted her once she entered the Jewish infirmary was like a punch to the gut. The terrible stench of rotting flesh turned Orli's stomach, reminding her of gangrenous wounds left untreated. Fecal matter lay frozen under some bunks in scattered hay. A new nurse who looked as skeletal as her patients was making her rounds apathetically, checking for signs of life in those who didn't move at her approach and begged for relief of any kind. Everywhere Orli turned, she saw emaciated bodies lay on rickety bunks, their eyes vacant, the life slowly ebbing from them. The infirmary was a grotesque mockery of a hospital, a charnel house where the sick were left to die.

"Where's Miriam?" Orli asked the nurse.

She only blinked at her dully; she didn't understand German.

"Miriam," Orli repeated without including any other words and pointed at the red cross on her armband.

That did the trick. The nurse pointed at the end of the barrack that was swaddled in darkness even in the middle of the afternoon. No candles for the Jewish infirmary, just a bit of light from the tiny stove to heat the entire barracks and whatever meager winter light the overhead skylights provided. And with a snowstorm like the one that was raging outside and piled the snowdrifts atop the roof, there was no light whatsoever.

Painfully reminded of her blinded charges, Orli groped her way in the midday twilight until she recognized the familiar body shape, but most of all the sweet voice with which Miriam always addressed her patients. Through the film of tears pooling in her eyes, Orli heard Miriam coo above one of her patients as she tucked the pitiful imitation of a blanket under her skeletal frame.

"Miriam," she called to the apparition her friend had been reduced to.

"Orli," Miriam greeted her, her voice barely above a whisper. Her eyes, once vibrant, were now dull with despair. She still grasped her in the tightest of embraces and rested her head on Orli's shoulder. With tall Gerda by her side, Orli had all but forgotten just how tiny her little Miriam was. A tiny little sparrow carrying the weight of the entire world on her fragile shoulders. "How good it is to see you."

"Mengele is finally gone for his Christmas leave else, I would have come earlier."

"It's all right, Orli. You don't have to explain."

"How are you holding up, Miriam?" Orli asked softly, her eyes taking in the horrifying sight. "They have cut your medicament supplies, haven't they?"

"And the rations, too." Exhausted beyond any measure, Miriam passed the back of her hand over her forehead. "For the most part, people come here to die now." She was silent a beat, but then brightened in spite of herself and took Orli's hand. "Enough about us. Tell me how you are doing?"

"The infirmary itself is well-stocked and warm," Orli said and bit into her lip that was suddenly trembling. The memories were much too fresh, much too painful. "It's Mengele's ward that is the epitome of horror. He's at the ramp every day, on the hunt for his twins, dwarfs, and anyone with deformities. He plucks them out, puts them in the ward, charms them with smiles and sweets and warm, snug beds and then—" Her voice broke off mid-sentence.

Miriam watched in alarm as Orli's hand flew to her mouth to stifle a sob ready to tear off her lips.

"I thought it was only rumors."

"I wish it was."

"My God, Orli."

"Yes."

"And children, too?"

"Them, especially. Remember I told you how he loves his twins the best? Well, now we know why. They're perfectly identical specimens for the clearest results of experiments. He infects one with whatever comes to his mind and leaves the other one intact. And when the first succumbs to the illness, he gives the healthy twin a shot of phenol to the heart and then proceeds to cut them open to compare the organs."

"Good God," Miriam exclaimed, pale beyond measure.

"There is no God here," Orli said with a forlorn look around. "Devils and condemned only."

Miriam made no comment. There was nothing to argue that point with.

Annoyed with the despair that lay around them like winter snow, Orli swiped her hand and tossed her head to clear it from dark thoughts. "You need medicaments. I can get almost anything, tell me what you need."

"We'll be grateful for whatever you can get, really. They

drop like flies here, Orli. The death cart pulls up twice a day to gather corpses."

The despair in Miriam's voice cut Orli like a knife. She had seen death before, but nothing like this. These people were dying not only from their wounds or sickness, they were dying from hopelessness. The conditions in the camp had deteriorated so rapidly in the past few months, it was indeed a death camp now. And preoccupied with her own troubles, she hadn't the faintest idea just how much worse the Jewish population had it.

"I'll come back with supplies first thing tomorrow. I'll think of something, Miriam. I promise I will."

"I know you will, Orli." Miriam smiled at her and somehow, the icebox parading itself as an infirmary grew warmer a tad. "You always do, you never give up."

Free from Dr. Mengele's ever-watchful eye, Orli gathered her little physician flock around her right after the patients had had their dinner. Seated around the table, Gerda and Velma had their eyes on Orli as the three munched on their bread and cheese—still a delicacy despite being rock-hard and the pale greenish spots of mold staining its surface. In the mugs in front of them, water with a few drops of alcohol. Physicians needed their medicine too, to get them through the horrors of Birkenau days.

"I visited Miriam today," Orli began, a plan already conceived in her mind, but without her camp sisters' support, there wasn't much she could do. And what she was about to ask them was risky—extremely risky indeed. "They aren't doing well there."

"Who in this place does?" Velma asked over the rim of her dented aluminum mug.

Just like Gerda, she had grown her hair out, but didn't stop at the neck length as Gerda did but wore it in a braid wrapped around her head like a crown. Naturally thin, unlike the tall and sturdy Gerda, Velma didn't much care for extra rations and whatever foodstuffs she received from grateful discharged patients she either shared between her other charges or traded for kerosene—the only luxury she permitted herself was to keep her braid lice-free.

Orli considered Velma for a moment. She was cautious but selfless, too. Now, only if her selflessness outweighed her instinct of self-preservation...

"The Kanada girls do," Gerda offered with a chuckle but without malice. "I passed by their little heaven today. You should see the shearling coats on them!"

"For the life of me I can't imagine how they can wear those clothes. They must be still warm from the new arrivals that just got gassed," Velma said with visible distaste.

"Don't blame them," Orli said quietly. "And don't envy them, either," she added with a look at Gerda. "Their warehouses are right next to the crematoriums. They live in that nightmare daily and nightly. That's why the SS cut them some slack, just as they do with the *Sonderkommando*. Without being permitted to take whatever they want, they wouldn't last long there."

The women lowered their eyes. There was no arguing the point. With every kosher position came nightmarish duties that wrenched the person's very soul out of them. They had found out that much themselves. Warm and well-stocked, tending to children that were about to get slaughtered by a madman's hand.

"Speaking of lasting," Orli probed carefully. "Miriam's patients have little chance there. The state of the infirmary is close to the one in which I started here, in Auschwitz, where I had to break a cabinet to make a splint and close wounds with fire because there was no stitching kit."

The women's eyes widened in spite of themselves. They

had never heard that story before, which wasn't all that surprising; Orli was never one to complain. She suffered in silence and solitude, without burdening others with her grief when they had enough of their own.

"Take whatever you need to her first thing tomorrow." Gerda was the first to recover herself. "We're well-stocked. And Mengele is gone—we can write off whatever we want until he comes back."

"Yes, naturally, take whatever," Velma joined in at once. "And if they need help, I can always go there for a few hours."

Orli nodded slowly, thankful for the thoughtfulness and care. But it wasn't quite enough. "And what happens when Mengele is back?" she asked. The words hung heavy in the air, like a guillotine blade ready to drop. "What I was thinking is more of a permanent solution."

Both women pulled forward, interested.

Relieved by their reaction, Orli wetted her lips and continued: "Remember the typhus epidemic we had last year? How Dr. Kitt sent the entire infirmary to the gas just because one SS man caught it?"

"What does that have to do with us?" Gerda asked.

"We set up an infectious ward here. For the typhus cases," Orli suggested, a smile growing on her face, warm with a glow of hope.

"We don't have any typhus cases," Velma said, confused.

"But the SS don't know that." Orli arched a brow. "And what they don't know can't possibly harm them. Right?"

Now, Gerda was smiling too, catching onto Orli's plan.

"I suggest we take Miriam's patients—those who we can help, of course—and treat them in our 'infectious' ward," Orli said. "The SS won't go near it, and Mengele, he doesn't care for the patients all that much. All he's interested in is his experiments. He probably won't even notice that it's there."

"And what if he does?" Velma asked as she chewed on her

lip. "He isn't like most of them. He's been to the Front. He might be a madman and a sadist, but he isn't a coward. What if he goes inside?"

"Then he sees all of those very sick women," Orli replied. "He's not a coward, I agree, but he's much too preoccupied with his 'research' to inspect every single one of them and see who has typhus and who doesn't."

"But he'll see the stars on their chests. And then, it's to the gas with us all."

"Gerda, go to the Kanada again tomorrow, will you?" Orli had already thought about that very issue and had a solution for it as well. "Get red cloth from them. We'll cut red political triangles and sew them over our Jewish patients' stars. From a first glance and without a thorough inspection, they'll be none the wiser. Well? What do you say?"

Gerda and Velma exchanged glances. When they turned back to her, Orli knew she had her answer.

The next day, when the pale sun was just rising from the dark woods looming up ahead, Orli charged into the Jewish infirmary, her face aglow with the desperate and dangerous plan she, Gerda and Velma had conceived the night before.

"An infectious ward," she told Miriam while emptying her pockets of vials, bandages, and drugs. "In our German infirmary. We aren't monitored that closely. We can easily smuggle some patients of yours into our ward to treat them there and give them a chance to put some meat on their bones."

"No, Orli. Too dangerous. Mengele is obsessed with racial purity—it was the reason why he separated us in the first place. If he discovers that you hide Jewish patients in your infirmary, he'll slaughter you with his bare hands."

"He won't discover anything, he's too preoccupied with his

experiments to pay any heed to ordinary patients—they don't interest him in the slightest."

"What about other SS check-ups? The camp administration is fond of those."

"That they are, but after some of them caught it last year, they won't set foot inside a typhus ward." In the dim morning light, Orli's smile was as bright as a new day. "Miriam, it's genius, I'm telling you. We have to try it. We cannot just stand by and let them die."

Miriam considered as she chewed on her bloodless, chopped lip. Genius, yes, but dangerous as hell. If uncovered, it would be to the gas for them all—Jews and Germans alike. But, then again, didn't the industrial crematorium chimneys belch their ghastly smoke into the air day and night like hungry beasts feasting on human flesh? They were all brought here to die and the only difference was whether they died like cowards or heroes.

"Do it," Miriam said with sudden quiet, fierce resolution.

Over the next few days, the plan was set into motion. Making use of Dr. Mengele's absence, Orli and Gerda sectioned off a part of their infirmary with a sign, *"Warning! Typhus. Do not enter—highly contagious."*

The SS, after losing a few of their own to the disease, kept their distance, just as Orli had predicted.

And, under the cover of night, Orli and Gerda began to smuggle Jewish patients into their ward. Each night was a terrifying game of cat and mouse, the fear of being caught always lurking in the shadows. Emaciated women could barely walk, even aided by the German physicians; searchlights probed the camp grounds like all-seeing demonic eyes, but they persevered, driven by a desperate need to save those they could. Each patient they smuggled in was a victory, a small triumph against the monstrous regime. But with each victory came more fear, more danger. The stakes were high. If they were discovered, they knew what fate awaited them.

One night, as Orli slipped into the Jewish infirmary under the cloak of darkness, Miriam met her in the doors.

"I have a favor to ask."

"Of course. Anything."

"It's a big favor."

Miriam stepped aside, revealing a young girl, no more than ten. The girl was barely standing as she clung to the barrack wall. Her eyes, bright with feverish delusion, looked up at Orli.

"Mama? You came to get me..." she said in Yiddish.

The tiny voice, so weak and yet so hopeful, stabbed Orli's heart like a shard of ice.

"She's not contagious," Miriam rushed to whisper in Orli's ear. "Just very, very sick from malnutrition and..."

She didn't need to finish. The child's entire family had been gassed—Orli read that much in Miriam's pleading gaze.

The girl's fever-bright eyes searched Orli's face for a moment before the hope in them died, replaced by an understanding far too profound for such a young soul.

"Mama couldn't come, but she sent me to help you," Orli whispered, crouching down to the child's level. Her hand, roughened by labor and the biting winter, brushed the girl's clammy forehead.

The Jewish infirmary was a grim spectacle that night. It echoed with the low moans of the sick and dying, a chilling soundtrack to the macabre theater of Auschwitz. The girl, merely a small addition to the canvas of suffering, was shivering uncontrollably, her thin blanket providing little comfort against the winter's cruel bite.

Rising to her feet, Orli looked at Miriam. A silent communication passed between them, their shared fear and determination reflected in each other's eyes.

At last, Orli gave a curt nod, understanding the urgency. "She'll live. I'll see to it."

The child was quickly moved into their secret ward. Her tiny body seemed even smaller on the cot—a stark contrast to the imposing image of the SS outside, their shadows dancing on the icy ground like sinister specters.

Days turned into weeks. The girl—Lotte—became a beacon of hope in their clandestine ward. Despite her emaciated state, she clung to life with a ferocity that was both heartbreaking and inspiring. The darling of the ward, she became everyone's daughter and there wasn't a woman among its secret patients who didn't share a bit of bread or soup with their youngest barrack mate.

Only once did Lotte ask Orli about her real mother: "Will I see Mama again?" she asked, her voice barely above a whisper.

Orli paused, her heart aching. She looked down at Lotte, her small face pale and drawn. What could she say to this child who had seen the worst of humanity, whose innocence had been robbed by the cruel hand of war?

"Your mama is in a much better place than this, Lotte," she admitted quietly. "But in spirit, she's always with you. She's looking after you through Miriam, who gave you to us, through every one of your new aunties who feed you and tell you stories at night, and through us, who love you so very much. Wherever you look, you'll always find your mama if you just look closely enough."

Lotte smiled. "That's something our Rabbi used to say."

"I'm the furthest thing from a Rabbi, I'm afraid."

"Rabbi means teacher so, in a sense, you are. Thank you."

As Orli looked down at her, this little girl who had to age beyond her years, a sense of determination filled her. They were trapped in a world of darkness and despair, but as long as they had hope, they had a chance. They would fight—for Lotte, for all the Jews in Auschwitz, for their humanity.

And so, amidst the icy grip of winter and the shadow of death, a small flicker of resistance burned on, a testament to the indomitable spirit of those who refused to be crushed by the weight of their oppressors. Orli, Gerda, Velma and their secret ward stood as a silent rebellion against the horrors of Auschwitz, a beacon of hope in the darkest of winters.

TWENTY-TWO

A frosty gust swept through Auschwitz, rattling the barbed-wire fences. The snowflakes, ethereal and silent, cloaked the ground, burying the horrors beneath a deceptive veil of purity. Orli pulled her threadbare coat tighter as she trudged toward the Gypsy camp, her heart heavier than the winter sky. Dr. Mengele had returned and, while searching for anything to occupy himself with in the absence of the twins he had run out of, had discovered a new obsession.

"Have you ever heard of Noma, Dr. Reichert?" he had asked Orli one day after summoning her to his personal quarters.

Puzzled and on her guard as she'd always been around him, Orli shook her head, admitting her ignorance.

"I thought so," Dr. Mengele had said with a certain satisfaction about him. "People in the developed world rarely come across it, so it's no wonder you've never heard of it. And, in the meantime, it's been sitting right here, under our very noses, and we were none the wiser."

With those words, Dr. Mengele had suddenly leapt to his feet, pushing the door open to the examination room, equipped better than some hospitals—Orli was certain of it. Whoever had sponsored this madman's research spared no expense.

"Take a look," he had said, motioning Orli to the small child sitting on the examination table with his back to them. "I promise, you've never seen anything so utterly fascinating."

Orli had seen just about the worst humanity had to offer while here in Auschwitz-Birkenau. However, even she couldn't help but gasp and step back involuntarily at the terrifying sight that had presented itself to her eyes. Half of the child's face was virtually missing, crooked teeth visible through the hole in the cheek that by no means was supposed to be there. Little had been left of the nose as well: it had been reduced to a black, rotten stub merging with the upper lip in an unnatural manner. And, above it all, two of the most beautiful, black liquid eyes, downcast as though in shame, for the little boy knew his appearance was revolting to people.

"Did you do that to him?" Orli had whispered quietly.

Visibly amused, Dr. Mengele had pulled back in mock horror. "Me? Why, Dr. Reichert, you certainly think of me as some sort of a monster."

Orli had only stared at him in deathly silence.

"Have you not been listening to a word of what I just said?" He had finally huffed in surrender. "I just told you, it's a disease. Flesh-eating bacteria of some sort that only attacks the most vulnerable, such as those with extreme malnutrition and extremely lowered immune systems. I have requested all of the research that could have been pulled, not just from Germany but all of the occupied territories, and what do you think I ended up with?" He had gestured toward the desk on which a few scattered photocopied papers lay. "A few pitiful articles dating mostly to the last century when the scientists were still interested in Africa. Some of them even claimed that Noma only infected Negroes, but, as you can see from our Gypsy boy here, such a theory has just been disproven by yours truly." His eyes gleaming under the bright light of the overhead lamps, Dr. Mengele had leaned toward Orli. "Now, imagine what a paper I can write if I dedicate all my attention to Noma for the next few months. Naturally, we'll need more case studies."

It was those "case studies" that Orli was presently looking for as she trudged through the snow and frozen mud toward the Gypsy camp, cursing the weather, Mengele, Noma, Auschwitz and everything else that was wrong with the world. To be sure, he'd be collecting these cases not to cure them—if there even was a cure for it—he'd just poke and prod them until he got whatever he wanted out of them and then—phenol to the heart and the death cart for the children that had already suffered enough.

"I'll remember every crime of yours," Orli whispered under her breath that gusts of wind kept stealing. "I'll remember every child you tortured and when I come out of here—"

A soft whistle reached her through the wind. Orli swung round toward the sound, her heart pounding as she scanned her surroundings. *Did someone overhear? No, impossible. Not in this weather—*

It was then that she finally saw an inmate smoking behind the barracks, half-hidden in its shadows. *Sonderkommando*, it occurred to her as soon as she scanned his hulking frame and noticed rubber boots. Only one particular work gang wore them in Birkenau: the special commando assigned to gas chambers and crematoriums. Chosen for their strong physical build, they spent their days dragging corpses out of the gas chambers, hosing the chambers down until not a trace of bloody foam and excrement was left inside, and piled the corpses on the crematorium gurneys, several at a time, under the close supervision of the SS guards.

Some inmates claimed the *Sonderkommando* slept in good beds with real mattresses on them and ate like kings. Some told how those very *Sonderkommando* had to drag their own family members out of the gas chambers and push them into the oven's raging inferno. One thing was agreed upon: the SS valued them for the work they did and treated them much better than anyone else in the camp. Which didn't mean they hadn't been damaged beyond any repair by the ghastly work they were performing daily. Orli saw that much in the *Sonderkommando* inmate's eyes that had called out to her as soon as she'd approached him. They were haunted and dark, a testament to the camp's horrors. He was a living ghost, one of the damned forced to usher their own people into the abyss.

"How goes it, Doc?" he rasped, his breath misting in the cold air.

"It goes," Orli responded guardedly.

"Heard you got an infectious ward in your German infirmary." The statement—not even a question—hung in the air between them.

"We do," Orli replied evenly, despite everything tensing inside of her.

"Typhus, eh? That one's a hell of a bitch."

"It is."

For a few moments, it was a staring contest between them. The *Sonderkommando* fellow took a final drag on his cigarette, so close to his lips it must have burned, but he didn't show it, just flicked his fingers and sent it flying in a perfect arch toward the neighboring barracks.

"The SS check it at all, that ward of yours?"

"The SS check everything," Orli replied. The conversation was taking a turn she didn't care for and she went to leave when the *Sonderkommando* man caught her elbow with his great paw.

"Don't be in a rush, Doc. I'm not a rat." He must have seen the mistrust in her eyes for he dug in his pocket and produced a small package, which he pressed into her hand, his fingers ice-cold against her skin. "Here, little gratitude for a big deed. You saved my little niece there. My *Jewish* niece, Liselotte," he said, his voice barely audible. "Thank you."

"Oh, little Lotte is your niece then... You're welcome." Orli looked down at the package. It didn't smell of food but was weighty despite its small size. "I didn't know she had any relatives left, else I would have told her to search for you when we discharged her."

"It's just me, the rest are dead," he said through clenched jaws as he stared with great hatred somewhere into the distance. "And she found me without any prompts. She's a persistent little thing, my Lotte." A shadow of a smile warmed his face for an instant before disappearing once again. "Back to my question, do the SS check it?"

This time, Orli didn't deny any knowledge of anything unseemly going on in her infirmary. "Why?"

"Need a safe place to store certain... supplies," he said, shifting his gaze, hard as granite, back to Orli.

"Like what?"

"Like something you're better not to concern yourself with."

"You're planning to bring contraband into my infirmary and tell me not to be concerned about it?" She arched her brow.

"Not that I don't trust you, Doc," he softened his voice. "It's just... better for you not to know anything, in case the camp Gestapo come and search."

"And they might."

"Anything might happen."

"Do you not have a safe place to store it?"

"We do. Several places. It's best not to put all of our eggs in the same basket, you understand?"

Orli puffed out her cheeks, considering. "It's a lot, what you're asking."

But hadn't she asked the same of Gerda and Velma? Fate truly worked in mysterious ways, it suddenly occurred to her.

"I know, Doc. I do. It's not food or newspapers or radio parts either. Not even jewelry. What we're storing, it's..." It was his turn to heave a sigh. "The only reason why I'm still alive and talking to you is because the SS has just offed the entire previous *Sonderkommando*. They do that a couple of times a year, you know, so as not to risk anyone staying alive long enough to testify against their crimes if we ever happen to get out of here. So, being the savvy fellows that we are, and knowing that sometime next fall our time will come, we began stocking up on things which will allow us, if not to fight back, at least to go out with a big enough bang to ensure the SS remember. And then, who knows? Maybe we get our hands on enough stuff to make a break for it."

"A break for it? You're insane."

"Aren't we all, Doc?"

Orli shook her head, released another breath, wiped her forehead. "I don't know. It's not my decision to make. I need to talk this over with my fellow physicians."

"By all means."

"I'll have to get back to you."

"Fair enough, Doc. I'll be waiting." He nodded his good-byes, his gaze lingering on her for a moment longer before he turned and disappeared into the snowy gloom.

That evening, as Velma slept soundly, exhausted from the difficult day, Orli and Gerda huddled together in their shared bunk, their breaths visible in the frosty air. The small package lay between them, its presence a tangible reminder of the heavy decision they were about to make.

"Corpse gold," Gerda said, poking through wedding rings, earrings, and chains with the tip of her pencil.

"If I knew what it was, I wouldn't have taken it," Orli bristled.

"What else did you think a *Sonderkommando* man could

have offered you? That's all they have access to. New arrivals get undressed, take all of their jewelry off—"

"I said, I wouldn't have taken it. I'll return it to him next time I see him."

"And what do you plan on telling him?"

"What do you want me to tell him?"

"I don't know. This is dangerous, what he's proposing," Gerda whispered, her eyes reflecting the dim candlelight. "The SS don't venture inside, but Mengele might."

"Mengele doesn't do searches."

"He might order one once he realizes we're hiding Jews under his very nose in a German infirmary."

"He might," Orli conceded. "But we're already risking everything by hiding people. Might as well hide a few things under the floor and in the walls."

Gerda was silent for a moment, her face a mask of contemplation. "All of the *Sonderkommando*'s coming and going may attract unnecessary attention. They visit the Jewish infirmary a lot with their death cart, but we hardly have any deaths. If they suddenly start showing up here—"

"They don't have to. I can meet with him elsewhere. I move freely around the camp on Mengele's orders. No one will find it suspicious. So can Enna. Everyone knows our little minx and her particular ways. No one will blink an eye if they see her with a man. And next time I visit their infirmary, she or Miriam can pass it to me."

"All right," Gerda finally said, her voice barely audible. "Let's do it. But we need to be careful. *Very* careful."

"You don't need to tell me, sister," Orli smirked. "I like my neck intact, without a camp hangman's rope around it."

"On some days, when you show up with propositions like this one, I begin to seriously doubt it."

"And yet you agree to it."

"What can I say? Madness is contagious."

. . .

That was precisely what Orli told Simon, the *Sonderkommando* fellow, when she met with him the following day.

"Also, take back your gold. It's unseemly to steal from the dead."

Not only did he refuse to take the parcel back but took great offense at the accusation. "Is that what you think of us? Stealing from the dead? We aren't Nazis, you know."

After seeing puzzlement on Orli's face—*how else would you get it?*—he sighed into the howling wind and softened his tone a bit.

"Some of the new arrivals aren't as delusional as the SS believe them to be. They heard rumors of the camps, they know exactly where they're heading. And in their last moments, they allow themselves a final act of resistance against their murderers. Instead of handing the Nazis their most precious items that pay for their war machine, they give them to us."

A flicker of understanding warmed Orli's face. "So you can pay for yours."

"Now you're getting it, sister." With a knowing grin, he dipped his hand into his pocket and retrieved a small wrap and an even smaller pouch, smelling strongly of some vicious tobacco. "For the dogs. Wherever you hide the goods I pass to you, sprinkle this stuff all around them. That way, even if the SS barge in with an unannounced search, their Alsatians will leave empty-handed. Or empty-pawed, as Lotte would say."

"How is she doing?"

"I bribed a Kapo to put her in the kitchen detail. So, she's doing better than most."

"Send her our love, will you?"

"I will. And now, scram. Else, they'll see us and think we're in love."

"Not with your ugly mug, they won't."

Orli was well on her way back to the infirmary and still heard the echo of his contagious laughter in the gusts of the wind trailing her like a dog. She discovered that she was smiling —genuinely, for the first time in months.

The following weeks were a blur of whispers and covert exchanges. Sometimes, it was Simon who whistled at her from behind one barracks or the other; sometimes, one of his commando mates. Sometimes, a girl would wander into their infirmary claiming an illness, just to slip something into Orli's pocket during an examination and wander back off into the white expanse after a bright, "Well, 'spose that was nothing after all. I feel better already, see you around."

Orli never asked their names, nor which details they worked at, only hid the supplies in the typhus ward's walls, floor, and in between the bunk planks whenever the patients waited outside for the beds to be turned. There wasn't much to turn if one didn't count straw pallets and threadbare blankets, but the Jewish women never asked any questions either once the practice had been introduced. As for the sudden presence of the tobacco smell in their ward, they had learned the explanation from Orli and Gerda to present to the SS in case they appeared: lice didn't fancy it in the slightest and hit the road so hard, it hit back.

The secret ward became their sanctuary, a silent accomplice in their clandestine operations. Without knowing any details and asking a single question, everyone was suddenly in on the biggest Auschwitz conspiracy to date. Only time could tell whether anything would come out of it or whether they would all be slaughtered before they could go through with whatever enterprise the *Sonderkommando* were cooking. But at least there was hope burning warm and bright in their hearts, and for now, that was more than enough.

Despite the risks, Orli and Gerda continued their mission, bolstered by the knowledge that they were making a difference, however minuscule. Each night, as they lay in their bunk, the weight of their secret pressing down on them, they found solace in each other's presence, their shared resolve a beacon in the darkness.

TWENTY-THREE

SPRING–SUMMER 1944

As was her duty for the past few months, Orli arrived early at the Gypsy camp barracks. But instead of finding Dr. Mengele there examining the Noma children with inexhaustible fascination, she discovered only children themselves. In their usual uninhibited manner, they surrounded her and began pulling at the hem of her striped dress, asking for Herr Doktor, or, at least, the candy he always brought with him.

For the first time, their parents, ordinarily unbothered by anything, used to spending their days playing music or just lounging about unlike the less fortunate inmates assigned to outside work details, gathered around Orli as well. They'd grown used to the somewhat privileged status among the rest of the camp population but hadn't lost their vigilance. In Auschwitz-Birkenau, any deviation from the established norm was a sign of something sinister afoot, and the sudden absence of their benevolent benefactor alarmed them.

"Is he on leave?"

"Sent back to the Front?"

"Ill with something?"

Questions rang from everywhere, a desperate plea repeating

in each of them: *Please, let there be an explanation for his disappearance. Please, let there be hope for them still.*

"I don't know, but I'll find out," Orli promised and ran out of the barracks and away from the swarm of bodies and clinging hands around her.

She discovered Dr. Mengele in his personal quarters, uncharacteristically idle despite the early hour, with a glass of brandy in front of him and a look of utter serenity about him as he swung the tip of his boot in time with the music pouring out of the gramophone in the corner. No medical journals scattered around him. No notepads with sketches of Noma deformities cluttering his desk. Everything had been cleared, swept away so clean, there wasn't a trace of it left for Orli's eyes to find.

With a growing unease, she cleared her throat to call his attention. She shifted from one foot to another, but nothing elicited any reaction from Herr Doktor. He was lost to her and the world around her, in some dreamy fantasy of his.

It took Orli two attempts to call to him before he finally recovered himself, blinked the reverie away and smiled at her with an extraordinary charm.

"*Ach*, Dr. Reichert." There wasn't even the usual mocking in his voice when he addressed her by the elegant title. "A splendid spring day, is it not?"

"It is," Orli responded guardedly, and fearing losing him once again when he turned his attention back to the opened window, she risked reminding him of his morning duties: "Herr Doktor, the children?"

"What children?"

"The Noma children."

He wrinkled his nose slightly as if he smelled something foul. "I have no use for them any longer. What good is it to study Noma when no one in Germany will ever suffer it? Let the African doctors sort it out if they like."

"So..." Orli looked around, visibly at a loss. "I just return to the infirmary and mind my patients?"

"For the next few days, yes."

Orli didn't care for the enigmatic grin on his face at all.

"May I ask what happens after the next few days, Herr Doktor?"

Dr. Mengele raised his brow as though it was obvious enough, but then suddenly burst into laughter and slapped himself on the forehead. "I completely forgot. You don't have a radio here. Haven't you heard from the camp grapevine?"

Mystified even further, Orli shook her head.

"The Hungarian government has finally come to its senses and shall start transporting their Jewish population to us," Dr. Mengele explained. He pulled forward. In his eyes, the predatorial gleam Orli had grown to know and fear so well. "Nearly half a million people, Dr. Reichert. Do you understand what that means? Can you even fathom how many twins, midgets, cripples and what have you we can gather from such a sum? I have already filed for the construction of a new pathology laboratory. The camp administration assured me that it would be ready in time for the first transports to arrive. Half a million people," he repeated, not really seeing Orli in front of him any longer.

He was drunk, she realized it then, and not on brandy. He was drunk on the heady idea that he would soon be able to slice and dispose of as many human guinea pigs as he wanted. He could infect, maim, prod, and stage whatever experiments would spring to his mad mind, and no one would be able to stop him. Not only that, they were actually building a new facility for him, their Angel of Death who would soon be harvesting his biggest collection of souls yet.

And there was nothing—absolutely nothing—she could do to save them from him.

With every single nerve cell screaming inside of her as though she'd been skinned alive, Orli stumbled back into the infirmary and dropped to one of the free cots, hoping a real typhus lice would jump on her and God would claim her sorry soul before hell on earth would break out.

TWENTY-FOUR

SEHNDE, GERMANY. DECEMBER 1961

One week before New Year's Day

You find her in her room going over her old notes and journals. The room has been tidied up, everything sorted through, catalogued in alphabetical order. Your jubilation must be showing as she smiles at you with that maternal smile and says that, yes, the pill has been working fine, just fine, and she feels splendid, so very light and finally at peace with herself and the world.

You ask her about nightmares. She smiles again and shakes her head. No more nightmares.

Not even about that summer?

Not even about that. All gone. Cured. Bless advanced American psychiatry.

This gives you a pause. You search her face, but she's as serene as you've ever seen her, not a trace of the former terrors that plagued her for nights on end, and even days when reality would become indistinguishable from the memories of the past.

Did it truly work then? And so fast, too? You're still suspicious, but she's already shooing you away, telling you to go back to your office and write a nice report on her progress; put things in order before the New Year. Asks you if they'll give you a bonus of any kind if you report her miraculous improvement. You admit that they might but are still reluctant to walk away for some reason.

She laughs at you quietly and asks you how you like her hair. Her husband is visiting later today. Yes, you're aware; you're the one who put him on the list of approved visitors. Her hair looks gorgeous indeed: high and glossy, like in a magazine. It's been a long time since she took any interest in her appearance. Or her poor long-suffering husband for that matter, who tried to love her back to life but kept failing, and that's the reason why she ended up here with you, on voluntary admission, in your newest facility that used therapy and journaling and medications instead of electroshock and ice baths.

She shoos you once again, claiming she needs time to get ready for Eduard. And you go and write that report, she tells you. There's nothing else you can do for her. And, just some advice for the future—don't blame yourself either. Blame is the acid that eats at one's soul until nothing is left of it—you should trust her, she knows. She would have been so much better if she didn't blame herself for all the phenol shots and the twins and blinded children and the Hungarians burned in pits that ghastly summer.

Her suffering has finally come to an end. But please, promise her, before you go, that you won't start a vicious cycle, that you won't suffer like she did.

You nod reluctantly and go, because she does look so very happy and at peace and you believe in miracles that very moment, or the American pharma—you're not sure which one, but there's a spring in your step and sunshine in your eyes, and even the snow outside is somehow warm and fluffy and everything is right with the world.

TWENTY-FIVE

AUSCHWITZ-BIRKENAU. SUMMER 1944

The sun had barely risen when the haunting sound of the trains screeching to a halt echoed through the chilling silence of Auschwitz. As the wooden doors were wrenched open, a sea of trembling souls, all from Hungary, poured out onto the Birkenau *Judenramp*. The air was heavy with their terror, the taste of despair was palpable. And above them, like some ancient, bloodthirsty deity, Dr. Mengele towered, his eyes scanning the crowd with an unnerving intensity. Dressed in an immaculately pressed and brushed white summer uniform, he wielded his horsewhip like a scepter, the mere direction in which it pointed signifying life or death for the unfortunates facing him.

Orli, his reluctant companion, had already been ordered into the swell of that pitiful humanity with the same gloved hand that was deciding someone's fate right now. Her heart pounding painfully against her ribs, she was searching the throng for twins, dwarfs, people bearing the unforgiving mark of deformity, anyone really standing out from the crowd—the "chosen ones" for Mengele's pernicious experiments. Each glance filled her with a chilling sense of dread. The perverse selection process felt like a grotesque carnival game, where the prize was nothing more than a prolonged life of suffering.

In the same ocean of exhausted, terrified faces, Orli's eyes met Simon's briefly. He nodded to her, the unwilling gas chamber attendant, a sign of sympathy from one Nazi slave to the other: *You stay strong, sister*. With that, he was back to gently prodding men away from women and explaining to them, with infinite patience, that they would be reunited soon —*as soon as disinfection was over. Unseemly for men and women to bathe together, no?*

Even the SS and the Kapos were strangely reserved that morning. Instead of clubbing the new arrivals over the heads and pointing with their fingers at the chimneys belching putrid yellow smoke, they stood with their hands clasped behind their backs and answered questions almost politely.

"Water? Of course, my good woman. They'll give you water right after disinfection. Water and warm soup and some coffee even, if you prefer it. For now, there's nothing to be done about it unfortunately, but there's a hose attached to the bathhouse. You can use its water for drinking and a general hose-off. We'll tell the *Sonderkommando* to roll it out for you."

Reassured and even impressed to an extent by the very civil-behaving SS, the Hungarian Jews followed narrow paths set up by the SS days earlier. Only Birkenau old-timers knew that one of those barbed-wire enclosed sections led straight to the gas chamber. *Knew, and could do jack shit about it*, according to Simon and his commando mates.

He swiped at the fat blue fly and spat on the ground when Orli asked him later that day about the SS and Kapos' odd behavior.

"Don't want panic on their hands, those *Arschloch* bastards. The Hungarians, they're from the cities mostly. Haven't heard anything about the camps, or, if they did hear, didn't believe it. Until now, they only knew one side of the Germans: elegant uniforms, polite speech, manners, culture—all that rot. And the SS are peddling it to them to keep them calm until they lock the gas-proof door behind them. Then they realize what's what, but it's too late, the fellow in a gas mask is already pouring his stuff down the hatch."

All around them, crickets were rubbing their hind legs like mad, joining in with the cacophony of human voices. From the sky, thick greasy ash flakes were falling, smearing on their sweaty skin—a film of humanity slaughtered like cattle that would stick to them until their final days. Not enough water in the world would wash it off, even if they scrubbed themselves raw.

"Is there anything I can do?" Orli asked through the ash-filled air, her eyes rimmed with red.

Simon stared hatefully into the distance—what could possibly be done about all this? But then, suddenly, he turned back to Orli, looked at her as though he saw her for the first time: "Can you go to Auschwitz at all?"

"Auschwitz?" Orli repeated.

"Yes. Can you invent something about being there on Mengele's orders?"

Orli's already wet back was awash with yet another wave of perspiration. He had something on his mind, and whatever it was, it was a suicide mission. Worse than hoarding supplies for him—she read that much in his eyes.

"I suppose I could," she said slowly, as if tasting her own words before uttering them, committing to something from which there was no return. "Where exactly do you want me to go?"

"Processing barrack. Where they take photos of the new arrivals."

"I don't think they do that anymore."

"Not for the new arrivals in Birkenau, no. But they still do for those sent to Auschwitz. It's a resort compared to our birch woods." The last two words he spat out mockingly. "They're mostly sending political ones there, from what I hear."

"All right." Orli stared at him. The oppressive heat and that stomach-churning stench in the air was making it difficult to think. "Why do you want me to go there?"

"Why do you think, sister?" His crooked grin was circled with black. Everything was black around and above, the day itself turning into night before their weary eyes. "They don't even register them, those poor Hungarian devils. Don't process them, don't tattoo them. They just kill them outright, as though they never existed. Even if the Allies win the war, even if we ever come out of here, how will we possibly prove to anyone that a crime on such a mass scale ever happened?"

It started to dawn on Orli just then, the idea behind those mad, justice-craving eyes of his. "You want me to steal a camera," she whispered the impossible.

"And film."

"Why don't you ask me for my right eye as well?"

"I have no use for your eye, no matter how big or black or beautiful it is." He swiped gently at the tear Orli didn't know was there and shook his head with a sudden look of guilt about him. "It's too much, what I'm asking you. I realize it. You're already doing so much, Doc. Don't risk your skin for a gas chamber attendant's folly."

"It's not for you that I'll be risking it." Through the walls of barbed wire, Orli watched as inexhaustible lines of people snaked around the compound until the crematoriums swallowed them whole. "It's for them."

Simon grinned and pressed her hand—firmly and respectfully, like that not of a lady but a war comrade. "I understand now why they call you what they call you."

"What do they call me?"

"The Angel of Auschwitz," Simon said and saluted her with two fingers at his forehead as Orli swallowed a lump that had suddenly lodged in her throat.

TWENTY-SIX

BIRKENAU

Two weeks later

Another day. Another ramp duty. More Hungarians stumbling down onto the *Judenramp* and turning their heads this way and that, with hands shielding their eyes from the blinding sun, trying to make sense of the place they'd found themselves at. Among them, Orli felt as if she had been transplanted from a black and white movie into a Technicolor picture. Bright prints on the women's summer dresses, red sandals on the children's feet, striped slacks and blue silk shirts on the men; and the hair —blond, red, chestnut, all curled, done up, smoothed with brilliantine, braided into plaits—just to be shorn off in a few short hours, and only if they were fortunate enough to live.

In the sea of weary, terrified faces, Orli's gaze fell upon a man with an air of quiet dignity, despite the fear in his eyes. A physician's leather bag in his hand, he stood slightly apart from everyone, quietly scanning his surroundings, taking it all in. Unlike most men in his line, he didn't hold a younger boy's hand, neither did he search the opposite line of women for his

wife and daughters. All alone, and already making the connec-
tion between the people disappearing into nondescript
rectangular buildings and the thick yellowish smoke pouring
out of the chimneys soon after.

Orli couldn't quite tell why she approached him. He didn't
fall into any of the categories Dr. Mengele was interested in.
Perhaps, because he looked a bit like Orli's father, or held
himself in the same self-possessed manner even with mere
hours to live—she couldn't tell. But instead of searching the
crowd for Mengele's twins, she pushed her way toward him and
asked him for his name.

"Dr. Kertesz," he replied, a bit surprised at being addressed.

"You're a physician then?" Orli asked with a glance at
his bag.

"A pathologist," he offered a tad apologetically. His German
was immaculate, just as his suit that had been pressed before
he'd set off on his last journey—Orli could tell. "Nothing but a
glorified corpse cutter, I fear." Another self-conscious smile. "I
bet you have enough of those here."

*You can't even begin to imagine, but not in the sense that you
think*, Orli wanted to say but didn't. "Come with me."

She was feeling strange and all out of sorts that day. All of
her attempts to avoid ramp duty and sneak into Auschwitz
instead had been unsuccessful, much like her efforts to warn
mothers of twins. Even if they spoke German, they didn't want
to listen to her, didn't want to separate their twins and change
them into different clothes. Having twins was good, they'd been
told. These SS gentlemen assured them of that much. And who
was she at any rate? Some mad criminal inmate in a grimy
striped dress who must have lice too. Move away before we
report you.

Slowly but surely, Orli's spirit was fracturing under the
strain. The kaleidoscope of blinding colors, the blissful ignorance of those marching to death, the smell of burning flesh, all

were etched into her mind, an indelible stain on her soul. She was haunted by nightmares, visions of twisted bodies and pleading eyes, their silent screams echoing in her mind and nothing to be done to save them, not a single soul.

Perhaps that was the reason why she grasped Dr. Kertesz's hand and led him through the ocean of bodies toward the front of the ramp. He tried to protest in his mild manner, didn't wish to get her in trouble. He wasn't worth any, he claimed, but Orli dragged him all the same as though, if not her life, but her sanity depended on it.

In no time, they were standing in front of Dr. Mengele—Dr. Kertesz with a hat in his hand and Orli trembling with her entire body as her eyes gleamed wildly.

"Herr Doktor, this is Dr. Kertesz," she began, fighting with her own breath that was suddenly catching in her throat. She was hyperventilating and knew it, but couldn't help it, even with the best will in the world. Something was breaking, crumbling, inside of her, sending shockwaves through her limbs that were twitching without her noticing. All at once, it was of paramount importance to save one, just this one person, and then she would be able to live with herself for a few more days at least. "He's a highly respected pathologist from Hungary. You were saying that the construction of the new pathology lab was—"

Mengele, with a twisted sense of delight, interrupted her with his raised hand. "I know who he is." The same unhealthy gleam ignited in his eyes that was always there whenever he found a particularly interesting case of deformity or sliced open a fresh twin corpse. "Dr. Mengele," he introduced himself with a slight incline of his head. "Welcome to Auschwitz-Birkenau, Doctor. It's our great pleasure to have you here."

"So is mine," the Hungarian pathologist muttered automatically.

"Dr. Reichert, escort him to our new pathology laboratory, will you?"

Orli nodded, a sense of sheer delight washing over her. She all but danced on her way there, forgetting momentarily the crematoriums and the smoke and the people they were swallowing day and night. Refusing to release the pathologist's hand —as if there was anywhere to run here—she babbled something incoherently, giving him a tour of the hell on earth he would now have to call his home, but even that was all right: he could get used to it soon.

"You're safe," she kept repeating like a prayer that had finally been answered. And so what that the only one who answered it was the one they called the Angel of Death? "That's what's important. You're safe, you're alive."

He must have wondered if she were mad. Orli didn't mind. Perhaps, she was; lost the last of her marbles sometime between the Hungarian *Aktion* that was killing thousands of Hungarian Jews a day and Mengele's ward of wonders, as he mockingly called it, that had swelled to enormous proportions in the past few weeks. They arrived faster than he could kill them. He would never run out of fresh material, never again, and she was the one to watch all that never-ending horror unravel for days on end. No wonder she'd gone mad—who wouldn't?

Inside the newly constructed pathology lab, Dr. Kertesz froze momentarily.

"What is this place?" he whispered, more to himself than to Orli.

She, too, looked around, taking in her surroundings for the first time. She had never set foot in here before and only now saw the grandiosity of the entire affair. Inside the main chamber, there was a new slab, all shiny stainless steel with ridges running toward the drain and it was equipped like nothing she'd seen before. In the corner next to the porcelain sink with gleaming faucets stood a glass cabinet, fully stocked, labeled, and organized to perfection—by Herr Doktor himself, no doubt. On the opposite side, under a window protected by a mosquito net, a desk with a typewriter and a filing cabinet next to it—all business as it should be.

But it was the room attached to the main chamber that stunned Orli the most. From the way it looked, it could have been transplanted from any middle-class German apartment. It seemed frighteningly domesticated, with a bed by the window, a full library lining one of the walls, a table and two armchairs and even a telephone resting on the small side table by the door.

"All right," Dr. Kertesz said after recovering himself somewhat. "All right," he repeated and lowered his medical bag on the floor, so heavily it was as though it suddenly weighed a ton. "I know where I am. I saw how people die here. One of the crematoriums is right next to us, is it not?"

Orli nodded. There was no point in lying. He wasn't one of the delusional well-dressed mothers who chased her off while pushing her twins forward despite all her warnings; he knew precisely what was going on.

"What is needed from me that placed me in such a favorable position? Something terrible, no doubt?"

After a moment of silence, Orli nodded again. This wasn't a simple pathology lab, this was a place where science was stripped of its nobility and used as a tool for torture.

The Hungarian lowered his head, and all at once, tears sprang to Orli's eyes, hot guilty tears that burned like acid. She hadn't saved him for himself; hadn't asked if he wished to participate in atrocities that would make anyone's hair stand on end. Without any consideration, she'd sentenced him to a life that was possibly worse than death—and now there was nothing she could do about it. Once he got his teeth into the best assistant he could have wished for, there was not a chance in the world Dr. Mengele would let him go. Much too precious were his skills.

"You can always kill yourself," she whispered on her way out. She couldn't face him any longer. Just being in the same room with him was torture in itself.

"I'm too much of a coward for that," he replied softly.

"So am I," Orli said and closed the door after herself.

TWENTY-SEVEN

Each day, Orli watched as thousands marched toward the gas chambers, their faces etched with a hopeless acceptance of the inevitable. The stench of death hung heavy in the air; the ominous smoke billowing from the crematoriums served as a constant reminder of the harrowing fate that awaited them. The crematoriums, designed to erase the evidence of the unspeakable atrocities committed there, were now unable to keep up with the relentless pace of death. Bodies were piled high in open fields, their final resting place nothing more than a burning pit of despair.

Orli's psyche was shattered, her spirit broken. The endless torments she bore witness to, the inescapable reality of her surroundings, were too monstrous for any mind to bear. The sheer magnitude of the atrocities was enough to make one question the very existence of humanity within these electrified barbed wires. She moved through her days as though through one never-ending nightmare, eyes red from the smoke, skin smeared with gray and smelling of death.

Next to her German infirmary, an entire barracks had been emptied by the SS. On Dr. Mengele's orders, it had turned into a quarantine section—on paper (or, rather, in SS words, pouring like poisoned honey from their serpents' tongues) to keep new arrivals separate from the general population until they were given a clean bill of health. In reality, it was a makeshift purgatory, the doors to which were slammed shut and bolted until the *Sonderkommando* burned the previous weeks' corpse-load. Until then, the new arrivals were confined in that coffin of a barracks, waiting for their impending doom. The heat was suffocating, the conditions inhumane. The people were left to languish in their own filth, their bodies growing weaker each passing day, their spirits crumbling under the weight of their despair. The SS didn't bother feeding them or even providing them with the relief of some water.

Passing by the quarantine block several times a day and hearing the pleas and cries coming from behind its walls, growing weaker by the day, Orli finally couldn't bear it any longer and found her way into the *Sonderkommando* domain—the crematorium, now screened and manned by the SS so that those awaiting gassing on one side wouldn't see the multiple pits where corpses were burned on the other. Through the reddish inferno that turned the sky into a dome of gray ash, Orli stumbled into a group of men wearing nothing but trousers held around their waists by ropes and rubber boots with thick soles. Recognizing her, they pointed toward Simon.

She was about to approach him, ask him if he could do something to speed the process up. How terrible the words sounded even in her own mind! But, in reality, the people were sentenced to death already and there was nothing to be done to help them. Surely even gas was better than slowly going mad from suffocating heat and thirst and hunger and watching their own children or grandmothers dying in their arms and their corpses slowly next to them until someone would open that blasted door and drag them out.

But as she watched Simon tending to his grisly task, turning the bodies stacked in the nearest pit with a long stick while their flesh bubbled, turned black, and then burst and leaked yellow fat feeding the fire; as she saw an SS man drinking beer as he stood nearby; as she witnessed Simon's fellow *Sonderkommando* mate pulling golden crowns from the mouths of fresh corpses that another couple of *Sonderkommando* men had just brought from the gas chamber, Orli suddenly couldn't force a single word out of herself.

They were drowning in corpses here, working the gas chambers, crematoriums and pits in shifts because there were just too many of them, far too many people to process, and here she was, asking for them to please hurry up because it was too painful for her to hear their cries. How much worse Simon's personal hell must be!

Without looking back, Orli stumbled out of that inferno and back into the main camp compound.

"We ought to do something."

Gerda looked up from the child she was tending to—one of Mengele's recent projects. The boy's twin was sitting on the cot next to him, paler than his brother, who was slowly being eaten up by whatever infection the mad scientist had injected him with.

"About the children?" Gerda asked.

Orli regarded the tragic picture Dr. Mengele's children's ward had been reduced to and shook her head. There was nothing they could do about the children. The sick boy was on his last breath. By tomorrow morning at the latest, these twins would end up on Dr. Mengele's new slab, where, under his supervision, the Hungarian pathologist would be dissecting them through the tears in his eyes. "About the quarantine barracks."

Just as exhausted as Orli with this incessant death parade

outside their windows and the helplessness with which they watched it until their eyes were about to bleed, Gerda turned back to the young boy and replaced a cool rag on his forehead. "The doors are bolted, we can't get to them even if we wanted to."

"I refuse to believe that."

"I refuse to believe they're burning thousands of people daily in the open fields, but it doesn't change the fact that they are."

The sick boy's twin's whimpers turned into desperate wails.

Orli winced. Ordinarily, a child's cry would promptly awaken an almost maternal desire to soothe and hold and promise that everything would be all right, she'd see to it and he was a brave little soldier and she knew he would be strong for his brother. Now, with her nerves strung tight to the point of breaking, she rose abruptly to her feet and told him to shut it right that instant.

The boy did so, staring at her with those big frightened eyes.

"He's just a child," Gerda said with a quiet reproach. "He's scared and he's suffering."

"I'm scared and I'm suffering, and I have more reason to cry than he. Shall I start?"

Orli didn't know what had gotten into her. She wanted to fight with everyone and hurl things and scream into the ash-tainted air until there was no breath left in her to take. She was overcome with a sudden urge to do something—*anything*—just to stop her mind from processing things, just to fix something that couldn't be fixed, just to preserve at least a shred of her humanity amidst all this chaos.

Muttering to herself like a madwoman, she fled Gerda and the children's ward and began circling the quarantine barracks, wild-eyed and breathing heavily. She threw herself against the walls and tried to scale the roof, but it was much too high, and even if she reached it, there was the matter of a skylight that would have to be broken for there was no locks on it.

With sweat running down her face, she dropped back to the ground, raising a small cloud of dust around her, stared at the planks for some time and then began to dig under the lowest one. She hadn't the faintest idea how long she was going at it like some demented mole. Someone's hands tugged at her arms —"Orli, Orli, stop, please. Look at your hands, they're all torn and bleeding"—but she shook the unwelcome embrace off together with the pleas and continued digging into the ground with a renewed force.

"Something ought to be done," she repeated with obstinacy that made little sense, and suddenly saw a second pair of hands joining hers under the planks stained with mold, dirt, and blood. "Miriam?" Orli looked at the girl through the grit and sweat in her eyes.

"Who did you expect? President Roosevelt?" Miriam grinned at her and blew a stray lock of hair away from her forehead. Orli saw that it was completely white. How old was this girl now? Eighteen? Nineteen? If Orli only had Miriam's eyes with which to tell her age, she would have guessed closer to eighty—so much pain and grief and suffering reflected in their deep dark wells. "Gerda sent for me. Said you've completely lost it and that I ought to stop you before the SS do, with a bullet to the neck."

"Why are you not stopping me?"

"Because you're digging a hole to get water and food to them, no?"

Orli paused for a second. "You don't think I've lost it then?"

"I think, out of this entire place, you're the sanest one."

They looked at each other and one's smile reflected in the other like in a looking glass. Then, they continued to dig in companionable silence until the hole was big enough to push Orli's aluminum mug under. Promptly, she untied it from her belt and ran for the faucet in the German infirmary, grasping whatever she could on her way. A pitiful attempt to alleviate the suffering of the condemned, but that was all they had, she and Miriam, and to hell with those who thought otherwise.

In the next few hours, they smuggled scraps of food, water, anything they could manage, into the quarantined section. It felt miserably inadequate, like trying to extinguish a raging inferno with a single, trembling teardrop. But it was all they could do, and Orli clung to it as her last vestige of hope.

"Thank you." Orli couldn't see the woman who uttered the words but felt her fingertips brushing hers through the makeshift underground tunnel.

"It's nothing. I wish I could do more." At that moment, Orli would tear her own heart out and offer it to this person she had never met.

"You're doing more than you know," the woman replied. "There's a saying my people have: whoever saves a single life saves an entire universe. And I have a feeling you saved so much more than that."

Her words poured like a healing balm into Orli's battered soul. Clinging to them, she continued her clandestine acts of kindness, even as the monstrous machine of Auschwitz churned on, its gears lubricated with the blood of the innocent.

As the days turned into weeks, the Hungarian *Aktion* amplified. The camp swelled with new arrivals, each group more desolate than the last. Their eyes, once filled with fear, now held a vacant stare, a damning testament to the horrors they had endured.

Dr. Mengele's pathology lab, now under Dr. Kertesz's reluctant control, became a theater of the macabre. The pathologist was forced to conduct inhumane experiments, each more abhorrent than the previous. His hands, once used to finding answers for grieving families, were now tools of torture. Whenever Orli stopped by on Dr. Mengele's orders, she invariably found him obsessively scrubbing his hands raw as though he wished to wash the blood off them that was visible only to him. He never complained. In fact, he scarcely spoke at all, except for a "yes" or "no" or "will do" and the usual "please" and "thank you."

When Orli lingered in his doorway one day and finally gathered enough courage to ask whether he hated her for what she did, he regarded her somewhat surprised.

"You saved me from the gas chamber. How can I possibly hate you?"

"You never speak to me."

A wistful, paternal smile warmed his tormented face. "I'm saving the words. For later. For my testimony. For when we all come out of here. Then, every single memory, I shall put down on paper. That's the reason I don't talk much, sweet Aurelia. I could never hate you, you're an angel. And now, go on your way and help someone else. There's always someone to help and you do it so well. Go, sweet child, go. In times like these, each moment counts."

Orli nodded and left him to his work, which he looked upon with a mixture of revulsion and despair, the once-revered pathologist now a puppet dancing on Mengele's strings.

The crematoriums continued to belch smoke into the sky, their eerie glow a constant reminder of the atrocities committed within their stone-cold walls. Bodies were still being burned in open fields, their ashes carried away by the wind, a woeful dirge to their tragic end. But Dr. Kertesz was right: something had to be done. And so, Orli marched to the Jewish ramp and once again threw herself into the sea of dead people walking. Though, this time, she had a new idea in mind, even more suicidal than all of the previous ones.

At the end of the ramp, on the opposite side from where Dr.
Mengele sorted the people into the living and the dead, suitcases taken from the new arrivals were piled up. It was an open
space guarded by a couple of the SS men who did much more
smoking and jawing than guarding the suitcases that would
soon be taken to the Kanada sorting detail, but their guns were
oiled and ready at their belts and they liked shooting first and
asking questions later.

Orli watched them for some time.

Waited.

Despite her best hopes, they never left stacks of suitcases
unsupervised. Scarcely paid them any heed but lingered much
too close for comfort nevertheless. And the crowd around Orli
was already shifting, moving away from her and closer to the
front of the ramp and Dr. Mengele. Soon, she'd be sticking out
here like a sore thumb. It was now or never.

There was an old rule to the camp: walk around with
purpose as though you have all the right to be there, and that's
precisely what Orli did. After wiping her wet palms on her
skirt, she took a deep shuddering breath to calm her nerves and
walked toward the pile with a resolute step.

"Inmate 502 reporting, on Dr. Mengele's orders," she
shouted so loudly, the SS men started momentarily.

"No need to bellow, you're not at the parade," one of them
muttered and spat on the ground. "What do you want?"

"Medicaments. Instruments. Anything we can use in the
infirmary and the pathology lab."

Had they been in any way related to the infirmary, or even
set foot in the new pathology lab, they would have laughed her
off the ramp on the spot, for the pathology lab in particular had
been stocked better than the best hospital in Berlin. But they
were ordinary guards and none too bright at that, Orli realized,
once they waved her lazily through.

"Go dig, little rat. But don't you go thinking you can smuggle food or gold or currency."

Orli made huge stupid eyes at them. "Whatever would I do with currency?"

"Don't be smart now," the second one said, half raising his whip in the air. "You're getting smarter by the hour ever since the Allies landed."

"I'm German," Orli muttered, feigning offence. "I would never celebrate the enemy threatening my homeland."

Their attitude improved somewhat after this declaration. They turned their backs on her and continued to smoke and gossip about old times when crates of schnapps weren't rationed and camp administration didn't cancel furlough requests left and right.

The Allies landed! With muted jubilation, Orli dropped to her knees and began rummaging through suitcases in search of what could change so much and for so many.

The Allies landed, and that meant freedom on the horizon.

The Allies landed, and that meant the SS would become even more rabid now in their determination to eliminate all the traces of their crimes. She wouldn't be surprised if they razed the entire camp to the ground.

With a redoubled effort, Orli dug.

Five days and still nothing. Five days and the guards would grow suspicious before too long; ask Mengele just how many supplies he needed or complain to their superior about it and he would raise a stink. They were all such fine bureaucrats, those compatriots of hers. Everyone guarded his own department as though he was married to it.

For five days, Orli submitted herself to the searches and left with arms full of medical supplies and an occasional box of bonbons which she claimed were cough drops—thankfully, the

SS didn't know any better. For five days, she threw herself into her desperate searches just to come up with nothing, but then, on the sixth, her hand clasped around a small leather case with a familiar German *Leica* embossed in the right corner.

Breaking into a cold sweat, triumphant and terrified to the core, Orli threw a quick glance over her shoulder. The SS were bickering about engine differences in the Messerschmitts and RAF fighters as if they were in charge of each respective plane building plant and paid virtually no heed to their "little rat."

Cradling the portable camera in her hand like a newborn, Orli patted herself frantically with the other in desperate search of a hiding place. Had it been winter, she could have stuffed it in her bloomers and the SS would be none the wiser, but it was summer and bloomers in summer weren't allowed, only someone else's underwear they'd been given two months ago, which was three sizes too big and held by a string and anything would fall out before Orli could make her first step.

She patted her chest, but that was no good either. Breasts, those had been reduced to nothing years ago, thanks to an Auschwitz diet, and would conceal nothing now. Finally, after running out of options, Orli decided on the last—and only— possible one. As inconspicuously as possible, she crept closer and closer to the edge of the ramp and, after another look in the SS guards' direction, dropped the Leica onto the tracks as close to the end as possible to prevent the risk of it being crushed in case the transport came before it could be retrieved.

Weighted down with a few bottles of cough syrup and alcohol, Orli marched toward the guards and didn't even mind the inevitable patting down.

"I got it," she whispered to Simon later that evening.

The sun was rolling toward the horizon, just as red as the inferno raging all around them. The SS amused themselves by rounding up young girls behind the crematoriums and setting their Alsatians on them until they would have nowhere to run except for the fire pits if they didn't want to be mauled alive. Maddened by the smell of churning meat and human blood, the dogs turned into savage beasts, with foam at their curled lips. Maddened by alcohol and power, their handlers howled in delight, betting on who would stumble into the pit first—the macabre race of human flesh torn to shreds and burned into ash.

Simon's gaze, full of cold hatred and revulsion, was riveted to the picture. He, too, was committing it to his memory. He, too, would one day have a lot to tell.

But telling wasn't always enough.

"I got the camera." Orli touched his hand to get his attention. It was hot to the touch and black with soot.

He turned to her, incredulous. "You did? It's been so long."

"I know."

"I lost all faith."

"I know."

"I thought we would never—"

"We will." Orli's smile was a feral grimace. In her eyes, the same inferno raged. "Now, we will. We'll photograph it all and show it to the world."

"So they will hang them like dogs." Simon, too, was now smiling, all white teeth against soot-smudged skin.

"It's by the end of the *Judenramp*, I dropped it onto the tracks."

"A team is going to retrieve the suitcases for the Kanada soon. I'll send word for them to get it."

"Take photos of it all, Simon."

"I will."

"And bring the film to my typhus ward. I'll hide it there together with the rest of your supplies."

He nodded, all taut muscle and steely resolve and revenge burning hot and deep within him.

Orli, too, was hot that evening, but it wasn't the fires that singed her flesh from the inside; it was the thought of sweet justice that would ultimately be served to their tormentors. Despite her crumbling psyche, Orli had persevered, and at long last, her efforts had paid off.

From that day on, Orli continued her secret missions, smuggling bits of food and water to the quarantined and hiding more of Simon's contraband under the floor of the typhus ward. Each grateful glance, each weak smile was a small victory against the insurmountable evil they were all trapped in.

On some nights, as the screams of the dying echoed around her, she allowed herself to weep. Her tears were a testament to her despair, a silent vow that she would continue fighting, for herself and for those who had lost their voice amidst the chaos. On some nights, she prowled the camp for her clandestine meetings with Simon to collect his contraband and on those nights, she felt most alive.

The chapter of the Hungarian *Aktion* in Auschwitz was a horrifying demonstration of the depths of human cruelty. For Orli, it was a crucible that tested her spirit, pushing her to the very edge of despair. But in the midst of the darkness, she found her resolve, a flickering flame of hope that refused to be extinguished.

TWENTY-EIGHT

SUMMER–FALL 1944

The sky was a dismal gray, heavy with impending doom. The air, thick with the stench of fear and despair, echoed with the hopeless cries that filled the Auschwitz-Birkenau concentration camp. In the distance, smoke billowed from the chimneys and open fields, painting a haunting portrait of the horrors that unfolded therein. Orli had forgotten what the world outside these gates looked like.

She and Gerda didn't speak much these days. Not that anything particular had transpired between them, but all at once the words lost all of their meaning in this charnel house with SS butchers at its helm. Unwittingly, on some instinctual level, they felt that words soiled the memory of those silenced forever. In their self-imposed penance for the sins that weren't theirs, they held a minute of silence for each of those perished and it was no wonder that their silence lasted for months. If the SS continued in the manner they did, they would have to be mute for years to come.

Others came and went with the news from the outside world. Orli tended to them and listened but cared little for the rumors that things weren't going all that well for the Nazis on either front. She didn't share their jubilations either. They had arrived from other places, places that weren't hell on earth, and spent far too little time in Birkenau to understand that this was their final destination, not a re-education, but an extermination camp—the place people came to die. The graveyard of ash and bone that stretched all the way to the forest was proof of this.

"We'll be liberated soon too, you'll see that we will!"

If Orli had a piece of bread for each time she heard those words, she'd feed her entire infirmary for a week.

With everything that had already happened and was presently happening around her, there wasn't a chance in the world the SS would surrender the camp with its inhabitants still intact. They would level the entire affair in order to erase the very memory of their crimes off the face of the earth.

It was the argument brought up the most among the new arrivals and Birkenau old-timers.

"Have you not seen what they're doing to the Hungarian Jews, you feebleminded cow?"

"Those are Jews. We're Aryans. The SS won't touch us."

"Oh, you reckon they will let us sign their guest book and send us off on our merry way while waving handkerchiefs at us as they're seeing us off?"

"Don't be daft. All I'm saying is that they might gas the rest of the Jews, but they'll surrender us to the Allies unharmed."

"So we can tell the Allies that they killed said Jews. We're witnesses; how difficult is it for you to comprehend?"

"We're still Aryans."

"So were all of those Wehrmacht fellows who tried to assassinate Hitler just weeks ago. Where are they now? Strung up nice and high with piano wires."

"Who told you that?"

"A most reliable authority that has access to the radio, both our German and Allied one."

"Even if it is so, we didn't try to assassinate Hitler. I'm here because I was stupid enough to offer a good time to an under-cover bull."

"Keep telling yourself that when you find yourself in the gas chamber."

Sometimes they turned to Orli for her opinion, but she was too preoccupied with present-day affairs to consider anything that lay ahead. In the walls of the typhus ward, a small ammunition depot was growing. Sometimes, on the pretext of collecting rare corpses from the German infirmary, Simon stopped by the ward and rested his hand on the wall as if on the shoulder of a dear friend, but then departed without claiming its contents.

Not yet. Not just yet. There were still transports arriving from Hungary even if what used to be a gushing stream had been reduced to a trickle.

"It is imperative to guess the last train," he would explain to Orli in his feverish agitation. "They'll take the strongest men from the last train to train as the new *Sonderkommando* and us... To the gas with us. But we won't surrender so easily, we'll fight back. We just have to guess the last train."

Orli, too, was on edge these days. Something was shifting in the air as though before a storm of the highest magnitude.

Everything was suspiciously quiet for a few days. Each morning, to the sound of the camp orchestra, work gangs left for their respective destinations. In the afternoons, Dr. Mengele visited his children, his pockets bursting with bonbons and sugar cubes. Each evening, Orli watched Dr. Kertesz scrub their blood off his hands as she labeled the packages with tissue samples for Mengele's research institute—eyes, kidneys, livers, and lungs of little boys and girls she had not long ago been telling bedtime stories to and tucking in with threadbare blankets. Her youngest charges, sliced, sorted into boxes and marked up to be shipped to Germany like some macabre merchandise.

And then, one day, suddenly, no Mengele and no ramp duty and the camp-wide lockdown that came crashing down on their heads like hail, drumming into them the realization that there was no safety in the routine no matter how ghastly. There was no avoiding the SS's plans to slaughter them all if they wished, no matter how much they tried to persuade themselves the opposite was true.

With the SS bolting the infirmary shut, Orli ran into the contagious ward but came to an abrupt stop in its doors. All of this contraband and for what? She was no *Sonderkommando* man. She hadn't the faintest idea how to shoot a gun, let alone hurl a grenade, a few of which were concealed under her very feet. She only knew how to fight back with her selfless desire to help, not with fists and weapons. She knew how to save people in her ward but had no way of protecting them now that the SS were outside, shouting orders at their underlings over the rumbling of the truck engines that kept growing and growing in volume until one couldn't hear their thoughts inside the barracks.

At first, there was tense silence hanging over the barracks like a poisonous cloud. After came the tears and wails of utter, animalistic terror. In that communal rat trap, inmates clung to each other, panted, hiccupped, and prayed. The air stank sharply of sweat tinged with fear. It quickly grew stale and stifling as the temperatures rose outside and the sun stood high in the sky, pouring its unforgiving heat through the skylights like hot lava.

Gerda found Orli by the window in the physicians' cubicle, or, rather, under it, where she sat cross-legged with her skirt pulled high over her thighs—anything to bring at least some relief from this relentless heat.

"Don't stare out the window," Orli said quietly to her. "I tried it once and was shown the barrel of a gun. I don't think they'll use it as a warning next time."

Gerda didn't need to be told twice. Swiftly, she dropped to the floor next to Orli and began fanning herself with the hem of her skirt.

"What are they doing there?"

"Damned if I know. A liquidation, judging by the looks of it."

"The quarantine barracks?" Gerda asked, growing even more alarmed. It was much too close to their infirmary, much too close to them, and in Birkenau death tended to be contagious.

"No. I don't think so, at least. When I looked out, the doors were still bolted, just like ours." Orli paused, staring into nothing. "Those poor wretches. How are they going to fare without water? Must be wandering where I am..."

Gerda pulled back in apparent disbelief. "We're locked in here ourselves without water, possibly living out our last hours, and you're concerned with the quarantine barracks? There's nothing we can do for them now."

Orli slapped the mosquito that landed on her thigh. "You're right." She rose to her feet, swaying slightly like a drunk—from the heat, not the Polish moonshine grateful patients smuggled to them from time to time.

"Where are you off to?" Gerda called to her.

"Girls are crying."

"Yes?"

"Let's go hold their hands at least."

Without any further explanation, Gerda rose to her feet. Somehow, it made perfect sense. They were physicians, not resistance fighters, nor even someone who could smuggle a bit of water and food to the neighboring barracks, and if holding hands and keeping their patients company was all they could do, they would do it.

For such is the very essence of every healer who was born to carry the difficult task of caring for the infirm: to throw themselves at death itself and fight it tooth and nail until the last drop of blood. In the end, they can close their eyes, at peace with the thought that they did everything they could and more, and would do it again a thousand times over, sacrificing themselves for the sake of others for as long as they lived.

That day was stifling and seemingly would never end. Inside the infirmary, women died a thousand deaths before, at long last, the bolt was removed from the doors and the SS departed in their trucks without a single word spoken.

Orli felt the entire barracks exhale collectively in immense relief but against the ink of darkening sky, the orange flames danced brighter than ever. They'd been spared that day. Others hadn't.

In the thickening twilight, Simon appeared in Orli's cubicle like some grotesque apparition, his face grayer than ash and smeared with it.

"Orli." His voice trembled as he spoke, his words barely rising above a whisper. The lines on his face were etched deeper tonight, the hollows of his eyes darker. "They liquidated the Family Camp."

A chilling silence hovered between them, punctuated only by the distant wailing that echoed through the night. The words hung heavily in the frigid air, their weight threatening to crush Orli. She had been fearing this day, and now it had arrived, bringing with it a fresh wave of despair.

"The Family Camp? The families transferred from Theresienstadt?" Her entire body trembled as she regarded him in disbelief. "Weren't they under Red Cross protection?"

From Simon, a derisive snort. "They were. Fat lot of good it did them."

Orli's very insides turned to ice. If the SS could off the most privileged of them, the rest of the camp population stood little chance of survival. In her state of shock, she didn't notice at first how Simon lowered himself heavily to the floor as though his very legs refused to hold him.

"Entire families," he moaned, rocking side to side as he clutched at the collar of his shirt as if it was suffocating him. "Mothers, fathers, children, their grandparents, brothers, sisters, cousins... All into the same chamber. Didn't even separate them this time. All stripped naked, watching their loved ones suffocate to death in front of their eyes while they could do nothing but die themselves. Mothers screaming for help as their children were coughing up bloody foam. It doesn't take as long for the gas to work on children. Their little lungs seize up first. And their parents watch them struggle for their last breath—" The last word stuck in Simon's throat, choked him with the weight of it.

Orli dropped to the floor as well, holding him, swaying with him as he sobbed silently, great waves of grief wracking his powerful body. It was the first time she had seen a *Sonderkommando* man cry. They were the gas chamber attendants, the crematorium ovens' slaves, forced by the SS into performing the worst labor imaginable and were used to seeing death up close. Orli didn't wish to imagine what it was exactly that he had seen to shatter him into the pieces she was desperately trying to hold together in her thin, helpless arms.

"And yet they... they began to sing," Simon continued, his voice breaking with the burden of his memories. "As they were herded toward the gas chambers, they began to sing their national anthem. Their voices were filled with such defiance, such courage. It was both heartbreaking and inspiring."

Orli watched Simon's wet face transform after that last recollection, harden somehow, as though turning into granite.

Moving slowly and deliberately, he reached into his pocket and pulled out a small roll of film. He regarded it gravely, a most dangerous artefact, a secret chronicle of the atrocities he had witnessed. "It's all here," he said. "I personally photographed it all through the window of the crematorium when our SS supervisor left to take a leak. The open fields, the stacks of bodies, the smoke from the open pits. My comrades. The SS."

Orli felt the power of the entire humanity as he lowered the small roll into her open palm for safekeeping.

"Hide it, Orli. Hide it the best you can. If they find it, they'll destroy it together with all of us. And the world needs to see what has happened here."

Orli looked at the roll of film in her hand—such a small, inconspicuous object carrying the weight of countless lost souls. She nodded, understanding the gravity of the task. "I'll hide it, Simon. I promise."

He nodded; he knew she would. "As for the other supplies you keep here, comrades will come later tonight to pick them up. Can you move the patients from the ward somewhere? It would be best if no one saw it before it all goes down, and after today, I feel it will, and sooner rather than later."

"I don't need to move them. They're all Jewish, illegally here—they won't say a word."

He nodded again and suddenly pulled forward and kissed her—not on the lips but on the forehead, like a sister. "You stay alive, Doc; all right? You stay alive and you get out of here and you tell them what happened. You dig out this film and show them."

"I don't like your tone. Sounds too much like a goodbye." Now, big tears, salty and hot, were rolling down her face as well.

"It is. I have no illusions about the outcome. We'll all die regardless. But if we take even one of them with us, we'll know that we didn't die in vain."

"Simon—"

"You won't try to stop me, will you?" He looked at her almost with reproach.

"No. I wouldn't have been stockpiling your supplies if I

wanted to stop you. I just wanted to say thank you. For everything."

"And you too, Doc." He kissed her hands, wetting them with his tears. All at once, the world around them was a blur. In those last few moments, time itself had come to a stop. "Will you take care of my little Lotte?"

"Of course, I will."

"She's a very bright girl, she'll live to do great things."

"I'll make sure that she does."

"Ask her to have children, please. For me. For our parents. For all of us who died here."

Orli nodded. She couldn't speak any longer. The words burned in her throat like acid. In a place where goodbyes were all but nonexistent, the last hug, the last look, the last promises exchanged almost wrenched a person's heart straight out of their chest.

"Fight well, brother."

In the door, he half turned and offered her a smile, the memory of which Orli would carry with her forever. "Live free, sister."

As Simon disappeared into the darkness, Orli wept until tears would no longer come and only dry heaves wracked her body. Then, she took a big breath, wiped her face with the back of her hand and rose to her feet.

Moving as quietly as possible, she went through the shelves of the medicine cabinet until she found what she was looking for: a metal can where a wrap of cotton was kept. After ripping away the middle of the cotton roll, she stowed the film inside and replaced the cotton back to cover the evidence. It was a fitting hiding place, a symbol of hope amidst a world of despair.

Under the cover of night, Orli made her way to the edge of the barracks. The air was thick with ash, without a single gust of wind to offer any relief. Orli knelt down, the hard earth flattened by thousands of feet, biting into her knees, and began to dig using the top of the can as a makeshift shovel.

She couldn't possibly tell how long she was digging for. For all she knew, she would soon reach Hades itself, but she cared little for her aching hands or her back that she couldn't even feel any longer. After what the SS had done that day, she wouldn't put blowing up the entire camp past them, together with its inhabitants locked inside. She had to bury this so deep, it would survive the hardest of blasts if it came to that. And then, perhaps, a century from now, when some Polish farmer culti-vated this land again and stumbled upon the relic of the past, he would open the treasure she had hidden and release the memory of millions of souls buried under his very feet and the whole world would shake with reverberations at that revelation.

Behind her back, two pairs of feet moved stealthily into the barracks and, after some time, out into the night, weighted down with weapons and deadly determination. Their eyes met momentarily and, in that single moment in which no words were exchanged and yet everything was understood, the *Sonderkommando* men's and Orli's very souls spoke to each other.

Fight well, brothers. Avenge us all.

We will, sister. Tell the world what happened here.

The ground was cold beneath her palms, each handful of earth that she placed back into the hole soothing her aching heart with the assurance of the justice that would be done. The small mound of dirt, the only evidence of her recent activity, seemed insignificant compared to the monumental secret it guarded. As Orli patted the ground flat, her heart echoed with the rhythm of the silenced voices that the film roll encapsulated.

She looked up at the night sky, the stars masked by the acrid smoke that constantly billowed from the crematoriums. The moon, a mere sliver above, cast a ghostly pallor on the camp, making the barbed wires and guard towers look like specters from a nightmare. But this was no dream, it was an existence more horrific than any sleep-induced terror.

Orli returned to the infirmary, her mind oddly hushed and at ease. The barracks were eerily silent, save for the occasional cough or whimper that sliced through the quiet after the day they had endured. Only the children in Dr. Mengele's ward slept fitfully, their bodies huddled together for comfort despite the suffocating heat. The sight was a stark reminder of their shared plight—individuals bound by a common misfortune, their humanity stripped away until only the instinct for survival remained.

In the cubicle she shared with Gerda and Velma, Orli sat down on their double bunk bed. She wrapped her arms around her knees, her mind replaying the haunting melody of the Hungarian "Himnusz" that Simon had described. She could almost see the faces of those brave souls, their voices rising in a chorus of defiance even as they walked toward their death. Their courage in the face of such horror was a testament to the human spirit, a spark of hope in the otherwise suffocating darkness.

And now, Orli was a guardian of their memory. The roll of film was a beacon in the darkness, tangible proof of their suffering. It was a silent cry for justice, evidence of the atrocities that should never be forgotten. It was a burden, yes, but it was also a promise—a promise that their suffering would not be in vain, a promise that the world would know the truth.

For now, it lay hidden beneath the earth, a secret guarded by a courageous heart. But someday, Orli believed, it would see the light of day. And when that day came, the silenced voices would echo once more, their stories resonating in the hearts and minds of the world. Until then, Orli would carry their song within, a haunting melody that would fuel her determination, an elegy for the lost souls of Auschwitz-Birkenau.

TWENTY-NINE

SEHNDE, GERMANY. DECEMBER 31, 1961

You're slicing the roll of salami as your wife dances between the stove and the kitchen counter, a festive apron over her new dress. On the radio, the countdown of the most popular songs, but your mind is far away. You promised Lotte, no work today, just like she promised you. And her work is much more demanding than yours. She's one of the first neurosurgeons—not female, but one of the first altogether—to begin performing lifesaving operations on the open brain, with only local anesthesia, instead of the general one. But she has never been one for convention, that slightly mad wife of yours. Raised in the newly found state of Israel by a band of brothers, if not bonded by blood, then by a common past, she had learned to pull a trigger and hurl grenades before she had learned how to tenderize meat as she's presently doing.

When you first met, at a medical conference held in Switzerland, where she first presented her theory on treating brain tumors, you asked her why she chose such a difficult field, which you were afraid to touch with a ten-foot pole. She only smiled at you, with her lips and her clear, bright eyes, and explained that after what she had lived through, little could frighten her.

She didn't lie. You married the most fearless woman in the world.

Lotte says it's because she had the best teachers. Sometimes the urge to tell her overcomes you, to tell about her "auntie Orli" from the camp, the one who saved your life all those years ago, but you always bite your tongue at the last moment. In the letters they still exchange, Orli never mentions psychiatric hospitals to spare Lotte the suffering of knowing how broken her childhood hero actually is; doesn't want to shutter the illusion of healing, of forgetting it all. Orli's husband mails them from his home address to keep up with the charade and who are you to interfere? Let Orli remain an invincible hero—for Lotte at least.

You arrange the salami on the plate and pause and smile when your wife reminds you that the cheese won't cut itself, but you excuse yourself all the same and go for the phone.

Eduard answers on the second ring. He's home alone tonight, he says. He already visited the only person he wanted to see and toasted champagne with her.

You ask him how she is, the woman that is on both of your minds today. Eduard considers the question. You hear him breathe on the other end of the line. She's better than he's ever seen her, he says at length. One of the nurses helped her do her hair for him. She also made up her face and wore that dress he liked the best. Gave him all of her notebooks as a present.

All of them?

All of them.

You don't like that last bit, but the doorbell rings and you hear Lotte greeting Fredo and Irma in the hallway and it's rude to be on the phone if it's not an emergency, and it really isn't—but it is, and for a moment, you stand there torn between two different worlds, and it's Eduard who makes the ultimate choice for you. For you both.

He tells you not to worry at least for one day. You worry too much. She'll be fine, you'll see that she will.

You promise to visit her first thing tomorrow and he laughs softly and kindly as he always does and you understand why she fell in love with him—he's a good man, a rare good man through and through—and he tells you once again to go and be with your family and wishes you all the best in the New Year and hangs up.

You stand there with the phone in your hand and for a second consider dialing the sanatorium, but then Irma and Fredo pour into the room and push a champagne bottle into your hands, and all at once, there are arms and laughing faces all around you and cheese in the kitchen that still needs to be sliced and you let yourself be led away.

THIRTY

AUSCHWITZ-BIRKENAU. FALL 1944

With the fall came a strange, heavy silence. The transports no longer arrived from Hungary and the *Judenramp* stood still, like a prop in a condemned, grotesque theater. The SS were oddly quiet too, going about their business as usual, as though they hadn't just obliterated the entire Jewish population of Hungary, as though the Warsaw Jews hadn't just revolted against them, as if the Soviets weren't approaching from the east and allies from the west. If Orli didn't know better from the Birkenau grapevine, she'd be convinced that Germany was winning the war. As if nothing was out of the order, they counted their prisoners every morning and evening, smoked as they watched them break their backs in their work details and jawed among each other about anything really but the war itself.

Unharmed and still very much alive, Simon and his men were going about their job as well—Orli saw them with her own unbelieving eyes now and then. And yet, it was her profound conviction, as must have been theirs, that the SS were lulling them slowly into oblivious compliance. The air was much too still, just like before a heavy thunderstorm. Suspicion hung in it like ozone; they could all smell it.

Only in the pathology lab, that ghastly domain of the Angel of Death, the air smelled strongly of disinfectant and formaldehyde. As Orli looked on, Dr. Mengele was taking down the vitals of a frail, pale twin girl. His unwilling assistant, Dr. Kertesz, was quietly taking notes in the corner. It was anyone's guess which concoction Mengele had jabbed her with two days ago, but the girl's health was deteriorating swiftly. Just that very morning, her fever had sharply spiked and an ugly yellow shade tainted the whites of her eyes that were rimmed with purple. Her abdomen was hard to the touch. Even without Dr. Mengele's comments, Orli knew that the girl's liver was failing.

Just as Dr. Mengele finished noting down the girl's rapid, unsteady pulse, there was the sudden sharp crack of a gunshot. Orli started, just like the Hungarian pathologist did, but Dr. Mengele remained unflustered.

The second gunshot was followed by a series of rapid-fire shots, and this time, even Dr. Mengele looked up, his cold eyes narrowing.

"Stay put and don't go near doors or windows," he ordered and swiftly exited the lab, unholstering his gun as he went.

After laying the girl down on the examination table to keep her comfortable, Orli and Dr. Kertesz moved toward the window against Mengele's orders and their own common sense. If it wasn't an approaching army—Allied or Soviet, it made no difference—it was something worth risking one's life for and they felt it on some instinctual level. Inside their chests, their hearts were pounding as they peered through the glass with wide eyes.

Neither of them could have imagined the picture that presented itself to their gaze. Through the haze already rolling toward the laboratory in waves, they saw one of the crematoriums going up in flames, a glowing inferno against the gray sky. Taking cover against the invisible enemy, SS guards were shooting in the general direction of it as they shouted for help to some of their comrades running away from the scene bent double.

"What in the world...?" Dr. Kertesz whispered and didn't finish. His tame nature just couldn't take in the idea of a possible revolt even when it stared him directly in the face.

"The *Sonderkommando*," Orli replied with reverence and wonder and heartache as she clutched at her chest, where her heart was beating itself to death. "They must have gotten word of the upcoming liquidation somehow."

"And?" Dr. Kertesz looked at her in pallid astonishment.

"They're fighting back." Orli's voice was a mere whisper.

"Those fools," the Hungarian muttered but kindly somehow. "Those mad, mad fools. They will get themselves killed."

In front of their eyes, an SS guard charged toward the crematorium with a machine gun but jerked suddenly, spun round, dropped to his knees, swayed slightly as he looked at the blood staining his smart uniform red and keeled over silently, his machine gun hitting the dust.

All at once, Orli forgot how to blink. For the first time in her entire life, she saw an SS man getting killed, and not by just another soldier but by an inmate, no less. Inside her ribcage, her heart swelled with a feeling she couldn't quite describe. It was a mixture of satisfaction and bloodthirst and pride and hope that surged through her bloodstream and went straight to her head like a good wine. Suddenly, she was drunk with the sight of the uneven battle and the scent of smoke and blood as though they were the richest of liquors in the world.

"They will," she said, breathless. "But not like helpless SS slaves. They'll die like the warriors they are."

Orli's heart pounded as she watched the scenes of rebellion unfold. She heard the whining of the trucks' engines; heard steel-lined boots spilling out of them, taking cover; saw the SS rapidly setting up a perimeter, their machine guns aimed at the chaotic scene. And on the opposite side of the makeshift front line, the *Sonderkommando* inmates were fighting back with a fierce determination as they used whatever weapons they had to retaliate. The weapons she had helped stockpile. The weapons smuggled by dozens of people who still believed in freedom in spite of it all.

Orli's chest swelled with emotion as she watched part of the crematorium's roof burst into a ball of flames and collapse to the cheers of the *Sonderkommando* men. With their own hands, they were demolishing the very symbol of their oppression, the place where they had witnessed their families die, and now, they danced on its ruins as the bullets flew past them in rapid succession.

All at once, Orli was seized by an overpowering desire to do something as well. She had no weapons and neither did she make much of a fighter, but there must be something she could do to contribute, to join the rebellion in her own way, no matter how little—

The sickly twin girl whimpered on the table, and suddenly, Orli saw a small window of opportunity; grasped at it with all she had. Despite Dr. Kertesz's protests—"What in the world are you doing? You'll get yourself killed!"—she scooped the child into her arms and bolted for the door.

There had never been a better chance for an escape than this. The camp's entire SS population were much too preoccupied with stifling the revolt to mind the rest of the inmates, and the inmates themselves much too stunned with the general commotion to pay any heed to anything else. Even the Kapos would just stand there with their mouths agape if Orli charged right past them, but there were no Kapos on her way. The burning crematorium and the pathology lab stood on the very edge of the camp and after that open fields with mounds of ground, where the pits had smoldered mere weeks ago.

Orli didn't much care for herself. Her own freedom and life didn't mean much. She had no one to run back to. Her ex-husband, whose report had condemned her to life in prison and various camps, had seen to that. All of her closest friends, who had shared the defendant's bench with her, were either dead or serving their time behind barbed wire. Her family—she hadn't the faintest idea if they were even still alive. She had lived her share and, frankly, had had enough of it. But the girl, she was still young, she had her entire life ahead of her, she still had a chance to recover if the Polish farmers she was presently running to took her to the nearest—

Orli yelped as something crashed into her from behind, making her tumble onto the ground together with her precious cargo. Swiping the girl under herself, covering the child with her own body, Orli felt teeth sink into her neck and hot breath singe the skin under her kerchief.

A dog.

An SS Alsatian; the hellhound, wherever he had jumped from, the cursed beast.

Her neck still locked in the predator's jaws, Orli moaned in despair—not at being caught; to hell with that, what did it matter?—but at being caught before she could save at least someone from Mengele's death grip.

"Release," a female voice commanded. "Heel. Good boy. You. On your feet and don't try anything stupid or I'll set him on you for real."

Slowly, Orli rose to her feet and looked directly into the barrel of a handgun an SS overseer was holding in her small, white hand. Next to his handler, the Alsatian was panting, his pink tongue lolling as he stared at Orli with his brown eyes.

Orli didn't blame the dog. Not his fault the SS had trained him to maim and kill instead of giving slobbery dog kisses and exposing his belly for rubs.

With her eyes still on the dog, Orli asked the SS woman softly and bitterly, "How do you manage to turn the best things in this life to such rot?"

A blow from the pistol butt on her cheekbone was her answer.

"You're lucky that you're Dr. Mengele's medic, you filthy sow! That's the only reason you're still alive. Move."

With the barrel of the gun poking in her back, Orli trudged back to the camp. To avoid gunfire, the SS warden took her through a maze of barracks, now all bolted from the outside, and into the camp Gestapo holding cell. The door was slammed after her and the lock engaged with one final clang, leaving her in complete darkness, with thoughts of immediate execution as company.

Orli didn't know how long exactly she'd been locked there—must have been a few hours at least. Her skinned knees had stopped aching and the girl in her arms had stopped whimpering and fell into a fitful sleep. In the distance, the gunfire had eventually died down. Silence had once again settled over the camp.

As twilight drew nearer, one of the camp Gestapo men fetched Orli from the cell. Dr. Mengele was waiting for her outside, his face an impassive mask. He looked at the girl in Orli's arms, his gaze cold and calculating.

"Thank you," he said to the SS guard. "I'll take it from here."

Orli didn't find it surprising, the fact that even the camp Gestapo wished as little to do with the Angel of Death as possible.

They made their way back to the pathology lab on foot, through the camp that was still on the lockdown, enveloped in thickening darkness and silence. By the time they reached the pathology lab, Orli began to wish Mengele would say something, but he remained as mute as a statue, refusing to as much as acknowledge her with a single look.

Little was left of the crematorium. Its ruins still smoldered faintly against the indigo sky, but the fire was mostly extinguished. Under the sickly yellow of the searchlights now aimed at the front of the pockmarked entrance, the bodies of the *Sonderkommando* men were laid out. Orli thought that she recognized Simon among them, but her vision blurred and she wasn't sure of anything any longer.

The day was much too long. She was suddenly very tired. All she wanted was to lie down and close her eyes—forever.

Inside the pathology lab, Dr. Mengele pulled the chair out and sat in it, motioning for Dr. Kertesz to take the girl from Orli's arms.

"May I ask what it was that you hoped to accomplish?" He finally addressed her, his voice dripping with icy contempt.

Orli said nothing, her gaze fixed on the lifeless eyes of the twin.

"Did you wish to set her free?" Mengele continued, a cruel smirk playing on his lips. "From me."

That wasn't a question. He knew well enough what he was, what Orli thought of him.

"Fair enough. But it's a bit cruel to separate the twins, don't you think?"

Once again, Orli stared at him in mute defiance, her eyes speaking volumes as her lips remained sealed.

"You want them free, you'll have them free. Dr. Kertesz, fetch me her sister."

The Hungarian pathologist hesitated, but he knew better than to disobey Dr. Mengele. Leaving the girl on the cold slab, he went out and soon returned with the other twin, a healthy, vibrant contrast to her sister.

Dr. Mengele looked at them both, a perverse satisfaction in his eyes. Without a word, he pushed the chair back, strolled toward the glass cupboard, filled a syringe with phenol and, as

Orli looked helplessly on, administered a lethal injection to both girls.

"Are you happy now, Dr. Reichert?" he asked, his gaze fixed on her. "They are free now."

Orli could only cry silently, her tears a silent testament to the horrors she was forced to witness.

Mengele watched her, his expression unreadable.

"It was a stupid thing those men did today. Giving hope to the condemned; that's much more cruel than anything I have ever done. No one is leaving this place alive. The only thing here that can truly set anyone free is death," he said, his voice echoing in the sterile silence of the pathology lab.

Orli could only look at the limp bodies of the twins, their lives snuffed out in an instant. Without a sound, she wept for them, for herself, and for all the innocence that had been brutally extinguished in this pit of horror. Moving as though through a nightmare, Orli approached the slab and reached for the girls. Tears streamed down her face, washing over the dried blood and grime that marked her days of servitude. She held the lifeless bodies close, a silent promise of the love and warmth they had been denied in their short lives. And as she wept, something inside her broke—a dam of enforced compliance that had been slowly eroding under the weight of the atrocities she was forced to witness.

Mengele watched her with an air of detached curiosity, as one might study a particularly fascinating specimen. His eyes, as cold and gray as the ash that littered the camp, flickered with a perverse kind of satisfaction. Orli was nothing more than a plaything to him, a marionette he could manipulate to dance to the tune of his sadistic whims.

Finally, she looked up, her eyes red-rimmed but resolute. She gently laid the twins down on the cold metal table, their faces serene in death. Their innocence and the brutality of their end only reinforced the grim reality of their existence—they were no more than lambs led to the slaughter in this accursed place.

Orli turned to face Mengele, her posture rigid, her expression one of defiance. "You're wrong, Herr Doktor. Giving hope is not cruel. Inspiring others to fight for what is right is not cruel."

"How far did it get you, that inspiration of yours?" He regarded her with contempt and almost pity—had he been capable of it. "You'll die here, Dr. Reichert; don't you realize that yet?"

Orli nodded, newfound serenity settling over her like a halo. "I might. But that's not what matters."

"And just what do you think does? Enlighten me, be so kind."

"What I did while I was here matters, just as what you did. Not to me—you are correct, I shall be long dead—but to those who come out of here, and they will. You can't kill all of us. They will come out and they will tell their stories and those stories will change the world for the better. We both shall be long dead, but people will remember our deeds. I know that when my time comes, I shall die with a clear conscience like those men over there did." She paused before she shot the last question like a bullet through his forehead, "Will you?"

For the first time, he had nothing to reply to her.

Orli nodded and smiled wistfully. *Just as I thought.*

As she walked away, leaving the Angel of Death in the silence of his own making, she felt a sliver of satisfaction. She may be a prisoner, she may be at the mercy of a monster, but she had not let him break her spirit. In her heart, she was free, and that was a freedom Mengele could never take away from her.

THIRTY-ONE

WINTER 1944–45

Winter had settled over Auschwitz, casting a bleak and unforgiving veil upon the tortured souls that remained. As the Soviet army approached from the east, more and more inmates had been shipped back to Germany—or at least such was the rumor—leaving mostly the skeleton staff back at the camp.

The factories that had been employing slave labor folded first. Their owners stacked their suitcases with bloody cash, their pockets with passports with new names in them and vanished into the white landscape without a trace. Their workers had wandered aimlessly about the camp and soon disappeared on the first transports heading out of Auschwitz.

Next came the turn of the remaining crematoriums. Oddly enough, they hadn't been in use since the *Sonderkommando* revolt, either because the *Sonderkommando* had all but ceased to exist after losing many of their men to the day-long battle and the SS didn't fancy doing their dirty work, or the SS feared another revolt—it was anyone's guess. They had been blown up with enough charges to level the entire constructions to the ground.

Orli and Gerda surveyed the ruins the following day, their faces reflecting a mixture of fascination and concern.

"So, that's that," Gerda said.

Overhead, a plane flew with a low rumble, followed by rapid anti-aircraft gunfire.

"Reconnaissance?" Gerda asked, her breath coming out in small, translucent clouds.

"Seems to be."

"Soviet or RAF?"

"I saw a star, so either Soviet or American. RAF have circles on them."

"Imagine if they bombed us on the last day?"

"Daft cow. All you know is how to jinx." Orli spat and knocked on the barracks' wooden wall.

Gerda laughed, not taking any offense. The crematoriums lay in ruins and allied planes flew overhead, the day was much too beautiful to quarrel over silly name-calling. Over the course of the last few years, they had grown closer than sisters and it showed. Even the insults between them were almost terms of endearment.

All of a sudden, Gerda wrapped her arms around Orli and smooched her on her cold cheek. "Happy New Year, you pitiful scarecrow."

"One yourself. Anyway, it was a few days ago."

"No. This is the real New Year. For us."

Orli shook her head before resting it on Gerda's shoulder and smiled when Gerda put her chin atop it. "Happy New Year."

In the following days, when the wind blew from the east, they could hear the echo of the front-line salvo and smell faint traces of the gunpowder it carried. Each time it happened, the SS stood rigid and listened closely, their eyes trained on the horizon like those of foxes that hear the distant barking of the hunting party.

Soon, fires began going up in the camp itself, and for the first time it wasn't corpses that burned. Weighed down by heaps and heaps of paperwork, the SS scrambled to erase any trace of the evidence of their crimes, committing the names to fire, much as they had committed their owners only a few months ago.

Making use of the discipline that was growing laxer by the day, Miriam snuck inside the infirmary several times a day. All of her patients were Jewish. Whatever would happen to them now?

"Nothing, I presume." Orli pacified her the best she could. "There are no more gas chambers, or crematoriums for that matter."

"There are still bullets though," Miriam countered as she stared through the open door into the vast expanse of the almost-empty camp. "And one can always rely on the SS to invent new ways to kill people."

"I think they're saving the bullets for the Ivans."

Miriam stared at the burning heaps of paper and said nothing.

The next day, she disappeared. Orli hadn't the faintest idea where or when; all she knew was that the Jewish infirmary stood empty, yet still when she went to check on her very first bunkmate. Only a wooden clog dropped in what must have been a great hurry lay abandoned in the middle of the barracks and a trail of footprints led out of it into the great unknown. It had been snowing since the morning. Great, fluffy flakes were slowly covering up their last trail leading toward the woods.

"Where do you think they've gone?" Orli paced their German infirmary, biting into what was left of her nails. "The woods? To be shot?"

"We would have heard the shots," Gerda said quietly but without conviction.

"Where then?"

"How would I know? The SS didn't report to me the day prior."

Velma only shivered and scratched at her scalp. Together with the factories, the kerosene had disappeared. Lice crawled all over her braid, just like they did in Orli's and Gerda's short hair.

"Cut it off already, Rapunzel," Gerda teased her good-naturedly but received only a look of indignation in response.

"Over my dead body! They took everything from me here. This is mine, something I made, something I saved and nurtured in this graveyard where nothing else lives. I'm taking it back home with me."

Oddly enough, both Orli and Gerda understood such strange camp logic.

They discovered soon enough exactly where Miriam's infirmary had disappeared to. One night, right after the roll call, Orli and the rest of her staff were ordered to march out without as much as taking a blanket with them to keep them from freezing in the brutal Polish winter night. With only the cover of darkness shielding them from the enemy planes, they trudged through the snow-covered landscape alongside their fellow prisoners, away from the villages and deep into the woods. It was there that they had stumbled upon the first bodies—quite literally.

Orli was the first to fall onto what she had presumed to be a fallen log, only to yelp in fright when her eyes met the frozen ones of the corpse on which she had landed. Scrambling onto her feet, she peered closer into the night, lit by the pale light of the moon grinning at them like a skull floating in the indifferent sky. All around them, as far as the eye could see, bodies were scattered where they fell, killed not by bullets as Miriam had predicted, but by the brutal temperatures that made Orli's very bones ache and settled so deep in her stomach, she could swear her intestines were cold to the touch.

"Do you think Miriam and Enna are among them?" Velma voiced what Orli and Gerda didn't dare to.

"No. It can't be," Orli said. The freedom was so close they could almost taste it. Dying right now was simply not an option —or, at least, so Orli believed. "They're both young and strong. And Miriam, she almost died in the very beginning, long before you three arrived; she has already pulled through once and she will now. I know it. And Enna, she's always been the most resourceful of us all. We never thanked her openly, didn't want to embarrass her, but she traded her own body just so our patients would have something to eat. How selfless is that? No. I refuse to believe that they'll give up now."

Gerda nodded together with Velma and stumbled when an SS rifle prodded her in the back. "Keep up with the rest if you don't want to get a bullet in your skull."

Hurriedly, Orli took Gerda's elbow and steered her away from the trigger-happy SS man and his threats. Keeping her head low, Velma followed close on their heels.

The entire night they were forced to keep up with the SS-imposed death march, their bodies weak and emaciated, their spirits barely flickering.

"Where do you think they're taking us?" Orli asked, struggling to unglue her frozen lips. Her jaws had been aching from the cold for hours now. Even her teeth had ceased their incessant chattering and that wasn't a good sign.

"Ravensbrück," a voice to her right.

In breaking dawn, Orli made out a Kapo in a warm winter coat and, strangely, without a signature baton.

"Well, you—ladies, that is," he explained, being oddly good-natured, much like all criminals at the first signs of their judgement day approaching. "We'll part ways with you along the road."

"Where are you heading to?" Orli asked, making use of his newfound chattiness.

"They say Dachau. Good deal. I came from Dachau, initially."

"And I came from Ravensbrück." Orli discovered that she was smiling grimly.

"A nice roundness to our journey then, is it not?" The Kapo barked a laugh.

Orli could have done without any roundness but nodded nevertheless. At least now they knew where they were going.

With the next day, little relief came. The winter conditions were unforgiving, a cruel reminder of the agony they had endured. The biting wind cut through their tattered clothing, and the frozen ground beneath their feet offered no respite. The prisoners, weakened by malnutrition and the horrors they had witnessed, struggled to keep pace. Those who stumbled or faltered were met with the merciless crack of a rifle, their bodies left to freeze in the snow.

Orli and her barrack mates pressed on, her heart heavy with grief for those lost and for the uncertain future that awaited her. She had been separated from Miriam and Enna and her patients, who had become like a second family to her, and the memory of their faces haunted her every step. Dr. Mengele had remained in the camp with them. However, a flicker of hope remained within her as she clung to the belief that he would spare them in the last moments before liberation and that she, too, could still help those in need. Hopefully, he'd find it in himself to release Dr. Kertesz too.

Days dragged as long as weeks as they trudged through the desolate landscape. Finally, the gates of Ravensbrück loomed in

the distance, a foreboding symbol of the further suffering that
awaited them. Orli's heart sank, but she pressed on, her spirit
unyielding.

As Orli entered the camp, she was met with a mixture of
despair and disbelief. Little was left of the once-picture-perfect
affair, with its aviary and white huts and gravel paths. Now, as
far as the eye could see, makeshift tents rose from the muddy
landscape like some demented circus with its skeletal inhabitants trying to warm themselves by the small fire pits in the
open space. Bundles of torn rags of indiscernible color had
replaced once-immaculate striped dresses. Women sat on the
icy ground slowly freezing to death and made no attempt to
even look up when a new influx of arrivals pushed through their
ranks. Any will they once had to live was now gone from their
eyes.

It was here, in the middle of this communal grave, that the
SS abandoned them with a simple, "Find yourself a place to
sleep." Like lost children, Orli, Velma and Gerda turned their
heads this way and that and lowered themselves slowly to the
ground among other wretches just like them.

"Is lunch still at twelve?" Orli asked a woman nearest her.

Two sunken eyes peered at her from under a bundle of rags.
The woman's entire face was a death mask, covered with grime
and sores and scarcely breathing through the gaping hole of a
mouth.

"Lunch?" she rasped and broke into something between
cackles and coughing—Orli couldn't quite tell. "Haven't seen
that in two weeks."

"What about dinner?" Orli was growing progressively
colder and not just from the ice seeping into her bone from the
ground frozen stiff beneath her. "Do they still give you a piece
of bread at least?"

The woman barked another laughter. "Bread? Last time I
saw bread was when they threw a few pieces into the crowd... I

wasn't close enough to get any... But maybe that's for the best."
She was speaking with long pauses between sentences as
though the act of talking itself was taking too much of whatever
precious energy she had left. "They threw themselves on that
bread... Several women were mauled to death... That was
about a week ago... Maybe longer. One can't tell here
anymore."

"Is there water at least?" Gerda whispered, her horror
growing as well. Orli could see it fermenting in her friend's
eyes.

"We eat snow."

They sat for a while staring at each other, two former physicians with distinctive armbands around their biceps that looked
like a mockery now. They hadn't eaten in days, and had hoped
to get at least some warm watery soup into their empty stom-
achs upon arrival, but there would be no soup and not even a
shelter from the elements. Night would soon fall, and it was
anyone's guess if they would survive it.

Her head swimming with hunger and exhaustion, Orli
rubbed her feet, aching with cold and bloody blisters, but didn't
undo the newspaper insulation for fear of someone snatching it
from her. Women were desperate here, anything was game.

"I'm starving," Velma said.

Orli's own stomach hadn't stopped cramping in days. All
she'd been thinking about was food—any kind of food really, no
matter how moldy or rotten, just to mash something with her
teeth that were aching too, just to swallow something that
wasn't a handful of snow.

Behind Gerda's back, a woman keeled over. Those sitting
around her regarded her indifferently, then slowly started to
remove her clothing. They wrapped it around themselves,
adding to the layers of rags that were already piled upon them,
and left her lying in the frozen mud, a bag of bones that once
had been a living, breathing human.

"Is there a *Sonderkommando* here?" Orli addressed no one in particular.

"Hasn't been in months."

"What do you do with corpses?"

Another apathetic shrug. "They don't bother anyone. It's cold. They don't smell."

Orli had thought she'd seen it all in Auschwitz. However, nothing could prepare her for this deepest pit of hell she'd descended to in Ravensbrück, where women killed each other for a few crumbs of bread and where the dead lay together with the living until the living turned into the dead.

"Where are you off to?" Gerda asked as Orli rose to her feet.

"I'm not going to sit here and wait to die, I'm going to walk around and see if I can find someone we know."

"Wait for us then." At once, Velma was on her feet too, reaching for Orli's hand with her ice-cold one. "We're going with you." She, too, felt that death would claim her faster if she waited around for it. She would also rather meet it on her feet like the soldier she was.

For a time, they wandered aimlessly, stepping over those dead or sleeping and asking those awake or still alive if they recognized their friends' names and numbers. Most of the time, they were greeted with silence or a single shake of a head. Only in rare cases someone more or less alert pointed them in a certain direction, which they followed slowly but diligently, tracing their lost sisters in this land of lost souls.

"Auschwitz infirmary? Their tents are over there, by the wire. They overtook it gradually after all the old-timers from the transit camps died. They had a girl with them who traded favors with the men when they still had bread on them."

"Enna," Orli and Gerda said in unison and pushed forward with a renewed energy, smiling to each other, not even surprised that there was a men's section added to the all-women's camp.

The wall of makeshift tents erected along the barbed-wire

fence was indeed marked by the symbol of a black cross, maybe painted with charcoal, but a cross nevertheless. There was a semblance of order about it, much to Orli's and Gerda's relief. Here, small blackened mugs hung on a wire above the fire and corpses didn't cover the ground as they did everywhere else.

They had to poke their heads into a few tents before they finally discovered their friends.

"Orli!" Miriam called to her from the darkness of the tent, where she was tending to someone's frostbite. "Girls, look! Our Orli is with us again! And Gerda and Velma, look, here they are!"

Crawling through a narrow passage created by women shifting out of their way, they hugged one another while still on their knees and patted one another's bony backs with a mixture of concern and relief.

"I never thought I would see you again," Miriam whispered, her voice barely audible above the clamor of the camp. "You've returned to us like an angel."

"Angel, my foot." Orli's eyes filled with tears as she embraced her dear friends. She wiped them with the back of her hand, laughing. "A traveling vagabond is more like it."

"I like the new coat," Enna said, lifting Orli's blanket she had shamefully taken from one of those who hadn't made it through the death march. "New spring collection?"

"Very funny, you wench! You're very popular in the camp, you know. It's only thanks to your reputation that we have found you."

"I don't like to brag, but I am. Was, at least, until all of my admirers first ran out of food and then died altogether." Enna, a mere shadow of her vivacious self, made a certain face at Orli, trying to turn it all into one big joke, but Orli's lips trembled with the realization that they were possibly living out their last weeks in this place without food or water, or hope. But at least they were living those last weeks together, and that somehow made it better.

"It's all right," she said softly. "Together, we'll pull through. You'll see that we will—we have to."

"Hey, Orli!" Gerda called to her from the opening of the tent. "Guess who else is here?"

She lifted the flap of the tent and Orli nearly burst into tears of joy and relief at the sight of Lotte, their little Lotte, Simon's niece and the only child they had managed to save from Auschwitz's claws.

"Lotte?"

"It's me, Auntie Orli."

"She's our youngest nurse-in-training," Miriam declared with certain pride in her voice and added the same prophetic words Simon had uttered when Orli had last seen him, "She'll grow up to do great things, this little one. You take my word for it."

Orli simply nodded and kissed the bright little head of the girl that had turned into a symbol of resilience for so many of them. *Yes, she will. I know she will.*

The final weeks in Ravensbrück were a testament to the indomitable human spirit. More prisoners evacuated from the nearest camps were herded into crowded tents, pressed together for warmth. But the bitter cold seeped through the thin fabric, piercing their frail bodies. Hunger gnawed at their bellies, and desperation clung to every breath they took.

One by one, their numbers dwindled. The harsh winter claimed lives with merciless efficiency. Hypothermia and starvation were silent assassins, stealing away the remaining fragments of life from their broken bodies. Orli and her modest makeshift hospital staff fought tirelessly, offering what little comfort and solace they could, despite the fact that they couldn't possibly save them all.

With the spring, new orders for evacuation came, but this time the SS followed them half-heartedly. There were no mandatory roll calls or orders to move out. They simply pointed in the western direction—"Mauthausen and Bergen"—and then in the eastern one—"the Soviets, your choice"—and marched off without a single look back. Some of the inmates followed them. Some, including Orli and her hospital staff, decided to stay put after a short and concise discussion.

"I can't take another march on foot," Velma said.

"Neither can I," Gerda agreed, retying the strings that held the remnants of newspapers around her legs—the only insulation from the cold they had.

"We've been boiling leather belts and soles for weeks now and having 'belt soups' as our main nourishment," Orli chimed in. "The Soviets shall at least feed us something more substantial."

"I'm with Orli on that one," Miriam agreed with a smirk. "Besides, I'd rather be free sooner rather than later."

"The SS say they rape women."

"The SS say a lot of things."

"Frankly, I'd rather have a Red on top and food in my stomach than the SS around and no food."

"Wouldn't expect anything else from you, Enna."

There was a lot of shooting going on in the distance for the next few days, but then the deafening roar of machinery shattered the oppressive silence of the camp. The Soviets had arrived, liberators of the damned.

Gerda, Orli, Miriam, Velma, Enna and Lotte stumbled out of the tent, their eyes squinting against the blinding light of freedom. The gates of Ravensbrück swung open, revealing a world they thought they would never see again.

As the women walked out of the camp, their bodies frail but their spirits unbreakable, tears streamed down their faces. The joy of liberation mingled with the sorrow of those left behind, forever etched in their hearts. They stumbled forward, their steps uncertain and hesitant, as if the weight of their past still clung to their weary bodies.

The sight that greeted them beyond the camp's gates was in stark contrast to the horrors they had endured. Vibrant fields stretched out before them, blanketed in a pristine layer of snow. The air carried a freshness they had long forgotten, a reminder of life's resilience even in the face of unimaginable darkness. They dropped onto that luscious carpet sprouting the first blades of grass and turned their faces toward the sun. If they didn't have to move for the rest of their lives, it would be fine with them.

By midday, Orli, Gerda, Miriam, Velma, Enna and Lotte found themselves surrounded by Allied forces, their uniforms a beacon of hope and salvation.

A young Soviet soldier with kind eyes approached them, his voice filled with compassion. "You're free now," he said, extending a hand to help them stand upright. "You can go, wherever you want. You're free."

The words echoed in their minds, a chorus of liberation that reverberated through their souls. They clung to each other, tears of relief mingling with smiles of gratitude. Orli's heart swelled with a mixture of emotions—survival, loss, and an overwhelming sense of purpose.

THIRTY-TWO

In the days that followed, under the supervision of the Red Cross, Orli, Miriam, Gerda, Velma, Enna and Lotte received medical care and nourishment, slowly regaining their strength and the flickering light of hope. In no time, Orli, driven by her unwavering dedication to healing, found herself assisting the Allied medical teams, tending to the survivors of the concentration camps. The Red Cross physicians protested, but there was no stopping Dr. Reichert as soon as she could stand on her own two feet without swaying.

"You're skin and bones yourself," they chided her in those first few days of Orli joining their staff. "Why don't you stay put in your bed and let us tend to you?"

"Because she's Orli," Gerda responded, a grin tugging at the corner of her mouth. Unlike Orli, she didn't mind lying in her cot propped on one elbow and gossiping with the girls for the first time in years, actually resting and chatting without fear of being shot for it. "No one tends to her. She's the one who tends to the others, because according to her good nature, others always have it worse than her and she'll just have to pull through because that's what she's been doing her entire life. She doesn't know how or when to ask for help."

"You ought to know when to ask for help, Aurelia," the doctor in charge of their wing said. He was Polish, not long out of the German prison himself—a rare member of the Polish intelligentsia that had miraculously survived the Nazi purges and outright slaughter. "Else, your body—or, even worse, your spirit—shall break eventually, and sometimes, there's no return from that."

Orli nodded absently and asked where she could find someone from the allied intelligence instead.

There were no allied intelligence agents to be found. Everyone was still at the front, beating the last of the Nazis out of Berlin, or already searching for the escaped war criminals, but Orli hadn't spent years in captivity for no reason. If anything, it had taught her patience and perseverance. In May, she talked to the Soviet SMERSH, but their agents had little interest in Hungarian Jews. In July, while passing through an American occupation zone, she camped out in front of their intelligence headquarters until they finally admitted her.

A male secretary of barely eighteen diligently wrote down her lengthy and very detailed story about the Hungarian *Aktion* and the film hidden next to the infirmary, though it appeared he did so mostly out of boredom than real interest. Orli still hoped that he would pass it along, but then the news of the Hiroshima bombing exploded in the American zone and Orli realized that they were much more interested in their new weapons than some hidden film.

She had little hope left when she finally crossed into Trier—the town where she'd grown up and considered her native, even though she hadn't been born there—and entered the French military headquarters.

"Is there any hidden film documenting the extermination of

the French citizens?" the captain in charge asked after a very long perusal of her camp discharge papers.

"Not that I know of," Orli said after a pause.

"If you come across any such information, come find me immediately. We could really use it in time for the trials."

The Nuremberg trials. That was all anyone talked about when they weren't talking about rationed food and the bombed-out ruins they now had for a shelter.

"What about Hungarian citizens?" Orli hadn't walked through the entire country to be dismissed so easily.

The captain from the French occupation forces only shrugged. "I suggest you try the Hungarian Embassy. When it reopens..."

"Reopens where? In Berlin? You suggest I walk there?"

"I'm sure they'll repair train tracks by then. Or you can call them."

"From where?" Orli gestured toward the window behind which the carcass of her city loomed against a painfully blue sky. "I don't know if I even have a home, I don't know if my family is still alive. I came to you before anything and you—"

"But, Madame, what do you expect me to do?" He spread his arms. "It's simply not my jurisdiction."

"The Jews are never anyone's jurisdiction. That's why it was so easy for the Nazis to kill millions of them, because no one wished to lift a finger to help."

With that, Orli walked out and slammed the door after herself.

Her homecoming turned into a rotten affair. She suddenly wished for her girls' company. At least with them, she had so much in common. Here, among her former neighbors, she was suddenly a stranger; someone who sought out something they couldn't comprehend and was much too angry about things that mattered little in their personal opinion.

For a few days, she stumbled about the streets, which were

vaguely familiar and yet so very alien; read the notes left on the doors hanging by a single hinge or littering the broken pavement or scribbled on the remnants of walls.

Willi, we left for Heidelberg. Come find us there. Your parents.

Heinrich, I took the children to my mother in the village. Go there when you're back from the Front. Irma.

And under them, faded and barely discernible, *Came on leave but couldn't find any of you. Please write your new address. Your son Joachim.*

None addressed to Aurelia. They must have thought she was already dead. Or were dead themselves.

Mutti, Vati, it's me, Aurelia, she scribbled with a piece of a coal she found lying in abundance at her feet. The bombed-out street was half broken stone and half charcoal. *I'm alive.* She stumbled after that part. Too many years had passed. She suddenly felt like a weary traveler returning to the country the language of which she no longer spoke. She forgot how to speak to her own parents; how devastating was that? *I'm going to—*

Here, she stumbled again. Just where exactly she was going? Did it even matter?

Yes, a voice said inside. *It did. The battle for justice hadn't ended with the liberation. It was only beginning.*

And there was only one place where all of the criminals and all of their victims would come together in the next few months. Either Allied prosecution would need the evidence or former *Sonderkommando* men, who would be there to testify, would want to uncover the film for which one of their own had died. The Nazis hadn't killed them all. Nearly, but not all. And those few that were left, Orli would find them.

To Nuremberg, she finished in a firm hand. *I'll be updating my information through the Red Cross. Find me through their lists. I'll be looking for you also. Love, Orli.*

THIRTY-THREE

1947

Months turned into years, and slowly, life began to take shape once again. Orli, Miriam, Gerda, Velma, Enna, and Lotte each rebuilt their shattered lives, finding solace in the beauty and resilience of the human spirit. The scars of their past were not easily erased. Nightmares haunted their sleep, and the memories of the atrocities they had witnessed lingered like specters. But through the borders and frequent letters, they clung to each other, offering solace and understanding, their unbreakable bond forged in the crucible of suffering.

Enna returned to her native Slovakia and was married within months to some bigwig in the new government—"No surprise there," Gerda jested in her good-natured way. "She always had a way with men. They could never resist that little minx." Enna wrote often and in the photos she attached, the tall strapping fellow in a smart suit never looked into the lens but always at her. The adoration in his eyes was unmistakable.

Velma returned to Germany and was volunteering in the Red Cross in between her medical classes. Oddly enough, she chopped off her Auschwitz braid as soon as she graduated and made a chignon out of it. A macabre artefact to keep, but on some level, Orli understood the motive behind it. It was a memory one could take out of a box and shove it back in at will when the sight of it became too overwhelming. Sometimes, she wished she could do the same with her brain—take it out and shove it in the closet and lock the door and throw away the key. But there was no closet in the world big enough to contain the immensity of all the memories she kept, and so, she carried it all with her and purged it onto paper, going from one psychiatrist to the next in the hope of ridding herself of at least some of it.

Miriam, forever grateful to Orli for her unwavering support, found solace in the embrace of her newfound freedom. Just like Lotte, she moved to Israel and proceeded to work in the medical field; *un*like Lotte, she refused to pick up anything resembling a weapon. She'd seen enough uniforms to last her a lifetime. Wearing one, even if fighting for her new land's independence, was the last thing she wanted.

"Once a healer, always a healer," Orli would smile and shake her head whenever she read the letters that arrived biweekly, as though on a rigid schedule. Eduard Wald, her new husband and a fellow victim of the regime whom she had met in a sanatorium established specifically for the victims of the Nazi persecution, would chuckle and silently agree. Love was the last thing on Orli's mind in those post-Auschwitz years, but somehow this man, who had asked her if he could sit outside and share a terrace with her—"I won't talk and won't bother you, I promise; just can't sleep—" had transformed from a fellow insomniac and a comrade she'd shared companionable silence with as both gazed at the stars and listened to the chirping of the crickets in the otherwise still night air into the only person other than her girls who actually understood what she'd been through.

It had begun with a shared cigarette—Orli had forgotten her pack that night—and ended with a conversation that lasted until the new day dawned, salmon pink and cool with morning dew.

Eduard had listened without interrupting, and touched her hand at all the right moments, and wasn't ashamed of the tears he shed—for her, for her girls who had made it and those who hadn't, but never for his own life that had gone to pieces during Hitler's regime. He, too, always thought that everyone else had it worse than him. Perhaps that was why Orli had fallen in love with him, the kindred spirit, the selfless soul, her fellow fighter for universal justice with a fire in his heart that no Gestapo could ever extinguish.

They married in 1947 and, with a smile on her face, Orli scribbled her new last name—Wald—onto her marriage license, forever shedding the old one, together with the last memory of her first husband, Fritz. Whatever had happened to him, no one knew. He'd vanished into oblivion, together with his SA uniform, and no one was left to mourn him. A just end for such scum, according to Gerda. Orli never argued the point.

Gerda, too, refused to let the shadows of her past define her future. Well, selective past that was. Closer than anyone to Orli distance-wise, she positively refused to talk about anything relating to Auschwitz whenever she visited but wouldn't shut up about yet another baby she had delivered in the practice she had resumed right after the war. Orli respected her wishes, talked politely about the babies; even wished that she, too, could simply erase the memory of the camp from her mind, but the tumor of it had wrapped its metastatic tentacles around every vital organ and there was no ridding herself of it, no matter how much she tried.

Instead, Orli dedicated herself to the pursuit of justice and remembrance, using her voice to speak out against the horrors of the Nazi regime, if not in person, through her writing. At first, it was mere therapy, suggested by her very first psychiatrist, but soon stories turned into evidence as more trials followed the Nuremberg ones and survivors' former tormentors were made to answer for their sins. Her hands shook each time she read of familiar names and the accounts of the atrocities they had committed, but Orli never refused her fellow survivors and prosecutors to testify against the SS.

She struggled with the past that had broken her into pieces and tried to tell Eduard that there was little point in trying to put them together, but he did—of course he did—because he was pigheaded, just as she was, and refused to let go, just as she used to do. Maybe he was the reason that she lasted as long as she did, much like her patients in Auschwitz, simply because there was someone to love them and care for them when they couldn't find the strength to do so any longer. She thought herself to be irreparably broken and yet, for all of those she'd saved and those she kept fighting for, she became a beacon of strength and resilience, a symbol of hope for those who had endured the darkest of days.

The legacy of Orli, Miriam, and Lotte served as a reminder —a stark and haunting reminder—of the depths of human cruelty and the strength of the human spirit. They walked out of the gates of first, Auschwitz, and later, Ravensbrück, scarred but unbroken, their hearts filled with a resilience that could never be extinguished.

And as time carried their stories forward, their voices became a testament to the power of compassion, forgiveness, and the unwavering belief in the triumph of light over darkness.

EPILOGUE

The sanatorium is particularly silent today. The only sounds you hear are your own steps muffled by the thick green runner, but audible nevertheless in this unnatural serenity of the first morning of the year. At the nurses' station, the only nurse on duty is still slumbering at her desk, her head resting atop her folded arms. The rest of the medical staff is gone until tomorrow. Only you haunt the sanatorium hallways like a Victorian specter doomed to eternal limbo.

Yesterday, you promised her husband, Eduard, you would check on her first thing in the morning, even though he assured you that it was unnecessary, that she would be perfectly fine. But something kept gnawing at you the entire evening and sleepless night and here you are, in your white medical gown, knocking gently on her room's door because you feel that you owe it to her, this constant vigil you imposed on herself in spite of her gentle reproaches and even gentler protests.

You don't like the silence behind her door. No matter her mental state, she always minds her manners and always opens the door, even if just to tell you to please leave her alone for she simply doesn't have enough energy for human beings at the moment. You call her name and listen again, holding your breath this time—she had tried taking her life before, more than once, and even jokes about it now, saying that she's just as bad at dying as she is at living—and gently turn the handle, already suspecting the worst and yet praying for a miracle.

Blast it, Orli! Just as you suspected, she's face-down on her neatly made bed, a handkerchief covering the spot on the rug where she must have been sick. No wonder, judging by the number of empty pill containers lined up in immaculate order on her nightstand.

With your heart in your throat, you turn her over, feel for her pulse, first on the wrist and then, after finding nothing, on her neck. You think you feel something, fluttering as erratically and weakly as the wings of a battered butterfly, and rejoice for there's still a chance. She's not gone just yet, you can bring her back, because you're not only her psychiatrist but a physician and a guardian, just like she once used to be for all of those people she cared for—

It is then that you notice a small note in her other hand. Your heart drops, already knowing what it's going to say, and consider pretending not to notice it; saving her first and then dealing with the consequences. But that feels too much like a betrayal.

Time is running out, but you unravel it slowly and read the words full of kindness and heartache. She thanks you for everything you've done for her but it's her time to go now and you shouldn't blame her and you shouldn't try to save her. She made the same mistake back in Auschwitz, trying to save some against their wishes, and suffered from a guilty conscience her entire life—and you're so very young and have such a promising career in front of you—she'd never wish anything of the kind on you.

Even in her final moments, thinking of others. You feel a lump in your throat and crush the note in your hand. You can still save her. The trouble is, unlike in the beginning, when you had just started treating her, you don't think it's mental illness that pushes her to the brink every now and then: it's her past that won't let go. She may have left Auschwitz's walls, but the walls of Auschwitz have never left her. They have kept her prisoner day and night, tormenting her with nightmares of the past.

You can still save her.

Or you can set her free.

You hold her pale hand and ask yourself, what she would have done. A few seconds pass and you think you have your answer.

More than anything, Orli Wald cherished freedom. She fought for it inside the camp walls and long after, when she gave her testimonies to avenge the victims and bring the perpetrators to justice. She was scheduled to speak at the Frankfurt trials. She has prepared her notes, and given them to her husband. He must be in on this too. It was he who must have smuggled this supply of the sleeping pills to her. He must have understood everything sooner than you did.

This wasn't spontaneous, what she's done. She's been preparing herself for it for weeks, if not months. She's put her life in order, made up her hair and face, put on her favorite dress, and toasted her last glass of champagne to the life that would go on without her.

She's smiling as you hold her in your arms. She's as serene as this painfully beautiful morning. You cradle her like someone infinitely precious and let her take her final breaths without any interruptions and still hold her after her soul departs. The Angel of Auschwitz is now with the angels as well.

A LETTER FROM ELLIE

Dear Reader!

Thank you so much for reading Orli's story, *I Have to Save Them*. If you enjoyed it and want to keep up to date with all my latest releases, just sign up at the following link. Your email address will never be shared and you can unsubscribe at any time.

www.bookouture.com/ellie-midwood

Even though it's a work of fiction, the people and events it is based on are real. Orli Wald earned the name of Angel of Auschwitz from the grateful inmates she saved from death while working as a medic, first in Ravensbrück and, later, in Auschwitz-Birkenau.

Denounced by her husband, Fritz Reichert, Aurelia Wald spent several years in prisons for her communist affiliation and, after she had served her term, was sent to Ravensbrück concentration camp on "protective custody orders," according to which she still presented a threat to Nazi-controlled society as a former communist.

It was in Ravensbrück that she began assisting the inmate infirmary staff with their patients—an experience which may have actually saved her life once she was transferred to Auschwitz. With the second camp of Birkenau still under construction, she was swiftly appointed as one of the Auschwitz infirmary medics, where she witnessed horrific injuries and treated patients as one of the physicians.

But it wasn't until she was transferred to Birkenau's women's infirmary that Orli truly saw the extent of the SS atrocities. Phenol injections, patients dying in her arms and lack of medicaments pushed her to the brink and, combined with her own illness, caused her first attempt to commit suicide Thankfully, she was promptly saved by her own hospital staff, who reminded her that she would be much more useful to the patients alive than dead.

Her bravery and quick thinking truly shone through in her final years in Auschwitz. She indeed came up with an ingenious idea to establish a fake infectious disease ward in her German infirmary, which undoubtedly saved many lives that otherwise would have been lost to Birkenau's gas chambers. She also joined the camp resistance and helped them with the preparations that eventually led to the historic *Sonderkommando* revolt that unfortunately ended in tragedy; yet, it certainly gave hope to the rest of the inmates who witnessed it.

Orli indeed was forced to work under Dr. Mengele's supervision. It was the memories of his horrific experiments that haunted her the most throughout her life and was the reason why she never had children of her own and generally avoided even looking at them—that's how painful her recollections were. She wrote several stories about her time in Auschwitz to help herself process it and also leave an eyewitness account for future generations.

Unfortunately, after several attempted suicides and despite the efforts of her loving husband and doctors who cared for her deeply, Orli Wald finally succeeded in taking her life on January 1, 1962 in a psychiatric sanatorium in Sehnde (Ilten), Germany, at the tragically young age of only forty-eight.

Unlike many of the perpetrators, unfortunately, Josef Mengele was never brought to justice and avoided capture, hiding under false names in different countries in South America. He died of a stroke in 1979 and was buried under a false name of Wolfgang Gerhard in Brazil.

When I first heard of Orli and her heroic actions, I did all I could to get my hands on those precious stories she wrote to get a first-hand insight into this truly remarkable woman's life, but, sadly, most of them are either out of print or in the hands of private collectors and are unavailable to the general public. It was then that I approached my wonderful publishing house about writing her story so that people would know about this incredible heroine. I couldn't be happier when they said a huge yes to the book that you are holding in your hands now. Thank you so much for reading and keeping survivors' memories alive!

Ellie

www.elliemidwood.com

 facebook.com/EllieMidwood
 instagram.com/elliemidwood

ACKNOWLEDGMENTS

First and foremost, I want to thank my incredible editor, Claire Simmonds, for helping me bring Orli's story to light. She truly made Orli's character come to life and, through her invaluable insights, helped me turn the very first rough draft into the novel that you're holding in your hands today. I wouldn't have been able to do this without her unwavering support and encouragement.

To everyone in my lovely publishing family at Bookouture for working relentlessly to help my book babies reach the world. Richard and Peta, you made it possible to have my babies translated into twenty(!) languages. I know I'm an author, but I honestly have no words to fully express my gratitude to you.

Huge thanks to Jess and Noelle for organizing the best blog tours ever and securing the most interesting interviews for each new release. Even for an introvert like me, you make publicity a breeze. Working with you is a sheer delight!

Ronnie—thank you for all your support and for being the best husband ever! And for keeping all three dogs quiet when I work. I know, it's not easy given how crazy they are. I love being on this journey with you.

Vlada and Ana—my sisters from other misters—thank you for all the adventures and the best memories we've already created and keep creating. I don't know how I got so lucky to have you in my life.

Pupper, Joannie and Camille—thank you for all the doggie kisses and for not spilling coffee on Mommy's laptop even during your countless zoomies. You'll always be my best four-legged muses.

And, of course, the hugest thanks, from the bottom of my heart, to all of you, my wonderful readers. I can never explain how much it means to me, that not only have you taken time out of your busy schedules, but you chose one of my books to read out of millions of others. I write for you. Thank you so much for reading my stories. I love you all.

Finally, I owe my biggest thanks to all the brave people who continue to inspire my novels. Some of you survived the Holocaust and the Second World War, some of you perished, but it's your incredible courage, resilience, and self-sacrifice that will live on in our hearts. Your example will always inspire us to be better people, to stand up for what is right, to give a voice to the ones who have been silenced, to protect the ones who cannot protect themselves. You all are true heroes. Thank you.

PUBLISHING TEAM

Turning a manuscript into a book requires the efforts of many people. The publishing team at Bookouture would like to acknowledge everyone who contributed to this publication.

Audio
Alba Proko
Sinead O'Connor
Melissa Tran

Commercial
Lauren Morrissette
Jil Thielen
Imogen Allport

Data and analysis
Mark Alder
Mohamed Bussuri

Cover design
Eileen Carey

Editorial
Claire Simmonds
Jen Shannon